THE FLIGHT OF A THOUSAND SONGBIRDS

A FAMILY'S COURAGE LEADS TO A NEW LIFE

WILEY P. DAVIS, JR.

PINECONE PUBLISHERS

COPYRIGHT NOTICE

DISCLAIMER

The Flight of a Thousand Songbirds is a book partly based on actual events that have been fictionalized to tell the story of the journey carried out by three generations of a family defined by their choices. The names, characters, businesses, organizations, places, events, and incidents are imagined and used fictitiously. Any resemblance to actual persons, living or dead, is entirely coincidental and not intended by the author.

DEDICATION

In loving memory of my parents, Wiley Sr. and Hattie Davis, and my good friend Vernell DeSilva.

EPIGRAPH

"The Great Migration can get forgotten if we don't pay attention or bear witness to it. It's part of my personal history and the history of millions of African Americans who left those oppressive conditions for better lives in the North. It's important to put that on the page."

Jacqueline Woodson

ACKNOWLEDGMENTS

First and foremost, I am grateful to the Creator for my many blessings. I am forever indebted to my parents, Wiley Sr. and Hattie, for their tireless efforts in raising our family; bless their souls — a shout-out to my lovely siblings, Leslie, Gwen, Melba, LaMonica, and their families.

I want to express special thanks and sincere gratitude to Spencer Haywood for permitting me to use parts of his life story to write this book. Our friendship dates back to high school and college as basketball teammates. It was his remarkable story that inspired me to write this fictional novel. Noteworthy are several chapters where I leaned heavily on his real-life experiences to shed light on the fictional characters depicted in the book. The epilogue in the book is powerful and details the recognition that should have been afforded Spencer.

Spencer's story is uniquely different from the hundreds of sports stories about athletes rising to stardom in that he is the only athlete to rise from the cotton fields to become an Olympic Gold Medal hero, to a victory in the Supreme Court, to an NBA championship, and finally to the Naismith Basketball Hall of Fame. Players in the NBA who entered the league prior to four years after graduating from high school (better known as early entry) and, for that matter, early-entry NFL players owe Spencer a great deal of monetary gratitude for his sacrifice and contributions that gave them the opportunity for economic success much earlier in their careers. If you haven't already, I encourage you to watch Spencer's documentary, "Full Court," currently streaming on YouTube.

I am grateful to acknowledge and recognize my former high school coach, the legendary Will Robinson, who passed away several years ago. As he was affectionately called, Coach Rob was instrumental in shaping my life and the lives of countless others. He demanded academic success and strict adherence to team play that centered around structure and discipline. During my high school years, he dubbed me the nickname Tiger, and I was referred to that name by my teammates until I graduated. Coach Rob would tell the team, "If you learn my system of fundamental basketball, you will be equipped to play anywhere in the world." As a result, many of his graduating seniors earned athletic scholarships to colleges and universities nationwide each year.

I am sincerely grateful to George Alfred Kennedy, renowned author, and former State Department Official, for his energy and selflessness throughout the writing of this book. George was a constant source of inspiration that kept me motivated. I would not have written this book without his guidance and support.

I would be remiss if I didn't acknowledge my wife, Roberta, and my sister, Melba. I trusted their judgment when I asked them if they would carve out some time to read my first rough draft and give me an unbiased and brutally honest opinion about my story and my writing. I also want to acknowledge my son, Taharqa, and stepson, Lance, who inspired, motivated, and challenged me to keep expanding my interests.

Thank you to Ray, Phil, Ed, and Buddy from Regis University in Denver, my former colleague in Everett, Dr. Art Bird, and my tax accountant in Phoenix, Gene Weinstein. Also, thank you to golf commissioner Bob French, who reminded me to write enthusiastically, my good friend in Phoenix, CEO and author Mario Bayne, and Student Services Vice Presidents Henrietta Harris and Sylvia Manlove, whose support was invaluable.

Lastly, I want to thank Anna Celini-Kennedy and her Pen to Paper Publisher's staff for turning my manuscript into a book. I would have been stuck in the ABP (all-but-published) locker room without their knowledge and expertise.

I also want to thank the many cousins, friends, students, players, coaches, and work colleagues who impacted my journey and knowingly and unknowingly became sources of inspiration for my life and this novel.

PROLOGUE

The winds of change blow in many directions.

On January 1, 1863, during the American Civil War, President Abraham Lincoln issued the Emancipation Proclamation, officially known as Proclamation 95. This declaration decreed that 3.5 million African-Americans enslaved in rebel Confederate states would be free as of that date. However, Lincoln needed more juice to enforce the Proclamation. He would need the backing of a divided Congress to implement his new ruling. For this reason, Lincoln asked Congress for a constitutional amendment to strengthen the Proclamation and make it enforceable. So, on January 31, 1865, Congress passed the 13th Amendment and ratified it on December 6, 1865, and slavery was officially abolished in the United States.

The passage of the Thirteenth Amendment promised freedom to African Americans. This meant independence from white dominance, liberty from the whip, and the sale of family members. The Thirteenth Amendment ushered in a promise of hope, opportunity, and self-determination and finally rid African Americans of the yoke of oppression.

The passage of the Thirteenth Amendment was now in place,

and the Civil War was coming to a close when Union Gen. William T. Sherman issued what was known as Field Order No.15.

In early January of 1865, Sherman ordered a large portion of federal land along the coast of South Carolina and Georgia to be set aside for the exclusive settlement of African-American families who had been enslaved. It gave birth to the dream of owning "40 acres and a mule". This was a dream come true for thousands of families who wandered homeless and aimlessly after slavery was ended. However, during the summer of 1865, President Andrew Johnson, shortly after taking office after the assassination of President Lincoln, not only ordered land in federal control to be returned to the former white owners, but he dismantled the racial equality gains made during the Era of Reconstruction, which opened the door for Jim Crow laws to take permanent root in America's racial ideology. The dream of having "40 acres and a mule" to start a new life was killed before it could ever be implemented.

In the absence of land, many of the former enslaved African-American people, having little or no economic options, had to return to the same white-owned plantations they worked as enslaved people. Some worked for meager wages, while others worked the land as sharecroppers. It was this sharecropper life that the Colemans of Mississippi and Alabama knew all too well. For decades, most Blacks in the South remained poor and without property, so living a life as a sharecropper was no more than a means to subsist. By the turn of the century, a new system of racial segregation was put in place, which further tightened the screws on Black families.

James Crow Laws (legislation) were passed in the South and aggressively enforced between 1877 and the mid-1950s, requiring the separation of whites from Blacks and other people of color on public transportation and in schools to prevent any contact between whites and Blacks. Jim Crow laws were made famous by the "Separate but equal" decision of the Supreme Court in Plessy v Ferguson in 1896. However, in 1954, the Supreme Court reversed the ruling in Brown v Board of Education of Topeka, declaring segregation in public schools and other public facilities unconstitutional.

However, the Black Codes were enacted in 1865 and 1866 after the Civil War. The Black Codes had their roots in the slave codes, which were entrenched throughout the Southern states, where various forms of physical punishment were harshly used as a method to control enslaved people. The new and improved Black codes were re-designed by whites to restore social control previously exacted over Black Americans during slavery before being ended by the Thirteenth Amendment.

Against this backdrop, it revealed how the great-grandparents of Papa James Coleman lived under these challenging conditions as descendants of enslaved people. This harsh reality also gives context to why Papa James, after years of learning about and later living alongside the constant violence, intimidation, low wages, and endless nights of despair his parents and grandparents endured, dreaded the notion that his children and grandchildren could live a life vacant of opportunities. He decided to end the vicious cycle of oppression and risk making the journey North so that his children could have a chance for a better life. Like many Southern families before and after him, Papa James and his wife, Essie Mae, chose to abandon the infestations of Jim Crow and Black codes and their restrictive lives as sharecroppers and migrate North to Chicago. There, they would soon encounter different forms of discrimination and segregation. The Flight of A Thousand Songbirds was born from these conditions, and the journey is fraught with drama, disappointment, triumph, and love. Enjoy!

INTRODUCTION

In early May, dozens of species of small Songbirds numbering in the millions, ranging from warblers, orioles, flycatchers, and grosbeaks, migrate to North America to ensure survival. They follow nature's rhythms to find food, shelter, and comfortable nesting places. Songbirds undertake perilous journeys during their annual migrations. Traveling by night in the cooler air allowed them to fly longer distances without stopping to rest and to avoid danger. This fascinating journey of the Songbirds and their motivations to migrate has sparked debate regarding the remarkable similarities to the journey of African American families during the "Great Migration."

The Great Migration, during which approximately six million African Americans migrated from the rural South to urban cities in the North, Midwest, and West, represented one of the most significant movements of people in United States history. The Great Migration is often viewed in two phases, augmented by America's involvement in two world wars.

In 1917, the United States increased its World War I effort and decreased European immigration, resulting in Northern cities experiencing an industrial labor shortage. The first Great Migration phase, between 1910-1940, saw over two million African/Black Americans (used interchangeably) exit the South, traveling primarily by bus, boat, or train to escape racial violence and to ensure their safety and survival. To further entice Blacks to leave the South, recruiters advertised jobs in Black newspapers, in particular the Chicago Defender, which further incensed white Southerners. Subsequently, Black migrants became the badly needed labor force for Northern Industrial jobs.

The effects of the 1930s Great Depression were felt nationwide and slowed the Great Migration considerably, almost bringing it to a standstill. However, as World War II loomed and the need for wartime production rose, the United States needed to find a way to increase its labor supply to expand the defense industry. This demand opened up additional opportunities, and phase two of the Great Migration ramped up.

During phase two of the Great Migration, occurring between 1940-1970, over three million African Americans relocated North and further West to not only pursue these economic and educational opportunities but freedom from "Jim Crow" segregation laws.

The Flight of a Thousand Songbirds is a three-part fictional story based partly on actual events that encompass a family's journey and subsequent trials and tribulations. Defined by choices, the flight unfolded after the family migrated to Chicago. One of the principal characters is a father, KeShawn Coleman, the oldest child of the Papa James and Essie Mae Coleman family. He experienced legendary success in track and field as a world-class athlete before an injury doing what he loved derailed his career and sent him on an emotional spiral that nearly destroyed his life. His best friend and former teammate from college, Jamaican Moe Banks, extended an invitation to visit him in Kingston, Jamaica, a turning point at which KeShawn, from Chicago, met and fell in love with Dorothy, a lovely and endearing French-Jamaican woman. This love affair, alongside the support of his friend, allowed KeShawn to resurrect his life and become the change that spawned a child prodigy.

After resurrecting his life in Jamaica, KeShawn, desperately wanting his young son to maximize his basketball potential and convinced the Jamaican coaches could not provide the necessary training, made a difficult decision and sent his young son to Chicago to live with his Uncle Freddie. While attending high school, Xavier benefitted from the teaching of legendary basketball coach Charlie Parker and developed a close friendship with teammate Willie Mitchell.

Young Xavier made life-defining decisions while becoming a high school and college All-American, an Olympic hero, and a Hall of Famer. He fought battles that intensified as he wrangled for acceptance on the basketball court and challenged the right to earn a living in a court of law. Consequently, the professional sports landscape was changed, paving the way for thousands of players worldwide, allowing them to gain entry into the league before graduating from college.

Decades earlier, Xavier's grandfather's decision to abandon the oppressive hardships of discrimination in the Deep South to seek social, economic, and educational opportunities in the North was the Songbird that started a chain of life-altering events. The compelling journeys of Papa James, his son, KeShawn, and his grandson, Xavier, will surely capture your imagination and warm your heart. Relevant information is interjected throughout the novel to lend clarity and context.

" I have THOROUGHLY enjoyed your book about the three generations of the Coleman Family and each of their songbirds' flight from their beginnings. As I said before, it's a compelling read; I felt feelings throughout, conveyed by your gifted storytelling. In summary, WOW, Wiley!"

Melba Banks

1

HALL OF FAME: CELEBRATION AND AWARDS GALA

On a lovely August weekend in Springfield, Massachusetts, all eyes are cast upon the Naismith Memorial Basketball Hall of Fame (HOF), an annual event that attracts basketball royalty, ardent fans, and lookie-loos worldwide. It was a ceremonial time when the Hall enshrined the newest members into the Hall of Fame.

THE HALL of Fame was established in 1959 to honor Dr. James Naismith and promote and preserve basketball history. Naismith, a Canadian-American, is credited with creating the game of basketball in 1891 at the School of Christian Workers (now Springfield College) in Springfield, Massachusetts. In less than three months, the game spread across the country through a network of YMCAs, and the rest, as they say, is history.

THE TWO-DAY HOF celebration concluded on Saturday evening when the nationally televised ceremony formally enshrined the 2010 class of legends. Among the six inductees were Jamaican-born Xavier James Coleman, an Olympic hero, NBA Champion, and now a Hall of Fame inductee.

But as customary, the weekend celebrations began on Friday night, where the Mohegan Sun Casino in Uncasville, Connecticut, was the host venue for the star-studded Hall of Fame Celebration and Awards Gala. An event that recognized contributions from Hall of Fame officials, sponsors, and supporters. Inductees, their families and friends, and fans lucky enough to get tickets were entertained with music, food, and plenty of drinks. An annual feature of the Awards Gala was the red carpet walk up to the casino, a very special informal recognition moment.

As the crowd of fans gathered outside the casino, standing three rows deep and growing, they gawked, pushed, and shoved to glimpse the procession of cars that transported the inductees when, suddenly, a roar erupted. Three two-tone Cadillac 10-passenger stretch limos made the turn and slowly approached the red carpet walkway entrance. The first to exit limo 1 was Xavier, his family, and friends Willie Mitchell and Vernon Akquia. Impeccably dressed, to the sounds of applause and camera flashes, Xavier and his entourage made their way up the red carpet toward the Casino.

Along the walkway, a barrage of reporters stood, holding microphones that extended from their reach, trying to get the stoic Xavier to stop his approach and oblige their media interview requests.

Despite the passing years, Xavier had maintained a physical appearance that belied his age. Though he sported a well-groomed facial beard, he could have easily been mistaken for a current player. The weekend's Recognition Awards and Induction Ceremony had been a long wait for Xavier. He was eligible for induction over the past ten years, but each year, he was passed over by the selection committee, which offered enough excuses to fill a grand ballroom. Xavier often wondered why there were repeated snubs despite his enormous popularity and contributions to basketball;

perhaps animosity still lingered from his having pursued and won a Supreme Court case many years prior. Although there had never been on-the-record comments, there was chatter that Xavier's years of omission were retribution for challenging the league's undergraduate policy that prevented players from entering the league before being four years removed from high school.

What many claimed finally moved the needle in Xavier's favor occurred when Hall of Fame members and a slew of retired players turned broadcast analysts who played alongside or against Xavier began publicly questioning the Hall's selection process. Their disenchantment called out the hypocrisy of the selection committee, and the groundswell of contempt didn't stop there. Voices inside the Players Union, including those on a Hall of Fame trajectory, called out the selection committee's process.

In their media discussions, Union Leadership professed that Xavier Coleman had done more to encapsulate the spirit of the Hall of Fame than anyone else, past or present.

Having earned First-team College All-American honors, an Olympic Gold Medal, an NBA Championship, multiple NBA All-Star game appearances, and four-time All-NBA selections, all credentials were beyond reproach and more than worthy of immediate Hall of Fame selection. The negative feedback and disappointment directed at the Hall did not sit well among their leadership as the criticism, just or not, harmed their image and their annual fundraising activities. Short of an apology but hoping to repair their tarnished image, the Hall leaked Xavier's name as a strong candidate for induction during the next election cycle.

So today, having mixed emotions and breathing a sigh of relief, Xavier felt a sense of vindication and resolution, knowing the weight of worry was finally lifted from his mind. As he walked the red carpet holding his head high, Xavier embraced the moment and absorbed the love from the fans, knowing he would finally take his rightful place among basketball's elite, but he also wondered, "Why did his selection take so long?"

While he mingled in the crowded casino, accompanied by his

wife, Sophie, and their three children, Angela, Morgan, and Miles, Xavier graciously posed for pictures, signed autographs, and accepted congratulatory handshakes. He tried his best to respect fans' well-intended requests as he made his way through the crowd, but the constant siege of well-wishers limited his forward progress and began to test his patience.

As he smiled and shook hands, Xavier took advantage of his six-foot-nine-inch height to scan the room to check the whereabouts of his parents, KeShawn and Dorothy. He also tried quietly to find an excuse to bail on the crowd that encircled him but to no avail.

KeShawn and Dorothy Coleman are father and mother to Xavier, who is the youngest of their three Jamaican-born and athletic children. KeShawn, called "The King" while growing up, is the oldest of three siblings born near Mobile, Alabama, to Papa James and Essie Mae Coleman. The Coleman family migrated to Chicago as part of the great migration to escape the harshness of the rural South. During his senior year at Chicago DuSable High School, KeShawn earned All-American honors in basketball and track. He later attended Chicago State University, where, as a freshman, he led his team to win the school's first NCAA Regional Track and Field Championship. In his sophomore year, tragedy struck while competing in an NCAA Regional qualifying 110 high hurdle event.

A devastating knee injury that required immediate surgery cost KeShawn the lead less than 50 yards to the finish line.

The injury derailed his promising career and caused unintentional harm as he fell into an ugly state of despair and depression as his life spiraled out of control.

While on a rest and recovery visit to Jamaica at the invitation of his college friend and track teammate, Moe Banks, he met his future wife, Dorothy Livingston, by chance. Between Moe's friendship and Dorothy's presence in his life, KeShawn shed the negative aura surrounding him and began to engage a brighter side to his life. Benefiting from this positive perspective, he raised the curtain of darkness and opened the window that welcomed back the light of his infectious personality that previously defined him. After establishing stable employment, permanent residency, and months of dating, KeShawn married Dorothy, the angel of his life, became a Jamaican citizen, and raised a family.

XAVIER FINALLY GOT eyes on his parents as they were surrounded by a contingent of fans seeking pictures and autographs. Wearing a broad smile, KeShawn basked in the attention just as much as any of the inductees. Fans shared stories, reminding him of his legendary track performances in Chicago years back. One onlooker repeated a common phrase when he said, "The King is back," which brought a smile and hearty laughter from KeShawn.

Xavier's wife, Sophie, excused herself and left the children in the care of their father as she moved to meet up with Xavier's Mom, sister, and Aunt at the nearby registration table.

SOPHIE TURNER DUMAS-COLEMAN is the wife of Hall of Fame inductee Xavier Coleman. She was born in Paris, France, and after her birth father was tragically injured in a train accident, her mother, Vivienne Alice-Dumas, met and, over time, married a former professional Canadian Football player, Thomas Brown. Sophie attended UCLA on a track scholarship and represented France in the Mexico City Olympics, competing in the Heptathlon. After completing her graduate degree in Business Finance, she attended UCLA Law School, where she was a stellar student. While attending law school, she and Xavier maintained a long-distance relationship while he pursued a professional career in two different leagues. She married Xavier in a small ceremony in Los Angeles shortly after all the legal entanglements had been resolved and his basketball career was on solid ground. Together, they raised three children: Angela, Morgan, and Miles.

THE BALLROOM WAS PACKED with attendees, and while she waited for the wives to arrive, Sophie had lost sight of her children. Although she wasn't worried, as a mother, she wanted assurances that they were still in their father's company and not wandering around the ballroom. Sophie calmly looked around where she had last seen Xavier, expecting the children to be near him. She assumed his height would allow him to stand out among the crowd easily, but everyone seemed tall at this event. Finally, her mind rested when she got eyes on Xavier. He was standing across the room, still doing what he was doing when she left his side minutes earlier, engaged in conversation, and her children were standing nearby also in conversation.

Although the women in the casino were well-dressed for the occasion, Sophie's black eloquent wool gabardine Saint Laurent jacket, a surprise gift from Xavier two weeks before the event, was stunning and stood out. Sophie waited patiently at the registration table meeting point when Dorothy finally arrived, wearing a nicely tailored Ann Taylor pantsuit.

DOROTHY LIVINGSTON-COLEMAN, the wife of KeShawn and the proud mother of Jabari, Ania, and Xavier, boasts fluency in English, French, and Jamaican Patois (Creole). She was born and raised in Jamaica to bi-cultural parents. Her Jamaican father worked for years in Kingston at the Ministry of Finance and the Public Service in the Human Resource Management Division.

While her mother, a French citizen and educator, moved to Kingston as a young woman before her marriage. She taught the French language at a non-profit organization that promoted the

French language and the preparation for earning French diplomas and certificates. Dorothy's parents dissolved their marriage during her first year of high school, but they remained cordial. Before retiring, Dorothy, charming and gracious, worked full-time at the Beaches Resort in Ocho Rios in a staff management position. Management appreciated her tireless work ethic and valued her ability to maintain a professional persona while delivering quality customer service.

THE TWO SHARE an embrace and mutually admire their stunning outfits. Standing in line at the open bar were Xavier's Aunt Claudia and Gladys, and as Dorothy and Sophie walked over to join them, Dorothy laughed when she said to the ladies, "This line doesn't look like the registration table," and they all laughed.

While Dorothy scanned the crowded room for an empty table, she suggested the ladies take their drinks and move away from the congestion. The smell of food coming from the tray full of hors d'oeuvres became overbearing as a server approached the group and pointed out an unoccupied table near what appeared to be a coat closet. Grateful for the heads up, Dorothy told the girls, "Let's hurry. There's a table calling our name." Moving quickly, they asked the server to follow them and bring along the tempting tray of appetizers that probably wouldn't stay on the tray for very long.

Xavier, temporarily free from well-meaning attendees, meandered over to the table, followed by his three children. There, he found the ladies seated and engaged in conversation. He warmly embraced each of them, patted his heart, and thanked them for everything. Then he gave his Mom a big, emotional mother-son embrace. Dorothy then turned to the ladies and said, "This is my baby, and I am so happy for him; doesn't he look good tonight?" The women all giggled in approval.

The lights blinked several times, a tradition that signaled cocktail hour was ending. One by one, everyone at the table stood holding drinks in their hand and started the slow procession to find seats in the auditorium, as the Award Presentation would soon begin. Boasting a big grin, Xavier, holding his wife and mother's hands, said, "Let's find the rest of the clan so we can all sit together; we don't want to miss the show."

In the auditorium next to his family, Xavier's brother Jabari and sister Ania could be heard needling their nephews at the adjacent table. KeShawn smiled at them and said, "No matter how old you get, some things will never change."

The new inductees were introduced to warm applause and, one at a time, were called to the stage to receive their awards.

The event's MC, a well-known East Coast sports journalist for many years, said through the stage microphone, "Ladies and gentlemen, please put your hands together..." but before he could finish the sentence, the audience abruptly rose and began thunderous applause! "Help me welcome Xavier Coleman to the stage," the MC continued. Notwithstanding the cascading applause, a dapper-looking Xavier rose from his seat and approached the stage in a custom Giorgio Armani suit. Slowly, he lifted his size 16 genuine Robert August Alligator shoes on the four carpeted steps as the standing ovation continued. He was recognized, honored, and presented a custom-designed Class of 2010 Hall of Fame Ring. But more importantly, after removing his suit coat, Xavier extended his left arm to receive help putting on his hand-made, custom-fit, Naismith orange-wool (the color of a basketball) Hall of Fame Jacket, a jacket signifying his permanent place among the basketball elite. It was at this time the significance of the moment overwhelmed his thoughts. "Damn! This is real. I have the jacket, and I have witnesses," were a few words he murmured.

When returning to his seat to another rousing ovation, his father, KeShawn, stood to give him a handshake and an embrace. Still, when the picture of the father/son's embrace appeared on the overhead video screen, they received another resounding ovation. After a salute to acknowledge the crowd, the men placed a hand over their hearts before taking their seats beside an overjoyed family. Jabari, Xavier's older brother and the first child of the Jamaica Colemans to go to college on an athletic scholarship, was seated on the other side of his mom. Reaching over his mom, he gave his younger brother a fist bump and then asked if he could try on his new Hall of Fame ring. After visually examining the ring from all angles, Jabari casually slipped the ring on his right finger and, showing a sheepish grin, said to Xavier, "Is this mine?" Dorothy playfully slapped Jabari on the hand, took the ring off his finger, and returned it to Xavier. She proudly said, "This is yours to keep. You've earned this, son." Xavier smiled and kissed his mom; afterward, he playfully shoved Jabari.

The MC hurried back to the mic as the crowded Casino Ballroom started to empty and, in a booming voice, issued a reminder, "Tomorrow's induction ceremony is a ticketed and sold-out event. So if you have plans to attend, arrive early, and don't forget to bring your tickets." The Recognition Banquet was a colorful and fun-filled event, but the Enshrinement night was special. It was a night that inductees rightfully earned from their tireless dedication, sacrifices, and contributions to basketball, and the world would be watching.

While he walked proudly out of the casino with his wife and Mother on each side of him, Xavier recognized the waiting limo driver and summoned him to bring the cars around. After ensuring the limousine had its passengers in tow, Xavier sat across from his dad in the first limousine. Laughter and love resonated in the limo during the ride back to the hotel. Suddenly, the mood in the limo seemed to shift, and the passengers became eerily quiet. Captured in the moment, the Hall of Famer and his family were mesmerized by KeShawn's words.

The events of the evening and the slow ride back to the hotel allowed him to become introspective and reflective of days gone by when he spoke to the party. "I'm sure all those folks at the event were well-meaning and had good intentions. But I'm not sure they can appreciate the magnitude of our family's challenges, obstacles, moving parts, and long odds at each step along this flight. As he adjusted his glasses, KeShawn continued. "For this weekend's events to happen, the planets had to be perfectly aligned, and God's hands had to be all over this. Lastly, I'll say this: it would have probably blown their minds if they had any idea how this fascinating life's journey unfolded."

2

PAPA JAMES COLEMAN – THE MIGRATION NORTH

O*n January 1, 1863, during the American Civil War, President Abraham Lincoln issued the Emancipation Proclamation, officially known as Proclamation 95. This declaration decreed that 3.5 million African-Americans enslaved in rebel Confederate states would be free as of that date.*

BUT WHITE SOUTHERNERS, incensed by this amendment, were determined to maintain a stranglehold of dominance over Black families. They established the discriminatory "Jim Crow" and "Black Code" laws of oppression and segregation and used the Klu Klux Klan to invoke terror and intimidation tactics to enforce them.

Set amid several thousand acres of cotton fields along the twisting dusty road about a thirty-minute drive northeast of Mobile, off U.S. Highway 31, was the rural town of Cloverdale in Mobile County, Alabama. Void of street lights, signs, or arrows pointing you toward the Coleman house, avoiding this road at night was wise unless you lived in one of the sparse collections of wood frame structures along this dusty, dirt road. Just past a row of Sweetgum and Water Oak trees not far from Eightmile Creek, towards an open gate at the end of a dirt driveway, sat the home of Papa James and his wife, Essie Mae Coleman. Although the small two-bedroom wood frame house, built with help from a few neighbors, lacked indoor plumbing and electricity, the tin roof and wood-plank floors offered some reprieve from the extremes of summer and winter. Despite the lack of comfortable amenities, the cozy home was full of warmth and an abundance of love.

The Colemans lived here and worked as sharecroppers while raising three children, KeShawn, Freddie, and Althea. Despite the day-to-day challenges faced by the Colemans, they displayed, alongside their neighbors, a strong sense of resilience and solidarity. The family patriarch, Papa James Coleman, whose broad shoulders rested on his 6-foot-2-inch frame, while his hands bore scars and calluses that represented years of toil and labor. Papa James was strong-willed and calculated, yet generous, caring, and loving for his family.

A man of virtue and conviction, Papa James accepted life as it was, but he was unsatisfied. The present was acceptable, but only as a prelude to the change he felt was worth a lifetime of sacrifices. He knew in his heart there had to be a better way of living and believed his children deserved to have that opportunity.

Fueled by an unquenchable desire to improve his children's lives and prevent them from enduring a life of unfulfilled dreams, Papa James was willing to do whatever it took to change the family's fortune. He spent his entire childhood in rural Mississippi, where days of constant work, little pay, and endless nights of despair and hopelessness were the norm—a manner of life he was all too eager to shed.

Conservative in his thoughts but decisive in his actions, Papa James developed his strength of character and integrity through trial and tribulations while adhering to the principles taught to him by his parents. Those same principles of hard work, respect for family, and love of God were like a baton passed down from generation to generation. The principles served as valuable components as he developed skills to survive and make a life in rural Alabama.

Papa James was born and raised in Hattiesburg, Mississippi, in addition to seven brothers and four sisters, by God-loving parents, Big James and Alona Coleman, whose parents were also raised in Hattiesburg. Unfortunately, formal education was out of their reach during that time or unavailable to him and his family. As a result, most of the family's time was spent working in the fields as share-croppers.

The great-great-grandfather of Papa James, an African who was said to have been a tribal chief from the Yoruba region, was captured and sold as a bounty to slavers from America. Never knowing freedom after being brought to America, he was sold into slavery at auction in New Orleans and spent the remainder of his life enslaved alongside 16 other African men and women on the Burns Meaher's Plantation in central Alabama, where he labored, fathered children, and eventually died.

Like the majority of black families, the Colemans of Mississippi worked from sunup to sundown in the same never-ending rows of Mississippi cotton fields their enslaved ancestors worked before them. They toiled as contract laborers (sharecroppers) on rented farming land from white landowners. The money earned from their labor and crops was enough to pay the property owner's fees, and what little remained of their meager earnings supported a growing family. The Colemans knew this repetitive world all too well.

In these Mississippi cotton fields, working alongside his father and grandfather, a young Papa James acquired knowledge and learned valuable life skills, including work ethic, family, and Godly love. To navigate life on a farm to become resourceful and self-suffi-cient, Papa was taught tool making, splitting wood, building from scrap material, and caring for animals, but more critically, how to survive among white folks in the South.

Having only the bare necessities, the Coleman household used the fertile soil typical in the South, particularly in Mississippi, to grow a vegetable garden and enough crops to feed and raise a family. They had chickens for eggs, pigs for meat, and cows for milk. This was life in the rural South, where all you can do is the best you can do with what you have. Learning those invaluable lessons as a youngster in Mississippi was priceless for Papa James, but they served him well when he raised his family in Alabama.

Change was never easy and often came before you were ready, but on this moon-filled night, the kids slept in hand-made beds, tired and tuckered from another long day of school and fieldwork. The elder Coleman, Papa James, sat on his porch in deep contemplation, rocking back and forth in his favorite chair, occasionally rubbing his calloused and worn hands as he blew smoke from a clay tobacco pipe he fashioned a decade earlier.

Meanwhile, his wife of 20 years, Essie Mae, whom he met in Mississippi and married in Alabama, gently pushed her feet that barely touched the porch, to start the movement of the decade-old wooden porch swing — a swing that proudly hung as a reprieve from endless days of labor. While she swayed back and forth, only a few feet from the rocker, Essie Mae used the light from the moon to knit the never-ending holes in her children's socks.

The stillness of the night and the illumination from the full moon invited them to talk about yesterday and today and conjure thoughts about what a new tomorrow might bring. Papa, in a tone of sarcasm, said to his wife, "Essie, you know we have choices? We can stay put and try to make something of this life or do what others have done and migrate North."

Essie replied, "How this town looks upon Black folk just upsets me and makes me want to do something different. Why, just the other day, Maggie Littlefield told me that she heard that schools up North are better and jobs pay way more than what we make from renting these cotton and corn fields from Mr. Clauson." Essie then got quiet as her emotions became entangled among her thoughts. Essie continued after drying her eyes using a folded handkerchief that had dried many a tear. "James, no matter what you're thinking, just know that I love you, so whatever you think is best, well, I just want the kids to get a good education so they can have a better life and not have to work these fields all their days for peanuts."

The focus of Papa James and Essie, and any decisions they would make, was to benefit their three children, KeShawn, Freddie, who they sometimes called Junebug, and Althea, the youngest and the only girl. Even though her brothers rough-housed with her when they played, she was overly protected outside the confines of their home. Althea was Daddy's little girl, and he made sure the boys didn't get carried away in roughing her up during playtime. She was intelligent and had an innate ability to problem solve, but she could be a spitfire when the children were off playing, probably because she knew she had backup from her brothers.

When not in the fields or singing in the Baptist church choir, the children attended Mobile County Vocational Training School, located just north of Mobile on a hill by the Alabama River called Plateau Africatown, the first Black public high school in Mobile. The school emphasized reading and writing but needed more resources to go beyond the basics. The sports program also needed more resources. Using recycled, donated, and discarded equipment, the school offered a limited number of sports: basketball, baseball, and touch football. Freddie and Althea relished attending school and were adept at more subjects than their classmates. They even assisted the teacher to help other students who found the lessons challenging. KeShawn, on the other hand, when not busy being the best athlete in the school, liked to read and draw cartoon characters from images he found in newspapers that were thrown away. But he was also attracted to the school's vocational training, especially woodworking.

Between school, church, and work, the kids enjoyed playing with their friends from down the road and competed in anything and everything they could think of for fun. A few kids enjoyed fishing in Eightmile Creek using makeshift fishing poles, and worms captured the night before. KeShawn, who was similar in build to his father and was ultra-competitive, towered over most of the kids. He organized creative ways to engage his friends in all sorts of games where the outcome produced a winner. The games included foot races, jumping over saw horses, playing horseshoes, kicking the can, and shooting a hand-made basketball into a discarded bicycle rim mounted on a tree.

KeShawn didn't brag too much when he won, which was so often that everyone proclaimed him "The King." Despite giving the other kids a head start in foot races, he always won. Even Freddie, quick but shorter and stockier than his older brother, thus the name Junebug, couldn't take advantage of his head start. He always seemed to finish in an agonizing second place but vowed to one day beat "The King." Often, when the kids went their separate ways, tired of losing to The King, KeShawn could be seen shooting his makeshift basketball into the tree-mounted bicycle rim. He fantasized about becoming a star playing on a big-time court, as hundreds of fans called him "The King" in admiration. But for now, those fantasies that occupy his mind only serve to pass the time of day.

After many back-and-forth conversations that involved weighing information from newspapers and talking with their neighbors, and given the few remaining options in Alabama, Papa James and Essie Mae made a tough decision. To spare their family, especially the children, from decades more of degradation and despair, they chose to abandon the deplorable conditions of over-bearing discrimination and search for a new land. The Colemans desired a place more receptive to Black families: a place where dreams can become a reality instead of being squashed like bugs on a windshield. So, as his heart wavered, torn between choices, Papa's mind remained steadfast. He decided it was time to leave Alabama and migrate North to Chicago.

In preparation for the journey, Papa James, intent on building his much-needed travel nest egg, reached out to his neighbors and offered to sell his livestock, which consisted of pigs, chickens, and three milk-producing cows. The trepidation Papa felt after selling his trusted pickup truck for pennies on the dollar was enough to make him scream.

Deep down, Papa knew his neighbors knew of his plan to leave his farm. He figured that time was running short, and contrary to his vehement objections, the neighbors took full advantage of the situation and held firm on their low-ball offers. Caught between a rock and a hard place, Papa reluctantly accepted the low-ball offers. But at least he could relish some comfort knowing he unloaded his stock and returned home holding cash instead of empty promises.

While the children were outside, Papa sat at the kitchen table across from Essie Mae. He shook his head in disgust and lamented that he had not received nearly as much value for his property as he thought he should have. But what was done was done. The wooden table creaked as Papa tossed the wrinkled paper bag of money stuffed with equally wrinkled dollar bills and coins. The weight of the coins tore through the bag and fell to the floor. Papa quickly scooped up the runaway coins and handed the accumulated money to Essie Mae for recounting. Essie could only laugh when she said to Papa, "Look at these wrinkled dollars. Those folks must have had that money balled up for years." Then she added, "That's a shame. Maybe they will straighten out if I put something heavy on them." Papa just shook his head before saying, "Wrinkles and all this is all the money we have to our name. So let's be sure we find a good hiding place in the car when we're ready to leave."

Despite her displeasure in having to unfold the wrinkled dollar, Essie re-counted the money while Papa continued his conversation. "You know, if we're ever stopped along the way, you can count on being searched, and if they find the money, well, just like that, the money would be good as gone." He handed Essie an old sock and said, "Stuff the money in this, and we'll find a good hiding place in the car."

KeShawn, the oldest of the three children by a year, opened his mouth in surprise. In his haste to help Junebug fit his necktie neatly under his shirt collar when he unintentionally dirtied the back of Junebug's white shirt. Meanwhile, Althea, two years younger than KeShawn but tall for her age, displayed emotional maturity and mannerisms similar to her Mother's. Still, she enjoyed playing and teasing her brothers, especially KeShawn.

While the children waited in the front yard, Althea, who was told not to dirty her dress and white socks, sang and danced alongside her brothers as the longest trip of their young lives was only minutes away. While they waited for further instructions, the boys began playing a game to see who could throw something the farthest. The impromptu game was right up KeShawn's alley. He and Freddie threw rocks, pieces of wood, acorns, and whatever else they could find. And the winner was?

Papa insisted that no matter how uncomfortable they felt wearing their church clothes, traveling in their Sunday best had advantages. He reminded them that an appearance that reflected a lovely, law-abiding family going on vacation would discourage being mistaken for vagabond travelers, perhaps up to no good.

Before his mother came outside, KeShawn tried his best to remove the unintended dirt stains from Junebug's shirt despite the lack of soap and water. But his experiment failed, as the smeared collar looked worse than before. After he walked away shaking his head, KeShawn turned his attention to cleaning the car's windshield. The idea of putting water on a rag to wipe the dirt from his brother's shirt collar quickly faded when he thought he might get dirt and mud on his pants and shirt.

KeShawn, meanwhile, paid extra attention to cleaning the front windshield before he suddenly tossed the cleaning rag into the bucket of water and decided that now would be a good time to hop into the front seat to secure his place as the co-pilot. Knowing KeShawn's motives, Papa said, "Not so fast, son. Have you checked the tires? What about the luggage in the trunk? Are we all set?"

Frustrated that his plan received a setback, KeShawn reluctantly exited the car but left the front passenger door partially open for a quick return. He walked around the car and kicked each tire. He then tried closing the trunk, but there was a slight problem. The trunk wouldn't close all the way. So KeShawn replied to Papa, "I think the tires look good, but the luggage, well, I, um, the trunk won't close."

Though all the belongings from a family of five were stuffed into four suitcases, KeShawn assumed that when he piled the bulging suitcases in the trunk to secure their possessions, the trunk would close easily. But his method for arranging the luggage left much to be desired. "Papa, we got a problem, he said." Turning with a furrowed brow, Papa noticed the luggage bungled in the trunk in no particular order. He looked at KeShawn and shook his head, telling his oldest son, as he pushed his glasses up off his nose, "Son, watch and learn." Papa removed all the luggage from the mid-size trunk and rearranged the pieces individually. He put the most oversized luggage on the bottom and smaller luggage on the top. He then filled in the open spaces using smaller items. The new luggage arrangement miraculously allowed the trunk to close and latch easily, free from blocking the rear window. This brought relief and a smile to KeShawn's face as he replied, "Thanks, Papa. You made it look so simple."

The trip was expected to be long and bumpy, so Papa added another layer of security to the trunk as an extra precaution. The last thing he wanted to happen was for the trunk to come open unexpectedly, which could expose the family to unwanted scrutiny. Papa used hemp rope and string from a croaker sack to secure the trunk.

Growing increasingly anxious to leave, the family milled around the car in anticipation of leaving but kept their eyes on Papa's every move. After he helped KeShawn resolve the luggage/trunk issue, Papa strolled back to the house, where he paused in deep thought. He looked at a voiceless house amid reflections on the life his parents endured and how they raised him and his brothers and sisters in Mississippi. Now he stood, minutes away from moving on from a way of life that had remained a Coleman staple for generations. He was entrusted with protecting his family's lives and their future as they embarked on an uncertain journey of a lifetime. Such was the circle of life, and Papa walked off the porch for the last time.

KeShawn, always in perpetual competition with his younger brother, moved nervously away from the family and towards the car, anticipating that Freddie, who was also inching closer to the car, would try and claim the coveted front seat. KeShawn couldn't afford to lose his desired front seat. Fearing his strategic plan was in jeopardy, KeShawn pushed his brother aside and jumped into the front passenger seat of Papa's pride and joy, the black four-door Plymouth Sedan.

This was the car the boys washed every other day, rain or shine, driven or not. The Plymouth was the primary vehicle for driving to church and special occasions, so Papa assigned the boys the chore of keeping the car clean and shiny at all times. They didn't seem to mind this task because it allowed them to drive the car around the house before and after each washing. As KeShawn rolled up the front window, he locked the door and sighed in relief as he finally secured his place for the long journey. But in an attention-grabbing tone, Papa James ordered KeShawn out of the car and joined hands in a family tradition of prayer.

Freddie giggled as he playfully bumped KeShawn as he disembarked the vehicle with his lip out and head down. "The King" may have been down but was never counted out. So, just before the prayer concluded, the competitive KeShawn hopped back into the front seat and laughed at Freddie before saying to him, Amen.

Mama Coleman's purse hung loosely over her shoulder as she walked towards the car, and in one move, she shoved the hand-basket of freshly cooked fried chicken and biscuits to the backseat floor, hoping the food would last throughout the trip. The jugs of water were put up front between the feet of the big kid, who sat smiling in the front passenger seat. Under the backseat, wrapped in a badly worn sock and triple-tied using string, Papa strategically hid all the money they had to their name. Mama Coleman clutched her Bible as she sat in the backseat behind her husband and prayed aloud for a safe journey and a better life of hope and opportunity.

Like many Black families who preceded them, the Colemans were part of a movement of Black families who refused to continue working as plantation sharecroppers and chose to migrate North, out of the deep South. Chicago, Illinois, was their destination.

Part of a tradition for Southern families was relying on and sharing information from the migration network, news from Black newspapers, and from relatives who had gone North seeking better opportunities. The influential Chicago Defender was one such newspaper that regularly advertised industrial and railway job opportunities in Chicago. News articles painted an appealing picture of life in Chicago, one that was far removed from the consciousness of Black Southerners who only knew of one type of life. "Good paying jobs in the big city, Chicago needs you," headlined the advertisement.

The industrial North used those paid ads as an inducement to help fill the void of the city's labor shortage, and migrants were the target. The article said, "Because of Chicago's industrial economy, the city is a preferred destination for Black Migrants, offering job opportunities in factories and railroads." The constant bombardment of news offering lifestyle changes fueled the fire of opportunity, so the Colemans, having the mindset of "any place but here," were sold and wanted a piece of that opportunity.

Papa James shrugged his coat over his massive shoulders, and as the coat jacket draped him, he brushed dirt from the jacket lapel and utilized the side view mirror to ensure his necktie was straight. The last piece of his meticulous ritual occurred when Papa used Essie's hand-sewn handkerchief, given to him on his last birthday, to dab the beading sweat from his forehead before he put on his hat. Lastly, Papa backed into his car seat and gracefully slid his long legs underneath the steering column. After adjusting the side view and inside rearview mirrors, he adjusted his seat for maximum comfort. The weight of his foot was pressed on the gas pedal, and Papa surprised everyone when the car moved in reverse. Papa circled the house backward and told the family, "Take one last look because I'm never going backward again." KeShawn and Freddie, their eyes filled with tears, sniffled as they rolled down their windows and allowed the family one last look to wave goodbye to the only place they called home.

Turning left from the house, the car found the familiar one-lane dusty road that took them to church every Sunday, where they would join a congregation that worshiped, sang, and prayed for a better life. The wheels of the four-door Plymouth began rolling faster than they should, causing dust from the road to billow and resemble a brown cloud, forever blocking the rear views of yesterday's life.

Papa was mesmerized in thought, and his eyes were fixated on the road. He ignored requests from the backseat to look at the endless rows of cotton fields and watermelon patches because doing so would only stoke memories of tireless, under-compensated labor.

Looming large just beyond the bend where the children often played were towering Magnolia trees whose roots clutched deep into the earth while their branches stood as silent spectators to centuries of pain and suffering. The Magnolias also shaded the two-lane concrete road Papa anxiously wanted to find, a road that would lead him to the highway of a new beginning.

Using a single click of his index finger, Papa James engaged the left turn signal as the family laughed and giggled. They were northbound on U.S. Highway Route 31, heading out of Alabama, when abruptly and without warning, Papa startled the family when he pulled the car off to the side of the road and came to a sudden stop. Confused, their mouths were open wide, but no sound came out. Mama Coleman fanned furiously and, not wanting to sound fearful, said to her husband, "James, is there something wrong?" The family sat in momentary suspense, wondering why the sudden stop. Papa explained, "I recognize the pick-up truck that's been tailing us." Looking from the backseat window, Essie Mae asked, "Isn't that our old truck you sold to Clyde Littlefield?" Papa replied, "Yes, It looks like Clyde and the children. I wonder what's going on?" Clyde's pick-up truck pulled up to a stop behind the

Coleman's. Clyde's children hopped out of their truck and ran towards Papa's Plymouth, smiling and excitedly. While Clyde explained to Papa why they were following him, his kids laughed and giggled along with KeShawn, Freddie, and Althea, who stood outside their car, equally excited to see their friends.

"The kids were pestering me all day to stop by your house so they could say goodbye, but you had already gone." As he laughed, Clyde continued, "We saw this cloud of dust on the road, so I figured it had to be you. So I put the pedal to the metal, and your old truck did the rest." Clyde added, "I told the kids I had to catch up to you before you got going on the 31." After conversing, Papa and Essie Mae hugged Clyde and his children and thanked them for their friendship. Papa then instructed his kids to get back in the car. Calmness restored, Clyde told Papa, "James, you all be real careful on the highway; you've heard the stories." Papa replied, "Yeah, we intend to mind our business and stay alert." Essie told Clyde, "Tell Maggie I will write to her when we settle." Those were the last words spoken as the two Cloverdale friends went their separate ways. One returned to life as a sharecropper, and the other was intent on following his dreams to pursue a better life in Chicago.

After waving goodbye to their friends, Papa told KeShawn, "Before we get going again, use water from the jug and wet this here rag and clean the dust and dirt from the front and back windows." KeShawn, his chest out, felt good about this vital assignment he had been entrusted with. He quickly wet the rag and expeditiously completed his assignment. The smile on his lips spoke the unspoken as he returned to his co-pilot position, but not before poking his tongue out in fun at Althea and Freddie.

Again, Papa adjusted the car's mirrors, then approvingly tapped KeShawn on the knee for a job well done cleaning the windows. Through the rearview mirror, Papa gazed and winked at his adoring family. He once again pushed his glasses off his nose, twitched his hips, and thus began the Coleman migration in search of a new land.

The speed limit would serve Papa as a reminder to avoid drawing attention or triggering self-inflicted problems that could harm the family. The flight of a thousand songbirds commenced on the 917-mile, 20-hour perilous journey north to Chicago, and having no regrets, the Colemans never looked back.

Although he felt confident and determined to fulfill his promise of getting his family safely to Chicago, Papa intended to drive using vigilance and awareness. He was keenly mindful and was reminded by Clyde of the potential dangers that lurked along every twist and turn the highway took, for it was not uncommon in Alabama or anywhere in the South for state troopers or Klan sympathizers to harass unsuspecting Black families.

The plan was to follow U.S. Route 31, which would take them through the Alabama cities of Montgomery, Birmingham, Decatur, Athens, and Lewisburg and on into Nashville, Tennessee. The route would then take them into Louisville, Kentucky, then through Indianapolis, Indiana, before reaching Chicago, Illinois.

Each state was just as notorious for discrimination as Alabama, so bathroom and stretching breaks were kept to an absolute minimum. There were no overnight stays in Motel 6s or stops to visit historical sites. Papa's family was on a mission, not a vacation.

Serving as the co-pilot, KeShawn took his role seriously. He was the extra eyes and ears for Papa, so he couldn't afford the luxury of dozing off into a dream world like those in the back seat. Outside of the occasional snoring, the trip was smooth and issues-free. KeShawn, who had previewed the map with his mom before leaving, was made aware of crucial landmarks and road signs he needed to recognize. Suddenly and unexpectedly, in a voice filled with excitement rather than terror, KeShawn startled the sleeping family when he blurted out, "We are only 15 miles from Athens, and Athens is only 13 miles from the state line of Tennessee." KeShawn's alarm woke his mother from her dose, and she asked him, "Boy, what's wrong? You know better than to belt out like that." A wide-awake Mama Coleman then opened the road map and held it closer to the window to get a better view of the miles they've traveled. She replied, "Wow, I can't believe we've traveled over 350 miles since leaving home, I mean, since leaving Cloverdale," everybody in the car laughed.

After five hours of driving and only one restroom stop, Papa felt good about not having any mechanical mishaps or unwarranted encounters. After he adjusted his slumping posture and cleared his throat as if to speak, he took a cursory glance out of the side view mirror, followed by a more prolonged look. He noticed a State Highway Patrol Car about 50 yards behind him heading south, quickly made a U-turn, crossed the median, and began to follow him.

At first, the patrol car kept a distance, so Papa wasn't too concerned, but when it sped up too close – within one car length away, Papa thought he probably wanted to find out who the passengers were riding in the shiny black four-door Plymouth.

Demonstrating great restraint, Papa chose not to overreact to the trailing Patrol Car. Still, as the cat-and-mouse game continued, Papa took another peak out of the rearview mirror and wondered aloud about the motives of the Trooper, not sure if the black sedan or the Black occupants were the target. Papa instructed everyone to remain calm, stay quiet, and make no sudden moves. He didn't want any movements in the car to be misinterpreted. There have been numerous stories of Black families traveling in Alabama and meeting cruel fates for no apparent reason.

Papa's heart pounded as his adrenaline surged, and a lump in his throat formed. He quickly glanced at the speedometer, mindful that one mile over the limit would authorize the Trooper to turn on his blue and red lights and, much to his delight, pull him over for questioning or, more likely, harassment. And if Papa were stopped, many misfortunes could befall their dreams.

Althea sat nervously and scared. She leaned over and put her head on her mother's shoulder for comfort. This didn't bother Mama Coleman, who quietly whispered the Lord's prayer. KeShawn, operating as the co-pilot, struggled to keep his composure. His chest became tight as a drum, and he struggled to breathe normally. Despite Papa's encouragement, KeShawn was frightened and afraid to look back at the patrol car. So he sat petrified and stared out the front windshield. The fear of drawing attention terrified him as his right hand, which was locked on the door handle, lost color from his intense grip. In the back seat, Freddie, uptight and emotional, stopped eating and hurriedly stuffed his half-eaten piece of chicken, a meal he had relished since leaving Montgomery County two hours ago, back into the food basket.

Papa struggled to quiet his mind, which meandered like a winding road. He tried to determine what would provoke the Patrol Officer to pull them over. Papa thought about the rope used to tie the trunk down. Maybe the rope came untied and posed a danger, or the tires appeared under-inflated. Perhaps the hub cap had fallen off. But more importantly, he thought, why did the patrol car suddenly decide to make a U-turn as soon as we drove by?

After 350 miles and six hours of driving, the Colemans' journey north for better opportunities faced their first confrontational crisis. Papa quietly asked KeShawn, "Son, could you read the blurry road sign we just passed?" Still in a suspended state of fear, KeShawn replied, but in a mumbled tone that was barely audible. So Papa had to ask him to repeat what he said. KeShawn then cleared his throat and quietly repeated his message. "I think the sign said Ardmore, one mile ahead." Hearing that information gave Papa a slight reprieve; he again attempted to calm his mind. Papa finally unloosened his death grip from the steering wheel and deeply exhaled. He knew from reading the map during their only rest stop hours ago that Ardmore, Alabama, was the last town in Alabama before reaching the Tennessee state line. Nevertheless, the patrol car remained on his tail. Ardmore seemed like a thousand miles away.

The family felt trapped as the self-induced tension from the trailing patrol car continued to boil. They desperately needed more air to breathe, but rolling down the window to get relief was not an option. They were frozen and caught in a vacuum of fear.

Papa had experienced several testy situations during his lifetime, so he knew that as the head of the household and emotional leader, he had to remain calm in the face of adversity. He removed his tie and unbuttoned his shirt collar to regain his composure and control what he could. He called on all his experiences and mental tenacity to stay in the moment and weather this unusual storm.

Papa took a quick peek out of his sideview mirror and noticed flashing bright blue and red lights from the trailing Highway Patrol Car. Fearing his worst nightmare, Papa uncharacteristically blurted out, "Oh, shit," as he slowed the car in preparation to pull to the side. Shockingly, the patrol car, its lights still flashing and siren blaring, raced past the traumatized Colemans and made a U-turn at the highway median 25 yards ahead of them. As the patrol car slowly headed back southbound on U.S. Route 31, the Officer slowed his patrol car, rolled down his window, looked over at Papa, and offered a grimacing look before speeding away from the northbound, frightened family. His head momentarily buried in the steering wheel in relief, Papa pulled the car over, got out, and, leaning over, placed his hands on his knees and voiced, "Thank the Lord." He said to KeShawn, "Look on the map and find me the nearest rest stop in Tennessee."

3

ARRIVAL IN CHICAGO

Having endured the arduous thirty-hour drive from their sharecropper farm in rural Cloverdale, Alabama, crossing four state lines, the Colemans, mentally exhausted and physically tired, finally arrived in the big city they'd heard so much about, Chicago.

Although they'd arrived in the city that held the key to their dreams, the Colemans couldn't appreciate the magnitude of their journey because they felt overwhelmed by its size. Chicago looked nothing like the rural farming community they came from. The Colemans were speechless and wide-eyed as they gawked at the city landscape. But the joy of arriving in Chicago, with the Highway Patrol Car issue behind them, superseded their exhaustion and any apprehensions they felt.

At the first opportunity, Papa pulled the car over and asked the family to join hands and pray for their travel blessings and the promise of a brighter tomorrow.

Having left the arduous travel behind, Papa and his family had to shift their priorities. They needed to reach out to the one person they knew, find a place to unload the contents from the bulging trunk, decompress, and unwind their minds. Finding a place to live would come soon enough. But for now, contacting their cousin, who they haven't seen in two or three years, was the most urgent piece in their journey. Making a successful contact would be the catalyst to jump-start all their other plans.

Back in the car, Papa drove slowly along a street he knew nothing about; he asked KeShawn to look for a telephone booth. Unaware of his exact location, Papa clung to the only certainty that he was in Chicago, not Alabama. Chicago was a city so big that it could swallow you up and spit you out, and nobody would know. At the stop light, KeShawn pointed to what looked like a drugstore, and as luck would have it, there standing as a guard was a tall, red phone booth just a few feet from the drugstore entrance. Papa turned the corner and found a nearby parking space. He was only minutes away from making the most important phone call he had ever made.

After parking the car, Papa got out, took off his suit coat, folded it over his arm, and stretched his legs. He then barked some instructions when he said, "Alright, everybody, out of the car and stretch your legs. Essie, check and see if there's a bathroom inside they could use, and if not, find out where there might be one."

Papa made his way to the phone booth, where he pushed open the folding door and retrieved a crumpled piece of paper from inside his coat pocket, which had managed to survive the sweat from the drama on the Alabama highway. Scribbled on the paper in what seemed like a lifetime ago was a barely readable number that Papa had to squint to read. KeShawn stood outside the phone booth as Papa attempted the phone call using the dime Essie had given him. True to form, the dime fell innocently into the slot but mysteriously returned to the bottom of the tray without an explanation. Thinking about how far he had traveled and what his family had been through, Papa was undeterred and not about to let the reluctant dime discourage him. So, on a second attempt, the dime cooperated, and a dial tone was detected.

The voice on the other end of the SOS phone call sounded like a blessing from above. It was cousin Nate, the oldest son of Papa

James' Uncle from Mississippi. Nate migrated to Chicago not too long ago and was said to live in a high-rise apartment complex on the South Side.

After a massive sigh of relief, Papa finally felt reassured as he greeted his cousin. In desperate need of directions in this foreign city, Papa opened the phone booth door and asked KeShawn to recite the names on the street signs. Papa then described the streets where he was parked and the surrounding buildings to Cousin Nate. He then asked Nate for directions to his home. But after getting the street coordinates, Nate said to Papa, "Okay, James, I know where you are. No worries. But it would be easier if I came to you, so stay where you are. You'll be safe." Then Nate abruptly hung up the phone.

Papa left the phone booth, patted KeShawn on the back, and exhaled deeply before saying to his son, "Nate will be here soon." Freddie and Althea, too excited to wait any longer, ran up to Papa to find out what their cousin had to say on the phone. "Did you talk to cousin Nate? What did he say?" They all shouted. Papa gathered everyone together and shared the news. He explained, "I talked with cousin Nate; he's coming and will be here shortly. He said, "Stay put and don't leave this corner." But what did he mean by we'll be safe? A question Papa silently wondered.

What the Colemans didn't know about Chicago but quickly found out was that Chicago was not prepared to embrace the thousands of newly arriving Black migrants. This number was fueled by several factors, including factories' hunger for labor, a willingness to hire Black workers, and deplorable conditions in the South. In a decade, the migration saw Chicago's Black population grow from 200,000 to more than 800,000.

THE INFLUX of Black families was overwhelming to what had been a predominantly white city, and reacting out of fear, government agencies, businesses, and newly populated white suburban commu-

nities responded negatively to the Great Migration by establishing and reinforcing restrictive covenants and discriminatory housing ordinances to support residential segregation.

Those restrictive housing measures, using formal and informal tactics, created a residential color line that funneled newly arriving Black families into an already crowded segregated community on Chicago's South Side known as the "Black Belt" and set the stage for segregation in Chicago Public Schools—giving rise to a residential ghetto infested with poor living conditions, limited educational opportunities, violence, discrimination, and indifference from city politicians. There was, however, emerging within the Black City within a city, Bronzeville, known as the "Black Metropolis," that would eventually produce successful businesses, entrepreneurship, athletes, and cultural creativity in music, art, and literature.

SUDDENLY, a bright, shiny red two-door DeSoto pulled around the corner. Cousin Nate leaned out of his car window and hollered," Cousin James, hey." Nate took up two spaces when he hurriedly parked his car. As Nate approached his cousin, he took one last puff of a half-smoked cigarette and stomped it onto the sidewalk. Looking tired and wrinkled, the Coleman clan stood outside their car and stared at their cousin as he approached. The Coleman children were overly excited to see their cousin because he was the only person they knew in this strange city they would come to call home. Plus, they understood Nate was the conduit for their settlement in Chicago.

Nate gave Papa a warm embrace and a firm handshake as a huge grin revealed a dangling toothpick and a gold front tooth. Afterward, Nate patted Papa on the back and shouted, "Good to see y'all, cousins; welcome to Chicago. I bet all of you are tired and probably starving."

Tired and mentally exhausted from all the driving, Papa could only smile at Nate's assessment. As he returned the back slap, he said to his cousin, "I guess you would know. That drive up from Alabama was something else, but here we are," and chuckled. Nate then laughed as he turned, hugged Essie, and told her how good she looked.

Then, he looked up at KeShawn in disbelief at how much he had grown and how he resembled his father. Turning to Althea, Nate said, "You are just so cute. You know James, these boys will come calling, so you better be ready." Then he asked, "Is this Freddie? Look at you, boy. My goodness, how time flies. You all have grown so much since I last saw you; I barely recognize you." After greeting and sharing hugs, Nate said to Papa, "James, follow me; I'll lead the way to my place."

KeShawn asked permission to ride in Nate's care back to his apartment. Papa looked at Nate, then gave KeShawn the nod. Looking back at his family out the rear window of Nate's red DeSoto, KeShawn smiled and waved while Nate drove through an area populated by people who looked like him.

Not too far removed from life as a sharecropper, Nate had first-hand knowledge about how life in the rural south could limit your views of the world and be a barrier to new ideas and thoughts.

Offering a smile and a controlled laugh, Nate said to KeShawn, "This is Chicago! Have you ever seen so many buildings like this before?" He pointed and described the enormous complex of high and mid-rise apartment buildings and the multitude of single-family row houses. Then Nate switched to a half-serious tone and said to his wide-eyed cousin, "This is home to many of us in Chicago, and I suspect this will be y'all's home as well, but don't worry, y'all get used to seeing all these buildings."

Turning into one of several open parking spaces near the all-brick high-rise building, Nate pointed and motioned like directing traffic for his cousin to park next to him. KeShawn, full of excitement and oblivious to how tired he was, hurried over to unload the luggage from the trunk. Meanwhile, Papa paused to excavate his hidden stash of money from under the back seat. The Colemans then took the "magical" elevator ride to Nate's fifth-floor two-bedroom apartment.

When the Colemans entered unit 508, they were warmly greeted by Nate's wife, Lois, a charming woman who worked as a clerical assistant at the Chicago Housing Authority before giving birth to her children. Lois was in the middle of tidying up the living area when the out-of-town guest arrived. Her three kids, ranging in age from high school to the youngest, who couldn't be more than a toddler, sat on the couch and stared at the newly arriving relatives.

"You have to excuse the place," Nate said, picking up a few toys from the floor before asking his cousin to talk outside in the hallway.

Nate apologetically explained how they could make the crowded apartment conditions work out for a few days. But Papa would have none of that. He was grateful that Nate welcomed his family and could help them until they got situated. Nate told Papa, " Why don't y'all wash up and rest a bit? Then we'll get something to eat. Tomorrow, I'll take you to meet the gal I know who works at the Chicago Housing Authority (CHA) office." Nate continued, "She's a real nice person, and I'm sure she'll be able to help, especially since a couple of vacancies just came open in the row houses next to these apartments."

There were no immediate plans except to unwind as Papa observed the crowded room with a shrug. Turning, he said to his wife, "Don't worry honey, we'll find a place. These cramped conditions are only temporary." However, while holding onto the thought that tomorrow would be the start of a new beginning, what crossed his mind again and gave him a sense of peace was that his family was no longer in Alabama. So, sleeping in cramped conditions for a few days may be uncomfortable, but it was the path they had chosen. Plus, sleeping in cramped conditions was not new to Papa, nor was it the end of the world. Tomorrow's CHA meeting would come soon enough, but in the meantime, Papa helped his family get as comfortable as possible in an uncomfortable situation.

The following day, Essie and Althea, still a little tired from the trip and the cramped sleeping arrangements, helped Lois make breakfast and tend to the young kids. They decided to wait in the apartment while Nate, Papa, KeShawn, and Freddie traveled to the CHA office.

During the drive to the CHA office, Nate engaged in a "matter-of-fact" conversation with his cousins as he explained the realities of life for Black folks in Chicago. He drove slowly so his cousins could see the vast number of Black people walking, standing, and driving along the south side streets. Nate began to share his experiences since moving to Chicago.

"To my recollection," Nate began. "The South was whites over there, and Blacks over here, and everybody knew their places." He continued his viewpoint. "White folks told you in no uncertain terms how things were and who was in charge." Nate said, "We understood the color line and the consequences if you crossed that line. I thought things would be so much different when I got to Chicago. I thought our people would find jobs, get kids into good schools, maybe even buy a house, and be treated more respectfully." By the rise in his tone, it was obvious that Nate was agitated.

He went on, "Let me tell y'all something. White folk here in Chicago have an invisible line that keeps you in your place, and our place is right here in these streets I'm driving on. Most Black folk can't shop, buy a house, or go to schools across this invisible line." KeShawn interrupted his cousin and asked, "How do you know if you've crossed the line if you can't see the line?" Nate could only laugh before he answered half-heartedly and said to KeShawn, "Don't worry, cousin, white folk will quickly remind you where your place is." Papa then asked, "What about all the jobs? Is it true what the newspapers said? That the city has a lot of jobs for us?" Nate, his head cocked, looked out of one eye and said to James, "Sure, there are jobs, and then there are jobs." He explained, "Some of these slaughterhouse jobs are so dangerous that many folk don't wanna work there no mo. And the other factory jobs work you all day, just like in the fields." Nate continued, and then there are the railroad and bus jobs; they ain't so bad, depends."

After they reached the Chicago Housing Authority office, designed to aid Black migrants seeking relocation assistance, Nate introduced cousin James to the CHA office manager he had spoken about. A person with a good sense of humor, a sharp wit, and an ability to respond quickly in awkward situations. She has worked as the CHA office manager since moving to Chicago from Kokomo, Indiana, five years ago. Besides her vast knowledge of available housing authority units across the complexes, she knew every tenant by name. "James, this here is Ms. Hagen. Ms. Hagen, this here is my cousin, James."

Papa, no stranger to filling out applications, carefully followed Ms. Hagen's instructions and completed the housing assistance application. While he anxiously awaited for Ms. Hagen to return, Papa talked to his sons about Nate's conversation on the way over. He reminded them why they moved to Chicago when he said, "We're new here and starting a new life. We didn't come all this way to start trouble with folks. I don't want you getting involved in anything that will bring shame to our family, and from what Nate has told us, if you run afoul of the law, you will be in big trouble, and I might not be able to help you." As the boys listened intently, Papa continued, "So, I want you to promise me you will keep your nose clean and avoid trouble. And when you get to school, you will do your best to make the most out of your schooling. A good education can take you a long way." Papa James could sense the door of opportunities finally opening for his family. So he continued, "Another thing. Look out for one another. Some of these kids will try and take advantage of you because you are new." Papa finished his message by asking one question. "Did I make myself clear?" One by one, the boys replied, "Yes, sir."

Papa could see Ms. Hagen emerging from an office carrying his application in her hand. Ms. Hagen motioned for him to join her in the office, where he would meet the head CHA administrator. Papa sat and listened as the administrator explained housing regulations, tenant rights, responsibilities, expectations, and the terms and conditions for maintaining the lease in complete agreement and an understanding of his responsibilities. The deal was sealed when Papa shook the administrator's hand and followed Ms. Hagen out of the room.

After the approved rental agreement paperwork was processed, Papa was given the keys to a three-bedroom row house on the South Side in the Ida B. Wells Public Housing Project, where most migrant families settled.

IDA B. WELLS, a civil rights advocate, educator, investigative journalist, and news editor with the Memphis Free Speech and Headlight newspaper, was born into slavery in Mississippi. She gained her freedom when Proclamation 95 was enacted in 1863. After graduating from Shaw College and Fisk University, she taught school and became the first female co-owner and editor of a Black newspaper in the United States. She was one of the founders of the National Association for the Advancement of Colored People (NAACP).

Ida B. Wells was honored with an extraordinary citation by the Pulitzer Prize Board for her outstanding and courageous reporting on the horrific violence perpetrated against African Americans during the era of lynching. The citation came with an honorarium of $50,000 supporting her mission.

Numerous awards honor her legacy, including The Ida B. Wells Award, presented by The National Association of Black Journalists and Northwestern University; the Ida B. Wells Award for Diligence and Achievement, presented by the University of Louisville; and the Ida B. Wells Award for African-American or Black American Attorneys.

Ida B. Wells dedicated her career to fighting for African-American equal rights and against racial prejudice, violence, and injustice, especially faced by women.

AFTER PAYING the required rent and deposit fees, Papa's Alabama nest egg was nearly depleted, which made finding a job to provide for his family imperative. However, there was relief; they had a place they could call home and would no longer be regulated to sleep on blanket palettes or wait half the morning to take a bath.

The unfamiliarity of the city left Papa at a disadvantage, but finding work was critical, so he asked cousin Nate if he had time to assist him in finding work. Much more in tune with the Chicago landscape than his cousin, Nate took advantage of his remaining time off from work and eagerly agreed to help his cousin find work. Nate insisted that Papa leave his car at home and allow him to be the shuttle driver. Nate told his cousin, "I have a better idea of where the jobs might be and know how to get there. So come on, cousin, let me do this for you." Papa replied, "That's a fact, so I won't argue with you. Thanks, Nate."

The arrangement couldn't have worked out better. While they drove around the city searching for job opportunities, Nate and Papa reminisced. They talked about relatives still in the South, the Chicago school system, and Black life in Chicago.

After three days of submitting applications and getting rejections, Papa finally found employment. Due to a sudden afternoon shift turnover, the Chicago Transit Authority (CTA) was looking to fill multiple positions. Word on the street was that the CTA fired a group of employees for insubordination and excessive absences. Papa's application was accepted, and he was hired to work the afternoon shift as a machine mechanic. The job's wages were far beyond what he earned as a sharecropper in Alabama. Papa was thrilled and anxious to earn a living to provide for his family. But the machinist position was short-lived.

Two months into his new job and growing comfortable as each day passed, the Transit supervisor notified the workers under his supervision that the company was making a change. There was an urgent need for reliable bus drivers for routes on the South Side. When Papa was first told there would be position changes, he prayed that he would not be released. Because he was one of the last to get hired, he thought he might be among the first to get fired. However, as it turned out, the supervisor was highly impressed by Papa's work ethic and ability to quickly process information related to operating the complex rail machinery.

After working and learning the nuances of the machine mechanics position, Papa and three other new hires were told by the shift supervisor that next week, he would be transferred out and trained as a bus driver. He would be assigned to shadow a seasoned driver on one of the bigger, Fixable Twin Coach Transit Buses, whose routes were exclusively on Chicago's South Side. The pay rate, however, was essentially the same as the mechanics' pay. So, Papa had no complaints and happily accepted the transfer without reservation. He felt fortunate to be in a position to earn a decent living that would allow him to provide for his family and not have to restart the methodical job search process again.

Meanwhile, Mama Coleman, determined to find a school for her children, got a recommendation from Nate's oldest daughter, Courtney, a sophomore at DuSable High School. As a member of the school's Cheerleaders squad, Courtney spoke glowingly about the teachers and the school's prominent athletic teams. Outside any other school comparisons or favorable recommendations, Essie Mae Coleman enrolled KeShawn, Freddie, and Althea as transfer students in the Bronzeville neighborhood high school, conveniently located only three miles from their housing complex.

4

DUSABLE HIGH SCHOOL

uSable High School, located in the heart of Bronzeville, is named after Jean Baptiste Point du Sable, an African-Haitian explorer born in 1750. He is regarded as the first non-indigenous permanent settler of what later became Chicago, Illinois, and is recognized as the "Founder of Chicago." DuSable was a wealthy man who was married to a Potawatomi Indian named Kittihawa (Catherine) before he died in 1818.

THE DUSABLE HIGH SCHOOL PANTHERS, located in the Bronzeville neighborhood on Chicago's South Side, is where the six-foot-five-inch KeShawn and his brother, Freddie, and sister, Althea, transitioned to from the educational system in rural Alabama. As new students in town, the big city felt overwhelming, but the school felt just as intimidating. After enrolling in DuSable, a campus of over 3500 students, which was almost four times the size of their Alabama school, the Coleman's began the arduous task of adapting to the big school's culture. Although they were not intimidated, they were apprehensive about attending such a large school.

The only person they knew at the school was Courtney, Cousin Nate's oldest child. But Courtney had her own school life to navigate. As a result, she provided only token support during the Coleman transition. KeShawn, Freddie, and Althea, from their experiences in Alabama, figured they would be on their own during this pivotal inaugural year at the new school. However, what comforted them was knowing they had each other's back in times of trouble and any superficial or frivolous issues would be collectively resolved. All new students, as expected, go through a transition and adjustment period; however, intimidation and personal attacks are unacceptable nor tolerated.

KeShawn's adjustment to Chicago mirrored the emotional rollercoaster that gripped his siblings. On top of that, his introduction to high school basketball at DuSable did not get off to the start he had hoped for. The nervousness and apprehension were evident as KeShawn and his younger siblings walked the unfamiliar path back and forth to school, always on guard for sporadic harassment from fellow students. It was common for them to experience various emotions for being the new students. They would be teased unmercifully for the way they talked and for the style of clothes they wore. The adjustment period and learning the intricacies of this large high school was challenging but straightforward enough. Still, KeShawn, who was bigger and taller than the average student, made it clear in no uncertain terms that teasing had its limits. There was one incident right after lunch, the day before a three-day holiday weekend when Freddie's harassment and teasing had gone too far. Fed up watching his brother be the brunt of jokes and taunts, KeShawn, watching from afar, became incensed and had enough.

Coming to his brother's defense, he approached the overly obnoxious student, who was widely known to students and teachers for being a school bully. In a responsive fit of rage, KeShawn, using one hand, grabbed the bully by the neck of his shirt and lifted him off the ground. The sight of dangling feet and screams of fear echoed in the hallway. KeShawn held the bully against the lockers until he apologized to Freddie and the other students watching. Shocked at what was happening to him, the bully began shedding tears before promising he wouldn't bother another student if he were let down. The crowd of students looked on in disbelief as no one had ever challenged the audacious but fake tough guy. It was KeShawn, the new student, who, with one hand, had taken the wind out of the sails of the school's notorious bully and exposed him for what he was: a loudmouth fraud who thrived on intimidating smaller and younger students. From that day forward, no more malicious teasing or threats were directed towards the Colemans. Thanks to KeShawn, the new migrant students from the South had completed their rights of passage and received no more teasing and harassment. Lost in the irony was that most DuSable students were like the Colemans. They were products of the Southern migration North who sought a better life.

KeShawn, taller than most of the students in his junior class, faced unanticipated adversity when he went to the gym to play pick-up basketball with players on the varsity team. Instead of getting a welcome opportunity to join in on the game, he received a standoffish reception when he showed up alone and unannounced. KeShawn quickly learned that acceptance on all levels at DuSable was not automatic and would have to be earned.

After watching the guys go up and down the court in informal shirts and skins games to twenty-one, KeShawn became acutely aware that the talent level at DuSabe was different from that in Alabama. This harsh reality quickly dashed his thoughts of coming in and being "The King."

During informal pick-up games, KeShawn, despite his size, was often the odd man out and was shunned from joining in on the fun. This act of omission put into question his hopes of playing varsity basketball. KeShawn needed to find his competitive place among a group of players determined to defend their positions and keep him at bay. The inner-city brand of basketball predicated more on athleticism and skill, as each player constantly tried to outperform the other, which was something that KeShawn would have to adjust to if he wanted to fit in and make the team.

However, a moment of acceptance and good fortune came KeShawn's way when, one day, after most of the players had gone home and he was still unable to get much involvement in the pickup games, he was befriended by the team's star player.

Off by himself, discouraged and depressed, with only his thoughts to keep him company, wondering if he would ever find his place on the team, the ordinarily outgoing KeShawn quietly practiced shooting and dribbling. His attempts to imitate the shots and ball handling he watched during the pickup games left much to be desired, as his movements looked stiff and awkward. The more he tried to execute the new moves, the more he failed, aggravating him even more. Although the sweat that poured off his shirtless frame revealed broad shoulders and chiseled abs, his frustration got the best of him. After throwing the ball high against the backboard, KeShawn took one step, caught the ball above the rim, and, using two hands, slammed the ball back through the basket with such force it rocked the standard supporting the backboard. This act of frustration did not go unnoticed. Watching from the other end of the gym were two others. The custodian, whose jaw dropped to the floor, and another player who, like KeShawn, stayed late to work on his game.

As he dribbled over to KeShawn, he said, "Hey, big guy, my name is Les, Les Hamilton; what's yours?" KeShawn, slow to extend his hand, introduced himself. Les, also a junior and similar in height to KeShawn but much more polished as a basketball player, was impressed by what he had just seen.

The two continued to talk as they made their way to the water fountain before taking a seat on two folding chairs near the gym's exit door. By now, the custodian finally closed his mouth, turned off the lights, and said to the players, "Alright, guys. Time to go, and by the way, young fella, don't tear my rim off."

While walking and talking, they realized they were heading in the same direction when Keshawn asked, "Where do you live?" "I live in the Ida's," replied Les. At that point, KeShawn said, "So do I," they slapped hands and laughed.

Days passed, and KeShawn and Les continued building on their budding friendship. KeShawn was humbled and appreciated the kindness and respect that Les, who was projected to be one of the best players in the league, had shown him. The friendship with Les went a long way to help make the adjustment at DuSable High School less cumbersome. However, the other players on the team were not so quick to accept KeShawn as an equal. The raw potential they've seen from KeShawn seemed to intimate them and their positions on the team.

It wasn't very often that KeShawn and Les were not seen together either practicing, talking as they walked home from school, or sitting on the porch telling jokes that Freddie got a big kick out of hearing. One day, while they walked home from school, the conversation about family was brought up. Les disclosed that his family, like KeShawn's, moved to Chicago from the rural south two years ago. He said it took him longer than he wanted to be accepted by DuSable classmates and even longer by his teammates, and his adjustment to the urban style of fast-break basketball took half the season to figure out. What Les shared was comforting to KeShawn. He learned that his new friend didn't start his career at DuSable polished and refined as he does now. Plus, the fact he didn't get a warm welcome-to-DuSable reception either helped to relieve a lot of KeShawn's anxiety.

As the school year progressed, KeShawn and Les developed a close bond. They spent hours together during weekends discussing a range of topics, including some of the school's best teachers and those who should be avoided at all costs. But most of the talking was about basketball, track, Chicago, and girls.

Despite Les's tutelage and KeShawn's curiosity about becoming a two-sport athlete, KeShawn knew his basketball development was far behind the other players, and he would have to work his tail off just to make the team. And if he was fortunate enough to make the team, getting into a game would be another formidable hurdle.

Initially, KeShawn's teammates were critical of his lack of basketball knowledge and made fun of his unorthodox shooting style. He was raw and unpolished, yet despite being pushed, knocked around, and fouled intentionally, KeShawn never made excuses, backed down, or quit. He knew his time would come if he kept his head down and did what the coaches asked. On the other hand, the coaches were aware of KeShawn's close friendship with Les and the countless hours Les devoted to helping KeShawn improve and refine his game. The only question remaining was whether KeShawn would be ready to reap the fruits of his labor before the season ended.

The basketball teams in the Chicago Public League were challenging and competitive. Because of DuSable's mounting injuries and inexperienced players, teams took turns beating them up. Although KeShawn had shown tremendous progress from the first time he stepped on DuSable's gym floor, his game and situational awareness still lagged what coaches demanded. This led coaches to question his ability to transition to the big-city style of competitive basketball and help the team this season.

The style of play in his rural Alabama hometown, where schools scrambled to find enough players, looked more like organized chaos rather than fundamentally sound team basketball. At DuSable, players were expected to commit to playing a team-oriented brand of basketball, utilizing the game's fundamental principles of passing, footwork, shooting, and swarming defense. KeShawn's lack of exposure in those areas served as a restraint that kept him on the bench and added to his growing frustration.

Even though his progress seemed slow, with each passing practice, KeShawn made incremental improvement, which didn't go unnoticed by the coaching staff. But they remained reluctant to give him the game minutes he desired. The coaches faced a conflicted reality about KeShawn. Playing him before he was ready could scar him psychologically and ruin his love for the game. Besides, other players have been committed to the program for several years and believed they should play ahead of KeShawn. Despite the coach's hesitation to give him game minutes, KeShawn didn't allow the frustration to alter his penchant for improving.

Determined to get better, KeShawn showed up early and asked Les to join him after practice to work on refining aspects of his game that may be holding him back. Even though they stayed after practice, sometimes late into the evening, KeShawn enjoyed the one-on-one battles against his good friend. When they started playing one-on-one, neither warrior wanted to get after it too hard. To do so would mean putting their friendship aside. But nothing would ever be gained from that laissez-faire attitude.

It didn't take long before Les's competitive juices surfaced. He began showing his buddy who was the boss as he repeatedly stifled KeShawn's attempts to score while scoring against KeShawn's defense. However, Les doesn't know that KeShawn still has "The King" mentality, and being dominated, his friendship aside could only last so long as his competitive juices surfaced. Now it was game on! Les, one of the best players in the Chicago Public League, was relentlessly going after the Alabama transplant. He confused KeShawn using a skill set that baffled many other Chicago defenders. However, in one breakthrough moment, KeShawn caught the unsuspecting star off-guard when he rebounded his missed shot and, without coming down, stuffed the ball back in over the outstretched reach of Les, sending him to the ground in a sprawl. As Les sat there stunned at what just happened, he looked up at KeShawn and, offering a wide grin, accepted a hand from the floor and said, "Man. Since I've been in Chicago, nobody has ever done that to me. I think you're ready." KeShawn accepted the compliment graciously and called it a night, only to get ready to go at it again the next day.

That determination and grit to improve paid dividends. Word had gotten back to the coaches about the battles KeShawn and Les were waging; thank you, Mr. Custodian. It wasn't long after that epic after-practice battle that a turning point occurred. DuSable's championship hopes were quickly fading as injuries to several starters and the ineffectiveness of crucial role players began to take a toll.

Coach David Williamson, a no-nonsense but affable veteran who has coached at DuSable for nine years, holds firmly to his principles of fundamental basketball. He finally gave KeShawn the opportunity he had patiently waited for and took full advantage.

Despite KeShawn's mistakes on defense, coaches liked the energy he brought, so they stuck with him. As his confidence began to build, so did his playing time. Using his 6-foot-5-inch frame and tremendous athletic ability, KeShawn went to work and began dominating his opponents.

Working alongside Les, they controlled the inside by scoring and rebounding at will. Although KeShawn's outside shot was inconsistent, he was unstoppable from close range. But what impressed the coaches more was KeShawn's ability to affect the game. His inside presence of relentless rebounding and shot-blocking, something the team sorely lacked, was impressive. KeShawn's motor allowed him to put his talents on full display as he ran the floor and dominated the inside on both ends of the floor.

KeShawn's understanding of the game's fundamentals has satisfied the coach's most significant concerns. His patience and hard work had paid off, and the monster was unleashed. He wasn't given anything; he probably would have turned it down if he had been. Everything KeShawn got he earned, and those critics who doubted if he would ever see time on the court were choking on their words.

Despite playing only nine games, KeShawn left an indelible impression on his coach and teammates. He finally got the acceptance he had yearned for since arriving from Alabama. Now, KeShawn has joined Les as the talk of the school, while his teammates proudly mention him in glowing praise and in the same vein as Les.

The DuSable basketball style and system of play were complex and intricate. So, to fully immerse themselves in the system and build team chemistry, KeShawn and Les organized weekend work-outs and scrimmages over the summer. The duo was aware of the team's potential and wanted to take advantage of the opportunity to compete for a championship.

During his senior year, playing alongside two-time All-City and All-American star forward Les Hamilton, KeShawn showed he had arrived. His terrific scoring and rebounding delighted his team-mates and fans throughout the league. His talents caught the media's attention early in the season as DuSable enjoyed a ten-game winning streak.

After a close but controversial two-point road game loss to Kenwood, DuSable would not lose again. They closed their regular season on a tear, steamrolling their opponents and winning their final seven games by blowouts.

Entering the postseason as the top seed, DuSable drew a favor-able draw in the Chicago Public League Boys Championship Tour-nament. This placed them on a collision course with the vaunted Marshall Commandos. Solid performances from KeShawn and Les allowed DuSable to advance, as they dispatched both Curie and Kenwood by double digits, setting up the much-anticipated title game against Marshall.

The University of Chicago was the host site for the Chicago Public School City Championship game. The sold-out fieldhouse pitted the SouthSide Panthers of DuSable doing battle against the West Side Commandos of Marshall in what promised to be an old-fashioned inner-city barn burner. Notwithstanding neighborhood bragging rights, the stakes were much higher as DuSable would like nothing more than to return the championship banner to the South Side. The Panthers relied on their two dynamic wing players, while the Commandos' talented backcourt was as good as any in the state. After the national anthem was played, the cheering section from each school remained standing and began cheering in a full-throat of enthusiasm. The start of the game lived up to its billing. Both teams went back and forth, trying to impose their will as spectacular play was followed by spectacular play. But the combination of KeShawn and Les was wearing on Marshall. After scoring 15 points apiece, the Panthers went into halftime ahead by six points. The halftime intermission couldn't have come quickly enough, as the break gave fans, who had been at full throat, time to exhale and collect their breath.

The second half started just like the first half had ended, courtesy of draw-dropping plays that turned the game into a classic matchup of talent on talent. The stars on both teams were electrifying. Entering the final quarter, DuSable led by 12 points, but the Marshall fans, sensing a possible defeat, raised their cheer decibel to another level and willed their team to make a push. Marshall responded and stormed back to take the lead late in the fourth on a pair of baseline jump shots. But, as time on the game clock was winding down, Les took a no-look pass from KeShawn and was fouled in the process of scoring in the lane for an and-one layup as time expired. The three-point play tied the game and forced overtime. In the OT, KeShawn showed why he was considered one of the best players in the state. His slam dunk off a missed shot sent the delighted fans into a frenzy, and DuSable held on to escape with a hard-fought 72-68 Chicago Public League City Championship.

Despite protests and lobbying by school officials and District Aldermen and Alderwomen, a decades-old policy precluded Chicago Public League Schools from participating in the Illinois State Basketball Tournament, denying coach Williamson and his talented squad a chance to capture a state title. However, KeShawn and Les were unanimously selected to the Illinois All-State Basketball team. Their Public League Championship results created quite a stir on DuSable's campus and among college recruiters, as scholarship offers poured into the school's mailroom for the two prolific players. The sheer volume of daily letters overwhelmed the students working in the mailroom. The school administration designed a mail-handling procedure to protect and separate the school's regular mail from the college letters to accommodate the daily offers.

College coaches called daily to schedule a time to meet with the players and their coaches on campus.

During his time at DuSable, Head Coach David Williamson saw the good and the bad in recruiting tactics. Some recruiters were unethical, while some made promises they knew they couldn't keep. He admitted a few recruiters had good intentions, but their institutions were limited and unable to offer full athletic scholarships. Thus, coach Williamson was skeptical of most of the offers. His skepticism stemmed from the fact that despite the over-the-top sales pitches from well-intended recruiters, segregation and discriminatory policies remained in place at major universities and would be difficult to remove.

Despite experiencing tremendous success on the basketball court, something unimaginable two years earlier. KeShawn was also being urged to try out for the track team. The interest shown intrigued him. Something he regretted not doing during his junior year. So this year, his last year of high school, and at the urging of coach Williamson, KeShawn paused his decision to accept the basketball recruiter's outlandish scholarship offers and turned his attention to the track.

Although KeShawn wanted to run track, his lack of familiarity with basic track protocols and fundamentals made him unsure where to start. He just knew he wanted to try something involving running. "I'm not sure what I like best, but I've been running and jumping most of my life, so I'm willing to listen and learn," KeShawn said to coach Williamson.

Meanwhile, basketball All-American teammate and good friend Les Hamilton, unable to convince KeShawn to join him on an AAU traveling team, bypassed the track team and signed a basketball scholarship offer to attend the University of Washington.

5

HIGH SCHOOL TRACK AND FIELD

An overcast afternoon with mild temperatures and a stiff wind blowing in from Lake Michigan was the perfect setting for aspiring track and field students who gathered at DuSable's Armstrong Field for open track team tryouts. Much to the chagrin of eight-year veteran track coach Chester Mims, some in the crowd of eager participants took the "come-one-come-all track tryouts fliers" quite literally. They showed up dressed in rather unusual outfits, including gym and beach shorts; amazingly enough, some were dressed in street clothes.

After hearing the high-pitched shrill of coach Mims's whistle cutting through the air to grab their attention, all the participants hustled to the center of the oval track's infield grass. They waited for instructions and clarification regarding the afternoon's tryout procedures. At first glance, the tryout phase, which divided the participants into groups based on their interest in the field or running events, looked like organized confusion. Still, after a few baffling minutes, the groups were assembled according to preference and coaches' recommendations.

KeShawn, whose talent for running began at an early age, despite his success on the basketball court, found the field events apparatus, hurdles, stopwatches, and whistles amusing. At the same time, he walked around talking to other participants.

Despite his inexperience as an organized track team member, KeShawn was overly confident in his running abilities. He had a reputation for beating all the neighboring kids in Alabama who dared to challenge him.

But what awaited him far exceeded the kids from the farm. Instead, he would be competing against highly skilled and technically savvy athletes who trained at some of the state's best facilities and had been exposed to quality coaching for years.

Coach Mims assured KeShawn he would have the opportunity to try out in as many events as he liked; the coach was thrilled to have this enormously gifted athlete turn out for the team. KeShawn chose to try the hurdles and sprints first because of his natural attraction to running and jumping. However, there was just one little matter that had to be resolved.

Using a bullhorn to address the participants, the field event assistant coach clarified a few critical points, "For today only, you will be allowed to wear your costumes during tryouts. But going forward, this is the last day of the clown show. Appropriate track attire will be issued to all those invited back." He continued, saying to all, "In addition, to avoid injury, track shoes must be worn during the actual tryout." This last-minute announcement caused some participants to scramble and utter their disapproval. "We will do our best to find you a shoe match, preferably in your position group. If no shoes are available, you will not be allowed to continue. Am I clear?" Barked the assistant.

The coaches knew from prior experiences that running and jumping competitively on a cinder-filled track without spike shoes was a recipe for disaster. KeShawn or any other student would not be the one to test that theory.

The mandate only added to the confusion and uncertainty, but surprisingly, the open-market auction-style bantering and shoe size exchanges went relatively smoothly. When one tryout group finished their event, they exchanged the corresponding shoes with others in the respective tryout groups.

KeShawn, wearing gym shorts and a tee shirt, did not own a pair of track shoes, so he asked if he could run in his gym shoes or even barefoot, but his request was immediately denied. "What size shoe do you wear, KeShawn," asked the assistant coach. "I wear a size 14 gym shoe, so I guess 14 is my size," replied KeShawn.

Coach Mims instructed his coaches to canvass between position groups and try and find shoes to meet KeShawn's relatively large size 14. Sprint coach Booker Powdrill was directed to a relatively large-size shot put athlete who wore a size 16 shoe. After a brief discussion with coach Powdrill, who promised to return his shoes promptly, the shot putter agreed to allow KeShawn to wear his shoes for his trial races. The extra-large shoes didn't seem to faze KeShawn. He just stuffed pieces of notebook paper, curiously given to him by the assistant coach, into each toe of the sleek-looking, red and white Pumas. As he completed his improv, KeShawn looked up at the assistant coach, offered a wink and a smile, and said, "Now I'm ready."

For the first time in his life, KeShawn was wearing a pair of authentic track shoes, and although they were two sizes too big, he didn't care; he was too enamored looking at how nice the red and white Pumas looked and felt on his feet.

The call from coach Powdrill instructed runners to take their positions. KeShawn received last-minute encouragement from a Jamaican sprinter who had just won his race in the short sprints. He slapped hands with KeShawn in support and wished him the best. As KeShawn took his place on the track, teammates from all the other events, including the shoeless shot putter, stopped what they were doing and gathered around to watch the star basketball player run in his race. When KeShawn stepped into the unfamiliar starting blocks alongside nine other quarter-mile hopefuls, the starting blocks confused him. When he raised his hand to request assistance, the request drew snickers from a few onlookers, but that didn't deter KeShawn. Even though his race wasn't the most fluent or technically sound, KeShawn's raw and unpolished talent allowed him to win the quarter mile trial easily and the subsequent 110 high hurdles going away, leaving teammates in awe and disbelief.

After the tryouts, Coach Mims and Coach Powdrill approached KeShawn and offered one comment: "I take it you liked the shoes?" KeShawn smiled and replied, "Yes, I do." Coach Mims replied, "Then you'll have a pair of 14 shoes at tomorrow's practice."

Although the tryouts were in the rearview mirror, coach Mims finally assembled his track and field team and officially welcomed everyone; the track season was underway. The gifted KeShawn received a steady diet of training and technical advice daily as the coaches worked to refine his talents. The coaches were not particularly worried about KeShawn's early season dual meet performances. Those meets were used as competitive rehearsals for KeShawn. The goal was to have him ready to seriously compete heading into the final stretch of the regular season and the league championships. As he absorbed and processed the training information, KeShawn couldn't help but visualize the day he would put all his training together and stand arms raised victoriously in the winner's circle.

The coaches were amazed at how quickly KeShawn had improved his running technique. His use of the starting blocks was no longer an issue, and while his pace control in the quarter mile continued to improve, the sequencing of his hurdle steps was night and day from his first debut. Yet, the competition in the Public League Dual-Meets still outpaced him.

The timeline the coaches established at the beginning of the season for KeShawn's development was on schedule. His progress kept him from becoming discouraged by his lack of victories. The hard-working KeShawn often joked with his track teammates during practice and could be heard yelling to no one in particular, "I'm close, guys. The King is getting close."

Like his junior year in basketball, where his late development revealed exceptional talent, KeShawn, despite not winning, grabbed the attention of rival coaches and a few college scouts who liked his style and grace. Looming in less than two weeks were the city track championships. KeShawn's rapid development made DuSable coaches change their team's projections about competing for the City championship.

KeShawn was no longer close; he had arrived and saved his best for last. He performed remarkably during the City Championship, winning the quarter mile, placing second in the 110 high hurdles, and ran a fantastic anchor on the 4x440 relay. This was enough to earn entry into the season's final event, the Illinois High School Association State Track and Field Championships, a competition, unlike basketball, that was open to all qualifying Chicago Public League Schools.

The finals, held annually at Eastern Illinois University in Justice, Illinois, attracted the state's best of the best to compete for the highest honors in high school track and field. KeShawn had gone from having track potential to earning the admiration and respect of peers, coaches, and college recruiters nationwide.

He led a contingent of capable DuSable athletes who were peaking at the right time and were among the favorites to medal in three races: the quarter, the 110 highs, and the 4x440 relay.

Unassuming but highly confident, KeShawn drew strength from his time as a youth in Alabama, when he was the self-proclaimed "King," giving head starts to anyone who dared to race against him. He called upon that confidence to get him through these championship races.

Determination and persistence, prerequisites for success, paid off big time for KeShawn, as he won individual medals in the 440 and 110 highs and anchored the 4x440 relay, which posted a winning time of 3:08.40. This set a school record and broke the state record that had stood for seven years.

KeShawn's high school track exploits were legendary and became topics for heated debate in those "whose-the-best-ever-to-run track" weekend barbershop conversations.

6

CLASSROOM ISSUES

Deflecting attention from himself was something KeShawn had been accustomed to doing since childhood. He attributed his athletic skills to a gift from God passed down through his father. Still, his academic development, well, despite his mother's insistence, was not high on his list of priorities. But now, as his career moved forward, KeShawn faced the challenge of qualifying for college admission because of his average to mediocre grades.

While growing up in South Alabama, KeShawn never applied himself in the classroom. School for him, as it was for many others, was considered something to do when not working in the cotton fields. Graduating from high school was not a priority, and going to college was like saying, "I'm going to the moon." Despite his lackadaisical attitude toward school, KeShawn was always considered a quick learner, so at this critical stage of his journey, as scholarship offers from two different sports besieged him, KeShawn was keenly aware of his academic shortcomings but was open to learning how to improve as a student and raise his grade point average.

At the urging of Coach Williamson, KeShawn willingly accepted the help of two female Math and English tutors, who were very familiar with his popularity and sports success and eager to help him. In addition to his warm personality was his desire to improve his grades and develop good study habits. The tutors took a liking to KeShawn and wanted to help him succeed. They emphasized that the same repetitive rigor he used to become a successful athlete would be required if he wanted to see improvement in the classroom and keep on pace to graduate.

Despite his good intentions, KeShawn could not distance himself from the distractions that compromised his study time. He spent more time than he should have hanging out with friends, listening to the melodic sounds of Chicago's jazz clubs along the streets of Bronzeville.

He confessed to close teammates when he said to them one day after practice, "Listening to jazz was magical. It relaxes my mind and soothes my soul, allowing me to cope with the concerns and challenges surrounding me and life as it treats my family."

KeShawn's use of Jazz to escape the realities of his day was similar to how his dad, Papa James, would listen to the blues to distance himself from the despair and challenges of living in the South. There were many evenings when Papa James would sit on the porch and tell stories about how listening to the "Delta Blues" from some-time radios (they worked sometimes) allowed farmers to camouflage their feelings and get through the day. His stories always ended when he would say, "Ain't nothing but the blues, son." As a reference to dealing with Mr. Charley.

DuSable basketball coach David Williamson, as a promise to KeShawn's parents, served as a surrogate and kept a watchful eye on KeShawn. Coach Williamson knew KeShawns' academic shortcomings and the tricky college admissions process. A process that included culturally biased tests that gave white, affluent male students an unfair admission advantage. Test scores were the major hurdle for KeShawn and would have a vital impact on the schools available to him. Williamson kept all college options on the table, including attending an in-state two-year school if the situation was warranted.

However, as college recruitment ramped up for track and basketball, Williamson became proactive and scheduled weekly meetings between KeShawn, the tutors, and the academic advisor. Their discussions focused primarily on classroom improvement and understanding the lexicon recruiters used to enlighten or confuse. This included terms such as standardized college admissions tests, predictive analytics, placement tests, transferable credits, and eligibility requirements. These terms could be misunderstood and baffling when taken out of context, but Williamson was not intimidated. He instructed the tutors to research additional topics related to college entrance policies, including student rights and responsibilities and athletic eligibility requirements. Wearing a wrinkled brow and a look of determination, Williamson told the tutors, "KeShawn will not fall victim because he was uninformed, so let's get to work."

While he focused on his studies, KeShawn reflected on his high school success in dual sports. He had grown increasingly intrigued and often thought about what it would be like to participate in two sports while in college. During one of his weekly meetings, he asked Coach Williamson, "Coach, how hard would it be to play basketball in college during the winter and run track in the spring? Would the demands be the same as they were in high school?" Coach Williamson, not known to mix words or try to sugarcoat reality, said to KeShawn, "There is no doubt you have the talent to be a two-sport star in college, but my concern is your academic readiness or better put your academic strength." Williamson continued, "As you know, the time requirements in your sports season are consuming, now double that. Now factor in your professors in college, who will have their demands that impact your time." He continued, "You could be the greatest two-sport star ever to lace them up, but what does it mean if you're not eligible?" The blunt but sobering assessment from coach Williamson was a reality check for KeShawn and begged the question about his two-sport ambition's importance. Was the thought of being a two-sport college athlete to be taken seriously, or was KeShawn having a moment?

When coach Williamson initially asked KeShawn to delay accepting a basketball scholarship offer until after track season, it was met with skepticism and mixed emotions. But now, he can see the wisdom of that recommendation beginning to pay off. By delaying his decision, KeShawn wisely used the time to develop a rapport with the tutors, who helped him improve his grades and raise his grade point average significantly enough to qualify for admissions, allowing him to avoid additional testing. After all, KeShawn was an All-City basketball player and was still highly sought after by dozens of colleges, so the recruiters, despite their pandering, weren't going anywhere.

The track program was a fun experience that kept him in shape and out of harm's way. Plus, running track was a good diversion that allowed KeShawn to stretch out and expand his possibilities as he fulfilled a dream of winning races, something he always enjoyed doing more than playing basketball.

Even though the dilemma of KeShawn's dreams was troubling, he knew the importance of including his family in the discussion about tough decisions. His parents were wise and loving, and he valued their opinions. However, with Papa working the afternoon shift, making time for those discussions was complicated. So he asked his mother to make sure Papa set aside some time over the weekend to discuss and counsel him on the reality of playing two sports while in college.

Papa James had no problem devoting time to counseling his oldest son. After listening to KeShawn's rationale, Papa favored not wanting to kill a dream before it happened. Having the advantage of wisdom, Papa told his son, "If the opportunity presents itself, and you believe you are prepared, then by all means, you should take advantage and follow your dreams. Remember, having dreams is one of the reasons why we left Alabama." However, Mama Coleman had a different viewpoint. Her biggest concern was time for school and time for study. She cautioned, "If you spend more time playing sports and socializing, as many college students do, and less time studying, you will end up swimming in the pool of college dropouts." KeShawn could only laugh at his mother's analogy and said to her, "Mom, I promise that getting my college degree is just as important to me as it is to you." KeShawn then assured his mother that he would do whatever was necessary to avoid swimming in "that pool," KeShawn vowed if the time came when he needed classroom help, he would ask his teammates, coaches, and whoever else what they knew about student support services or any other programs that could offer him academic support.

Aided by coach Williamson and the invaluable help from the school tutors, KeShawn was notified that his grade point average and course credits predicted and qualified him academically, making him eligible for an athletic scholarship.

Thankful that the burden of college admission has been lifted from his shoulders, KeShawn narrowed his choice of colleges to those closer to home, supportive of his degree ambition, and allowed him the option to continue participating in two sports.

The DuSable student body president, Chauncey Fogle, a friend and track teammate of KeShawn, devised a clever idea. In a pre-arranged meeting with KeShawn and Coach Williamson, Chauncey suggested they develop a marketing strategy and make a big splash to take advantage of KeShawn's impending college announcement. "We can call it a college signing ceremony and hold it in the school's auditorium," offered Chauncey. After considering the idea, Coach Williamson voiced his concerns but ultimately agreed and said, "This idea could be good not only for KeShawn but for the kids and the athletic teams across the board." Coach Williamson said, "We can expand the ceremony to include a fall and spring signing day." Coach Williamson continued, " I do not doubt for one minute that as soon as this idea takes flight, other schools will be encouraged to do something similar for their athletes."

When DuSable students began to spread the word about the ceremony around campus and in the community, the impromptu event picked up speed. Coach Williamson contacted his friends at the Chicago Tribune and the Chicago Defender and invited them to attend and bring along their camera crews.

On Friday afternoon, the day of the big ceremony, teachers eager for their students to attend ended classes earlier than usual. Joining KeShawn on stage behind the drawn curtains for the much-anticipated announcement were the school president, Dr. Luis Ellison, Coach Williamson, and student body president Chauncey Fogle.

As the drama began to unfold, KeShawn became nervous and filled with anxiety. He found it challenging to sit still, so he paced on stage behind the closed curtain. He had never really thought about how the magnitude of such an event would affect him. The ceremony turned into something much bigger than inviting just a few friends and family over for dinner. Chauncey and his team had gone all out promoting the event on and off campus, and by the size of the enthusiastic crowd, they were being rewarded for their efforts.

Still showing signs of nervousness, KeShawn peeked out from behind the curtain and saw his mother in the front row holding her Alabama bible in one hand while tightly gripping Papa with the other. Then he saw Freddie, Althea, cousin Nate, and his family sitting amongst the overflow crowd. He also recognized sports news media from their season's coverage of the Panthers.

The outgoing support from students could be directly attributed to KeShawns's popularity and the efforts of the student body president, Chauncey, and his team of officers.

The massive turnout, which surprised everyone, even Chauncey, required an "all hands on deck approach" from the school to manage the crowd. Teachers, staff, and student volunteers quickly moved people to their seats while the school pep band blared in the background. In a show of support for KeShawn, who fulfilled his athletic dream, teammates, some wearing their letterman jackets, and other athletes from across the sports program occupied most of the front seats.

Everyone was seated and conversing when suddenly the band

stopped playing, and the stage curtain slowly began to open. The crowd roared its approval when they saw KeShawn sitting on stage between the two presidents and his coach. He wore beige pants and a blue blazer over his white shirt and necktie. After a few complimentary introductory words from the student body president, school president Dr. Ellison took to the podium and used the moment to offer remarks that reflected on the robust history of DuSable High School. A school that cherishes a long list of outstanding alumni, including but not limited to Nat King Cole, Redd Foxx, and Dinah Washington. He thanked the current student body and the tireless work of teachers and staff. Dr. Ellison then motioned for KeShawn to come to the podium. When KeShawn nervously approached the podium to speak, his voice went silent. Recognizing that he was overwhelmed by the moment, Coach Williamson joined KeShawn at the podium and asked the audience for another round of applause to give his star athlete more time to compose himself. The quick thinking of Coach Williamson worked. After clearing his throat, KeShawn adjusted his necktie and removed his notes from his coat pocket. The longer he spoke to the hushed crowd listening intently, the more confident he became.

KeShawn gave a special thanks to his proud parents, who sacrificed so much to make this dream come true. Two years ago, the family were sharecroppers, and today, their son was going to college on a scholarship. KeShawn thanked his coaches, basketball, and track teammates for helping him achieve an unimaginable dream. KeShawn then turned around, pointed at Chauncey, and asked the crowd to give him well-deserved applause for organizing the event.

Then, abruptly, the auditorium was quiet. Nobody moved, and nobody said a word. The moment everyone was waiting for had arrived. KeShawn broke the silence through the podium mic when he said, "I have made my decision." Followed by more silence. "I am staying in Chicago and accepting a scholarship to attend Chicago State University." The audience then erupted in applause, followed by hoots and hollers, and the band started playing.

KeShawn's teammates, giddy with excitement, were joined by the crowd as they chanted his name: KeShawn, KeShawn, KeShawn.

The ceremony concluded as cameras clicked and the crowd slapped each other's hands. Before he joined his parents in celebration, KeShawn, his shirt wet from nervous perspiration, embraced Coach Williamson and the school president, Dr. Ellison, then turned to Chauncey, gave him a huge embrace, and said to him, "Thank you, man. I had no idea the ceremony would turn out to be like this. When I looked out at the crowd, I got nervous. I felt like running off the stage, afraid I would mess things up. But I'm glad I didn't. We made it, Chauncey, and I thank you again."

Even though the drama of his school announcement was over and the thought of not being admitted to college was now in the rearview, KeShawn turned his thoughts to the future. Fall classes at Chicago State began in less than a month, but KeShawn continued to agonize over a decision to be a dual-sport college athlete. If he chose one sport, which one would that be? Torn by those thoughts that weighed heavily on his mind, caused him unnecessary stress. Essentially, he was overwhelmed. During high school, whenever he needed to get something off his chest, he could always turn to the one person he trusted and whose opinion he valued: his high school coach, David Williamson.

When KeShawn arrived back at DuSable for a meeting with Coach Williamson, he was warmly greeted. Students shook his hand and patted him on the back as he walked the hallway to meet his coach. The handshakes from the students, coaches, and players were a welcome relief and temporarily eased his mind from the issues that troubled him.

Coach Williamson's familiar, no-nonsense voice was like the sound of music to KeShawn's ears. He was back at the place where the magic began. Coach Williamson listened as KeShawn explained his dilemma. He gave KeShawn the license to unburden his mind and unload the weight-bearing stress from his broad shoulders. Coach Williamson then talked about family, college life, and, more importantly, what makes KeShawn happy. He told his former pupil, "If you're doing something and don't experience happiness, then why are you doing it?" He continued, "Once your priorities are in order, the rest will fall into place. I know you like playing basketball and are very good at it, but you love running track." This was a wow moment for KeShawn as Coach Williamson continued. "So that right there should tell you something." KeShawn could only smile as he listened to the wisdom pouring from his coach's mouth.

Finally, the pieces of a dream started to make sense to him, and with a certainty he lacked before the meeting, KeShawn said to his coach, "My priority is to get a college degree. That's important to me and was a promise I made to my Mom." Secondly, I don't need to stress out. I want to enjoy, not endure, my time in college." And as Coach Williamson leaned back in his chair, KeShawn continued. "So, I will stick to one sport, track and field." Coach Williamson could only smile as he listened to a man who had processed his priorities in less than an hour. As they stood, a somewhat emotional KeShawn embraced Coach Williamson and said to him, "Thank you, coach." Who replied, "I like your decision. Now go do what you love and make us all proud."

7

CHICAGO STATE UNIVERSITY

Track officials hoped the weather cooperated on the second day of the two-day NCAA Regional Track and Field Championship. After an intense and highly competitive first day, played out under heavy skies, multiple schools remained in contention to claim the championship. If the final day's events somehow escaped the wrath of the summer storms, the fans would be in store for a thriller of a finish. Earlier in the week, however, a severe thunderstorm across much of Terre Haute, Indiana, produced widespread power outages and damage to trees and power lines. But today, despite dark clouds and the possibility of more thunderstorms, the weather held steady. Loyal track fans across the region braved the weather threat and descended on Terre Haute's Gibson Track and Field Complex to support their schools. At stake for the winning team was an opportunity to represent the region at the national championships in Eugene, Oregon. However, teams knew that anything but a victory would eliminate any talk of a national championship.

Although the clouds didn't appear threatening, the moderately blowing winds were starting to intensify. Meet officials became concerned when they realized they had no contingency plans to implement if the weather turned ugly and the day's final events had to be canceled. Keeping that in mind, coaches and officials were motivated to complete as many events as possible. They decided to dispense with all unnecessary announcements and made every effort to move the meet along as quickly as possible.

The weather was on everyone's mind as it was poised to break at any moment. Meet officials wasted no time getting athletes adequately positioned for their events. While the coaches barked instructions, all available volunteers collaborated to expedite race and apparatus setups. However, the excitement of the final day superseded any weather concerns as the projected sellout crowd, carrying unopened umbrellas and wearing colorful rain slickers, cheerfully made their way to the prime seats.

Tension in the Complex in anticipation of the final races was so thick you could have cut it with a knife. A lot was at stake in the final events, and the fans knew the implications.

In the earlier events, which typified the emotional and competitive nature of the two-day track meet, Chicago State U earned some badly needed but unexpected points by placing fifth in both the javelin and shot put. A first-place finish in the 1500 moved them up the leaderboard and into championship contention.

The crowd was alive and enthusiastic, cheering in the heavy air, anticipating the day's final race. Most of those in attendance stood and waited for the track to be cleared for the 4x440 relay. Track fans love competition and show great appreciation for the field events and distance races, but the sprints and relay races — well, those races take on another level of track love.

It was only fitting that after two days of head-to-head individual and team competition, the championship hinged on the 4x440 relay. Thanks in part to KeShawn's two victories in the 110 high hurdles and the 440 intermediate hurdles and unexpected points in the pole vault, shot put, and 1500, the surprising Titans of Chicago State U were locked in a virtual tie for first place along with Northern Illinois, U of Illinois, and the meet favorite, Bradley U.

All four schools had world-class lead-offs and anchors on their 4x440 relay teams. One of the assistant coaches for U of Illinois was overheard telling his relay team while huddled, "Barring any unforeseen circumstances, the relay race winner will likely claim the championship and move on to nationals in Oregon."

Knowledgeable track fans know that each relay leg's performance is critical. The leadoff and anchor legs get the most attention, but runners two and three are just as vital for success because they are the only runners receiving and passing the baton. Highlighted by teamwork, speed, and strategy, the 4x440 relay, using a staggered start, offered a thrilling and exciting event that was befitting of closing out the day's events.

The Titans leadoff runner Moe Banks, one of the team's best quarter milers, was being counted on to use his blistering opening leg to set the tone. The sound of rumbling thunder could be heard in the distance as the leadoff runners took their mark and awaited the starter's call. The runners were off as the sound of the starter's gun lingered in the air. The few remaining seated fans rose from their seats and joined the chorus of cheers as the leadoff runners, required to stay in their staggered lanes, made their way around the oval track.

Despite the staggered start's deception, Moe ran his leadoff leg precisely as the coaches expected. But a hard-charging runner from Bradley U challenged Moe for the lead at the first baton exchange. Despite the challenge, Moe made the first baton exchange flawlessly. In the first curve of the second leg, Chicago State, maintaining a slight lead, was first to move out of the stagger towards the inside curb lane.

The crowd was thoroughly engaged as the runners moved along the back stretch as close to each other as was anticipated. As the runners approached the second baton exchange, Chicago State executed a smooth exchange and maintained its slight lead. The crowd sensed that if the Titans' third leg could hold a lead going into the final exchange to their anchor, catching KeShawn would be next to impossible. Despite his tremendous speed, the Titans' third leg had to dig hard to maintain his lead. He was being challenged by runners from Illinois and Bradley, who were accelerating and closing the gap as they motored down the backstretch.

The pressure to hold the lead and the crowd's surging cheers got the better of the Titans runner. In his anxiety, he failed to recognize his de-acceleration checkpoint just before the final curve and instead increased his speed, a concern discussed at length during pre-race meetings. By disobeying command, his tactical error put the relay team in extreme jeopardy. The strategy for winning was predicated on each runner following instructions to the letter. Now, the hopes of winning the race are in question. This untimely mistake came at the worst possible time. This wasn't a dual meet. This was for all the marbles and could very well cost the Titans the opportunity to claim their first-ever Regional Championship and advance to Nationals.

In the stretch run, the Titans' third-leg runner, seemingly in command only 75 yards before the final baton exchange with the waiting KeShawn, became noticeably tired and began to tighten. Runners from teams with similar title aspirations blew past him on the outside, and the lead was lost. KeShawn was bouncy and encouraging while he waited for the baton. As he watched his teammate falter and lose ground, he had to relinquish the inside waiting lane — a lane the Titans had enjoyed for two baton exchanges.

Now standing three lanes wide in fourth place, with the fifth and sixth place teams in a threatening position, KeShawn received the final baton exchange ten yards behind the leaders. Instead of running to maintain the lead, he was put into a catch-up position. Be that as it may, KeShawn had only one thing on his mind. Catch them!

Despite the urgency, KeShawn's mental and physical training throughout the season prepared him for such moments. And even though "The King" relished come-from-behind history-making moments like this, he understood that trying to make up ground too quickly would be a tactical mistake he could not afford to make. But in the back of his mind, he also knew he couldn't let the race escape him by being too cautious.

KeShawn needed time and distance in his favor to chase down those world-class runners who were ahead of him by some 15 yards as they motored along the backstretch. Catching them was not going to be an easy task, especially if he didn't find a way to close the gap earlier than he wanted. He decided it was either now or never if he intended to make up some of the lost ground. He made his first move and accelerated when coming out of the first turn, and the crowd responded in a frenzy. But as KeShawn rapidly closed ground, he remained fully aware of the checkpoint where he had to ease off pace. The runners from Bradley U, Northern Illinois, and Illinois U were throwing caution to the wind and ignored their checkpoints as they maintained their torrid pace.

In his mind, KeShawn knew he had to ignore the crowd's urging, as now was not the time to make his second move, even though he had lost ground at his checkpoint. Remaining patient and having faith in what his training had taught him was one thing, but accepting it became a challenge within the race as the lead runners slowly increased their lead. The leaders were running to win, but deep down, they knew KeShawn from Chicago State would not go away without a fight. It would be catastrophic to the runners and their fans if they were caught from behind after starting their anchor leg with a 10-yard lead.

KeShawn's mind sent him multiple signals on when to go as he fought to resist the urge to accelerate before it was time. He stayed true to the race strategy discussed during his pre-race meeting when his coaches reminded him, "If you find yourself behind, don't panic, just keep them in striking distance, but whatever you do, don't make your move too soon. I know it will be hard, but be patient because you'll need gas in the tank to bring it home."

KeShawn's long strides looked smooth and effortless as he moved along the backstretch, quickly eating up ground that separated him from the leaders. Heading into the far turn, still in fourth place, KeShawn made another move that elicited another roar from the still-standing, delirious crowd. Just before the turn, his arms pumping and his knees high, KeShawn caught and passed the runner from Northern Illinois. Now in third place, he set his sights on the leaders, Bradley U and Illinois.

Despite the crowd's constant urging to overtake the leaders, KeShawn maintained his discipline and resisted the temptation to make his move. He waited until he came out of the far turn before making another move. The crowd, roaring ever since the lead runner bolted out of the blocks three runners past, were beside themselves in anticipation of what was shaping up to be a fantastic finish. As the runners entered the final turn, each stride from the world-class runners increased the tension. KeShawn broke wide when he came out of the turn, and to the crowd's delight, he passed Illinois U. Heading into the stretch, a distance that at one moment looked like a mile away and in another only a few yards. The finish line was less than 100 yards away, and the lead runner from Bradley U, looking to seal the deal, clung to his lead. KeShawn went wide again, and at this point, the only thing on his mind was the constant reminder that he had been "The King" since his childhood in Alabama, and winning was something he had always done.

Coming down the stretch, KeShawn had his sights firmly set on passing Bradley U. He was confident in his preparation for moments like this as his eloquent strides narrowed the gap the lead runner had enjoyed.

Chicago State's relay team members were deliriously cheering on one side of the track, trying to urge their teammate to victory: "Go get him, KeShawn, go get him," they shouted. The ecstatic noise from the overflow crowd cascading from the bleachers was electric. As the pressure mounted, the Bradley U runner tried mightily to hold off the fast-charging KeShawn.

Victory and the Regional Championship was now less than 50 yards away as KeShawn narrowed the gap to just a few strides and continued his pursuit of Bradley U. "The King is coming for you," he murmured subconsciously. The runners were now stride for stride, breathing heavily like two Kentucky Thoroughbreds, with "the winner takes all" at stake. The Bradley runner was formidable throughout the regular track season and had never been caught from behind. So, overtaking him at this critical moment would be epic.

What happened next was stunning and unexpected. The Bradley U runner, only seconds away from victory, began to do the unthinkable: he tightened up. His fluid arm movements no longer resembled pumping pistons, and his knee action barely lifted his feet from the surface. His head tilted back, and his lead challenged. Fatigue and pain from his all-out assault on the one-lap anchor robbed his body. He was now in panic mode. The effortless running style he displayed earlier in the race crumbled. His body no longer responded to his mind's commands; as a result, he couldn't summon one more push to the finish line.

Capturing the lead for the first time on his anchor leg, KeShawn, holding his form, looked superb as he crossed the finish line, arms raised for the win, two strides ahead of Bradley U and three years removed from the farm in Alabama.

Celebratory chaos ensued. Jubilant Chicago State fans from the overflow crowd tried to rush to the track to celebrate, but track officials and security personnel held most of them back. Those who got through were ecstatic as they ran towards KeShawn and his teammates. The tension to hold the lead to the finish was too much for Bradley U. KeShawn Coleman, representing Chicago State U, was simply amazing and would not be denied on this dark, overcast afternoon. The moment was there, and he seized it.

In celebration, members of the Titan track team, euphoric and basking in their success, hoisted KeShawn onto their shoulders and carried him halfway around the track, much to the delight of the admiring fans who had joined them in celebration and to those who remained cheering in the stands. Amidst the jubilation, the sound of thunder was heard echoing closer and closer, causing meet officials to hasten their presentation. Officials quickly thanked everyone for their attendance, then crowned the jubilant track team from Chicago State U as winners of the NCAA Regional Track & Field Championship and presented Coach Stosik with the stunning 18" championship trophy.

8

TRAGEDY ON THE TRACK

There is no more significant challenge than trying to defend a title. The anticipation to have that opportunity awaited Chicago State University as their second track season began with much promise. Most crucial contributors returned from the most celebrated track season in school history a year wiser and anxious to return to the national championship. In a pre-season poll conducted by the media, the Titans were installed as the presumptive favorites to defend their regional championship and earnestly contend for the coveted but elusive NCAA National Championship.

However, unexpected distractions would engulf the Titans and jeopardize their goals. Instead of joy and happiness, the misplaced priorities of two team members caused them agonizing grief as they became dysfunctional and teetered on the brink of self-destruction. To avoid total disaster, the team rallied and regained their collective spirit after their veteran coach's harsh but necessary disciplinary actions changed the behavior of the team's star but disconcerting runners.

Over the summer, KeShawn, along with teammate and good friend Moe Banks, took advantage of an invite from friends and associates and traveled to Detroit to hang out and party at social hot spots known for dancing, drinking, and picking up women. KeShawn and Moe became regular weekend visitors at the Graystone Ballroom, Baker's Keyboard Jazz Lounge, and a club called The Flame. But this was the summer, so nobody at Chicago State paid much attention or felt slighted. However, as the fall semester began, the two teammates extended their summer tour of fun and frivolity well into their sophomore year. Pleas from some of their teammates to dial it down, and words of caution from their concerned professors were ignored.

While they continued their gallivanting ways, the first of four fall semester academic progress reports were issued with troubling news. The progress report was an early alert system designed by the athletic department to inform coaches of any potential academic problems that could eventually impact an athlete's eligibility.

Due to multiple absences, KeShawn's professors reported that he needed to catch up in his sophomore English and Speech Communication classes. There was no sugar-coating the facts. A failing grade awaited if he continued this path of self-destruction. This would earn him the distinction of becoming academically ineligible for the spring semester track season.

Assistant track coach Jordan Phelan was outraged when he reviewed KeShawn's progress report. KeShawn was the team's most valuable member, so Phelan immediately shared the information with head coach Phil Stosik. Something had to be done to prevent KeShawn from failing his classes. He was as good an athlete as there was and too crucial to the track team's success. For KeShawn to become a casualty because of grade issues would devastate the team's morale and championship aspirations.

Disappointed upon hearing the news, coach Stosik, in his sixth year as head coach and still wearing his hair in a ponytail, addressed the alarming progress report news with his prize superstar. Stosik had grown fond of his fun-loving, charismatic star performer during their one year together. But in a move consistent with any Chicago State athlete in academic trouble, Stosik advised

KeShawn of the action he was forced to take as part of the consequences for landing on the "unsatisfactory and not likely to pass" progress report list." In addition to KeShawn, several other athletes from the basketball and football teams were placed on restriction and required to attend mandatory 90-minute study hall sessions three nights per week and once on Saturdays. The study hall mandate would stay in effect until the following progress report was issued.

Although Moe Banks didn't land on the unsatisfactory list, he had too many unexcused absences from his morning Literature class, thus qualifying him to join KeShawn for mandatory study hall.

The time spent in the study hall, supervised by a paid adjunct faculty, and facilitated by three work-study tutors has proved beneficial. Four weeks later, when the following progress report was issued, KeShawn, Moe, and all but two of their study hall mates improved their classroom performance. The second progress report indicated a "satisfactory and likely to pass" level. Relieved that the good news would free them from the mandatory study hall, KeShawn and Moe, despite applause by coach Stosik, were given a stern warning. In a closed-door meeting, coach Stosik said to his two stars, "Any future disruptions or classroom issues will not be tolerated and will have severe consequences."

As the spring semester track season got underway, KeShawn and his teammates were impressive in early-season dual and tri-meet victories. But trouble awaited as outside distractions reared their ugly heads again. KeShawn and Moe reverted to their ill-timed fascination with street life. The distractions negatively impacted team practice and, subsequently, the team's performance. Titan teammates were puzzled and couldn't understand why the duo was so fixated on making weekend road trips to Detroit rather than focusing on becoming a better track team.

Despite the team's early-season success and KeShawn's domination in his individual hurdle events, he and Moe seemed insensible to how their bizarre social behavior impacted the team.

Kinks in the 4x100 and the 4x440 relay teams began to surface when, inexplicably, the relay team started having problems executing the baton exchanges, something that had been as natural to them as tying their shoes. This unusual baton exchange issue disqualified the Titans relay team in two consecutive meets. So, to address the problem, a frustrated coach, Stosik, used a week off between meets to schedule an impromptu weekend practice to address the relay team blunders specifically.

KeShawn and Moe, critical members of the 4x440 relay team having baton issues, were conspicuous by their absence from the weekend practice. What compounded the problem even more was their failure to alert the coaches or teammates regarding their plans to miss practice. They just decided to blow off practice. This lack of responsibility left Coach Stosik and his assistants livid. Word had gotten back to the coaches that his two athletes had traveled back to Detroit on Friday afternoon and didn't return to Chicago until early Sunday evening.

The mood at Monday's afternoon practice wasn't pretty. It was awkward and standoffish as the team harbored feelings of betrayal and disappointment toward their teammates. The friction and resentment were a stark contrast from the fun and excitement of the previous season's magical ride and jeopardized any hopes of defending their Regional Championship.

His team's disappointment and sour attitude were not lost on Coach Stosik. This was not his first time dealing with an unsettling situation. He was disappointed in his two athletes' repeated misconduct and lack of respect for the program. Stosik knew that the balance of the season hinged on how he approached his two malcontent runners. He had to be firm or run the risk of losing the respect of his team. So, Stosik initiated a well-conceived discipline plan to address the issue. He prepared a general message for his team but specifically targeted KeShawn and Moe. Choosing to avoid using blistering or profanity-laced language in front of the team assembled in the bleachers, Stosik calmly informed KeShawn and Moe they were being removed from the 4x440 relay team.

Standing quietly and motionless, the team's two best quarter-mile runners tried to process the shocking news. They were then instructed to line up and prepare to run a series of sprints. Coach Phelan's scowl of disappointment was evident by his facial expression, served as the starter. KeShawn and Moe were ordered to run seven 100-yard sprints, seven 75-yard sprints, and seven 50-yard sprints. Their only break would come from returning to the starting line after each sprint. Finally, as their teammates were still watching from the bleachers and expressing no signs of empathy, KeShawn and Moe were ordered to run eight laps around the track before they could even think about getting a water break.

As the two exhausted runners finished their laps, Coach Stosik dismissed the rest of the team for the day. KeShawn and Moe, tired, dragging, and profusely sweating, made a beeline to the water fountain, thinking the worst of their penance was over. Unable to satisfy their water thurst, assistant coach Phelan informed them to join the coaches on the bleacher seats for a meeting.

Exhausted, KeShawn and Moe sat quietly under the bleacher canopy next to assistant coaches, their heads lowered, and listened as coach Stosik read them the riot act. Although the meeting wasn't lengthy, there was no mistaking the harshness in Stosik's tone, and his message of disappointment was apparent.

He was fed up with his star athletes' selfish antics, their total lack of commitment to the team, and their choice of driving whenever they felt like it, sometimes at night, to a city four hours away just to socialize.

Stosik explained to them in no uncertain terms that their behavior was not only counterproductive but also flat-out inappropriate and unacceptable as college athletes and would no longer be tolerated. As a result, Stosik instituted, until further notice, another three-day mandatory 90-minute study hall requirement. KeShawn and Moe had exhausted their coaches' patience and were given a simple warning; "Either you get with the program or step aside and let the understudies take your places."

Feeling embarrassed and ashamed, KeShawn and Moe had no

valid argument to oppose the sanctions. They apologized to the coaching staff and, after vowing to correct their behavior, agreed they owed the team an apology and would be willing to stand before them at the next practice and ask for forgiveness, promising not to be a detriment to the team going forward.

The message from coach Stosik was another wake-up call for KeShawn and Moe. Unless there was a behavior change, the next move would result in being kicked off the team, and their scholarships could be revoked. The mere thought of telling his parents that he was kicked off the team because of social life choices was too much to bear. It didn't take long for KeShawn and Moe to adjust their attitude and come to their senses.

No further code of conduct violations occurred during the next three weeks, and the Titans returned to their winning ways. KeShawn and Moe led by example, proving to be the force their teammates had expected from them at the start of the season.

The two runners' stellar performances since the infamous meeting with their coach put the team on the brink of qualifying to defend their NCAA Regional Championship.

Drake University, located in Des Moines, Iowa, was the host school for this year's regional championship qualifying meet. Even though Chicago State set its sights on winning the national championship, they were mindful of what comes first: qualifying for and winning Regionals.

Anything less and the season would be considered a failure, and fingers would point directly at KeShawn and Moe. Chicago State had already demonstrated that dethroning them would not be an easy task, especially after back-to-back convincing dual-meet victories. Entering the meet, Chicago State was one of the heavy favorites to advance to Terre Haute, Indiana, where it would have an opportunity to defend its thrilling regional championship from last year. However, this year's competition, which included three senior-laden teams who would be taking dead aim at the Titans, promised to be just as fierce and competitive as last year.

The track at Des Moines was fast and rendered some impressive times.

On the strength of outstanding performances in the shot put, pole vault, and long jump, earning them valuable points, Chicago State bolstered their chances of finishing among the top three to advance. But a tragedy on the track struck unexpectedly during the 110-yard high hurdles race. KeShawn earned the ideal lane five position, a lane he much preferred, for having the fastest time in the region coming into the meet. He was flanked by the usual suspects from Bradley U and Illinois U, who seemed nervous and jittery as they warmed up next to KeShawn. All three schools could advance if they finished the race in the top three spots. To unsettle the favorite, KeShawn, Bradley U, and Illinois U hurdlers resorted to trash-talking, vowing to take down the Titans star. All the while, KeShawn, who experienced a lot of the same talk from runners trying to take down "The King" when he was at DuSable and as a youth back in Alabama, ignored the antics of the two nervous hurdlers lined up on his left and right side. Finally, KeShawn displayed a smile as he adjusted his starting blocks.

Holding his starter pistol in his right hand, the race starter blared out, "Runners take your mark," simultaneously, eight hurdlers settled into their starting blocks in preparation for the announcer to "set them."

After pounding their legs, the talented field of runners took one more glance up at the first of ten 42" high hurdles. The only noise at the hushed stadium was from the starter when he said to the hurdlers, "Set!"

The arm of the starter was raised to the sky, revealing a black and orange Alpha .22 caliber zinc-aluminum pistol. The runners were off as the noise from the pistol pierced the air. KeShawn got an excellent start out of his blocks, but after clearing the first hurdle, a second sound from the starter's pistol brought the race to a halt. Although he vehemently objected, the hurdler in lane eight from Duquesne University was signaled for a false start and was disqualified.

Undaunted by the false start, KeShawn and the remaining hurdlers returned to their blocks and repeated their pre-start rituals. KeShawn knew the distraction could be unnerving, so to keep his focus on winning the race, he ignored his competitors while kneeling as he re-adjusted his starting blocks. KeShawn replayed in his mind the tape of his routine of aggressively attacking the first hurdle. Confidently, he silently repeated his five-step process: visualize, take a deep breath, wait for the gun, take three steps, and lift. He knew he was prepared. The countless hours of practice have removed all self-doubt. He told himself during warmups, "Just trust the hours of training and follow the cadence, and the results will take care of themselves."

The re-start was on a clean gun, and once again, KeShawn exploded out of the blocks and quickly took the lead after the first two hurdles. He began to accelerate as the standing fans roared and cheered wildly. As the hurdlers approached the race's mid-point, KeShawn was rolling at top speed.

Running confidently and much in command, his beautifully choreographed three-step cadence propelled his lead leg up as his trail leg folded. KeShawn was poetry in motion and gave the impression he was dancing between hurdles. His grace and fluidity amazed the crowd as he attacked each hurdle. It became apparent that KeShawn was in a special class. Gliding over hurdle after hurdle like a hot knife slicing through butter, KeShawn extended his lead. KeShawn, "The King," enjoyed winning no matter the circumstances, but today, a simple top-three finish would be enough to secure the Titans a place in the regional finals.

Bradley U ran a comfortable second to KeShawn in lane four and seemed content just as long as he finished in the top three as the hurdlers charged toward the finish. However, in a desperate attempt to improve his position among the leaders, a hard-charging hurdler in lane three from Drake U lost his balance and stumbled badly out of his lane, inadvertently causing him to bump the runner from Bradley U.

The following chain of events seemed so unlikely and unimaginable that nobody could have predicted them in their wildest dreams. Drake U, out of control and faltering badly and in desperation mode, tried to get back into his lane just to finish the race. While in an off-balance position, he attempted to clear another hurdle but stumbled again, which sent him crashing back into Bradley U in lane four for a second time. The Bradley U hurdler, unable to control his balance from the second bump, clipped a hurdle that sent him toward KeShawn's lane five. Unaware of what was happening around him, KeShawn, two hurdles from victory, was clipped on his trail leg by the falling runner from Bradley U just as he began his lift to clear the hurdle. The crowd's reaction was a startled gasp as KeShawn was thrown off balance and banged his trail leg into the hurdle, which caused him to stumble badly.

Although two runners were already down, KeShawn tried to regain his balance to hold on to the lead, but his leg gave way, and he went down in a heap while the last-place runners avoided the fallen hurdlers and surged ahead to join U of Illinois to finish one, two, three.

Grimacing in agony with a painful expression on his face, KeShawn clutched his knee and tried to rub the pain away. But it was evident to those watching in horror that the way he was withering and agonizing, the injury must be severe. The hushed crowd, standing in disbelief, some holding their hands over their mouths while others clasped their hands behind their heads, stared at the track, transfixed in a momentary state of shock as they tried to process the chain of events that led to the tragedy on the track.

Coaches and medical personnel rushed to the track to aid and comfort the fallen runners until the emergency medical technicians arrived.

After looking at KeShawn's knee, the on-site medical staffer, who didn't want to offer a premature diagnosis but wanted to take all necessary precautions, called for a stretcher. But as he lay there on the ground, wincing in pain, still stunned and confused about what just happened, KeShawn said to his coach, "No matter how bad it looks, I'm not dead, so don't let them carry me off the track on some dam stretcher. Tell them to use a wheelchair if they have to; if not, I will just hobble off the track."

The Emergency Medical Services (EMS) team from the Des Moines Fire Department arrived in under five minutes and rendered additional aid. The technician's initial assessment determined that once they immobilized the knee, a wheelchair could be used to move KeShawn from the track to the ambulance.

Amidst the thunderous applause from the fans, KeShawn was lifted and placed into the back of the emergency vehicle. The wailing siren drowned out the remaining applause as the red and white Emergency Medical vehicle left the track. It carried a hurdler who should have been smiling on the podium, wearing a first-place medal around his neck. Instead, the vehicle took a sedated passenger and a sad and heartbroken coach to an uncertain future as it sped toward MercyOne Des Moines Medical Center.

MercyOne Des Moines had an impeccable reputation for having a trusted and compassionate team of doctors who cared for its patients, extending quality and around-the-clock care, including a 24-hour medical imaging service.

After a general conversation with the EMT on the way to the medical center, coach Stosik, wiping tears from his moist eyes and trembling uncontrollably, feared the worst for his fallen star but openly prayed for the best.

Family, teammates, and friends rushed to the medical center, crowded into the lobby, and waited for the EMS team to unload the precious cargo. As KeShawn lay there, stretched out on a gurney, his knee bandaged in ice, memories of his life began to pass before his eyes. As the wheels of the gurney slowly passed his crying and emotional family and followers, a groggy KeShawn reached out to touch their hands.

After he was moved onto the X-ray table, KeShawn gave a big exhale that allowed him to get his breathing under control, looked around at the spacious and brightly lit room that was large enough to easily accommodate the X-ray equipment, the staff, and himself, the helpless patient, and wondered, "What in the world is going on." As the technicians moved about the spacious room, the assistant placed an X-ray apron over. KeShawn's body and explained, "Don't worry; this is for your protection." He continued his reassuring conversation, saying, "Just like your lead apron, the walls and doors are also covered with lead. This is to protect you and the staff from radiation exposure." The medical technicians and all other parties in the room were protected, so they took their time to take multiple X-ray images of KeShawn's knee. The many years of experience in medical imaging and working at MerchOne, the technicians were aware of the visual images the doctors needed that would allow them to give an accurate assessment. An injury of this magnitude required X-ray images from all possible angles.

Two long hours went by before the doctors emerged from the examination room. After removing their gloves, they lowered their masks and shared their findings with the family and coaching staff. The medical doctor in charge, Dr. Dorian Babcock, who received his medical degree from the University of Iowa College of Medicine and has been in practice for over 15 years, said to the family, "Despite the swollen knee, we were able to determine from looking at the X-ray images that KeShawn suffered a torn anterior cruciate ligament (ACL) and a partial tear of his meniscus tendon.

The news on the severity of the injury was devastating and not received well by KeShawn's family. His mother, Essie Mae, and his brother and sister, Freddie and Althea, were crushed and tearful. Papa James stood silently and unexpressive. But he held out hope, telling his family, "Things happen for a reason, and if the almighty chooses to bless KeShawn, all will be well." Mercy Medical doctors told the family they would like to perform the surgery when the swelling subsided. But Coach Stosik interjected and said, "Chicago State has an affiliated medical team back in Chicago. So, as soon as KeShawn is stable enough to be transported, we will have the doctors in Chicago do another assessment before surgery.

Twenty-four hours after the tragedy on the track, KeShawn was transported back to Chicago. Chicago State University arranged his appointment with the orthopedic surgeon at the University of Illinois Hospital. Accompanied by his family and coach Stosik, KeShawn received consultation from Dr. Bob Jeffers, a well-renowned orthopedist at Chicago Medical Center who maintains an affiliation with multiple hospitals in the area. Dr. Jeffers received his medical degree from the University of Illinois College of Medicine in Chicago and had practiced for over 20 years. After a review of the X-rays taken in Iowa, Dr. Jeffers confirmed the assessment made by Dr. Babcok at Mercy Medical Center and scheduled surgery for the following morning.

Unsure when or if his star runner would fully recover from surgery, coach Stosik indicated to KeShawn's family that Chicago State would provide the necessary physical therapy treatments for KeShawn to get back up and moving like his old self. But it was too early to decide on his track future.

9

A CALL FOR HELP

KeShawn spent the next year after surgery in physical therapy and battling Chicago State University over medical bills incurred while going through his prescribed rehabilitation program. Coach Stosik had promised KeShawn that the University would cover all his rehabilitation expenses. However, the University limited treatment payments to a twice-per-week program instead of the required five days per week treatment plan prescribed by his surgeon, Dr. Bob Jeffers, at Chicago Medical Center. Because of the nature of the injury, Dr. Jeffers felt that if KeShawn diligently participated in a five-day-per-week rehab program for one year, he would have a better chance of returning to the track. However, given the limited two-day plan supported by the University, Dr. Jeffers was not optimistic that KeShawn could return to the level of excellence he had before his injury. The best case scenario Dr. Jeffers could confidently offer KeShawn, if he followed the two-day treatment plan, was full leg mobility and an opportunity to live a productive life.

The back-and-forth grappling and broken promises with Chicago State left KeShawn in inner turmoil. He could not reconcile the tragedy on the track that frightful afternoon that ended his promising career. As a result, he struggled psychologically as opposing forces of abandonment, bouts of depression, and low self-esteem ate away at him.

Contrary to the truth, KeShawn blamed himself for the unfortunate track accident that led to his injury. Like a revolving door, never-ending or beginning, the excruciating memories of the sequence of events constantly replayed in his mind, soliciting hard questions that returned no answers. "Why me? Why didn't I see the stumbling hurdlers? Did the doctors give me the best treatment plan? Why did the University limit my physical therapy treatments?" he asked himself over and over. As the toll of those memories haunted him, they took root in the corners of his mind, fueling doubt and uncertainty that prevented him from moving forward. Moodiness and isolation had replaced the charm and wit that once was his identity, leading him to drop out of Chicago State and enroll at Chicago Technical College. A year later, a heartbroken KeShawn walked away from a promising relationship with his college girlfriend.

Although KeShawn's future remained cloudy, he had no problem finding employment due to his tremendous popularity in the city. But the uncertainty left him wondering what direction his life was headed. KeShawn knew enough about finances to keep putting money aside earned from his jobs and wait for the right opportunity, whatever that might be. Although his popularity, job skills, and work experiences allowed him to find work, maintaining a job had become problematic. His sour demeanor only fed his depression, which in turn led him to disregard the work ethic he once was known to possess.

During any given week, while working as a carpenter apprentice, co-workers took bets that KeShawn would be late for work or not show up at all. His behavior's negative connotations finally reached a tipping point when he verbally confronted his supervisor. Fed up with his attendance and punctuality habits, the supervisor had no other recourse. KeShawn was terminated from his carpenter apprentice job. His once charismatic personality, which opened many doors for him, was fading fast and only gave false cover to a man hurting inside.

Trust issues and low self-esteem caused KeShawn to shun the company of others, and he no longer pursued meaningful relationships. The weight of that unfortunate track accident had become too much to bear and was swiftly moving him down the highway to nowhere. Those who knew and loved KeShawn empathized with his pain and tried reaching out, but KeShawn purposely avoided their attempts at friendship, further retreated into an impenetrable shell, and shut them out.

After retreating to his South Side apartment, where drawn curtains hid a man in emotional pain and without direction, KeShawn had nowhere to turn in his darkest hour. He finally admitted that if he didn't pull himself together, he would end up as another sad statistic at the city morgue. He acknowledged that he must free his mind from despair but was torn between spilling his guts to a professional stranger or reaching out to a trusted friend. His self-imposed exile not only ruined the relationship he had with his former college friends but also strained his relationship with his high school coach and surrogate, Coach Williamson. KeShawn and the coach had already fallen on bad terms because of the track behavior issues at Chicago State. His brother Freddie, who was always in his corner, would gladly listen, but as a grown man, KeShawn was reluctant to burden his loving family with his problems. If he barred his soul to someone he didn't trust, he risked exposing the hurt outside the benefit of a resolution. As this dilemma tormented him, KeShawn, and his fragile state of mind, wondered if there was anyone he could trust to help him snatch victory from the jaws of defeat.

As he sat in the corner of his one-bedroom apartment, his drapes permanently drawn closed, KeShawn stared continuously at his TV, which offered a lousy reception and senseless TV commercials that failed to relieve his depressed state of mind. The pain he felt was real, and the more he tried to analyze his dilemma, the more he only deepened his despair. The poor TV reception was another source that added to his frustration. KeShawn fidgeted with the aluminum-covered television rabbit ears, attempting to fix the blinking screen. But his despair still consumed him as he slumped back down into his oversized man-chair and deeply exhaled air of frustration. Suddenly, his ears caught the tail end of a barely audible self-help promotional commercial that mentioned, "..if you're not happy with your life, do something."

Anxious to know more, KeShawn reached over to turn up the volume, but it was too late. The flipping TV screen had returned to a Gunsmoke Western program. Nonetheless, having heard just enough of the TV promo, KeShawn took action. He opened his apartment drapes, which, for KeShawn, was like opening his mind and welcoming in rays of sunshine. The light to a path of hope gave way to the thought of the one person who knew him best, Moe Banks, his Jamaican friend and former track teammate at Chicago State U.

Moe had returned to Jamaica shortly after completing college. He was always a great communicator and never judgemental. At this stage in his life, KeShawn needed honest feedback and a boost of confidence. So, he gave significant thought to contacting Moe. The thought of calling Moe sounded like a good idea, but he wondered how to call Jamaica. "He's the one who always calls me," KeShawn murmured. Then, a thought occurred to him. "Maybe the operator can help me make the call."

After grabbing the black rotary phone from the lamp table, KeShawn dialed the operator, but just as the operator answered, the whistling noise from the tea kettle distracted his intentions, so he hung up the phone.

Laughing at the timing of the interruption, KeShawn retrieved his favorite coffee mug from a sink filled with unwashed dishes. The cup bore the logo name of Chicago State University, a stark reminder of days gone by. After giving the mug a good rinse, he drowned a peppermint tea bag using steaming hot water poured from the red kettle. Just as quickly, KeShawn retrieved a badly worn coaster and covered the cup. While his tea bag was swimming in the cup of hot water, a now confident KeShawn attempted a second call for operator assistance.

After several rings, a female voice asked, "How may I help you?" The soft, caring tone of the operator's voice comforted KeShawn and helped to ease his apprehension. "Yes, ma'am, I would like to make an international phone call to Kingston, Jamaica," he said. The operator replied, "I can help you, sir. Please stay on the line."

While the operator was placing the call, KeShawn took a breath to remind himself about his current state of mind. He didn't want Moe to recognize the pain and hurt in his voice, especially not from the first hello. He thought putting himself into a frame of mind that projected a strong and confident person, not some sobbing loser holding a basket full of issues would be best.

Moe knew KeShawn better than anyone outside of his immediate family. They were tight-knit and hung out together throughout college, where KeShawn was the big man on campus.

Even though KeShawn was reserved and a borderline introvert in public, his engaging personality was magnetic. Teammates and students alike were drawn to his penchant for storytelling. KeShawn was always accommodating and made everyone feel good about themselves. So, viewing him as different from those memories would be a shock, especially to Moe.

KeShawn and Moe tried to stay in touch over the years, but living in two different worlds and having other priorities made scheduling visits a low priority. It was, however, refreshing and a blessing when, on those rare occasions, Moe would reach out to his friend. They enjoyed long conversations on the phone, laughing and joking, talking about something, and sometimes talking about nothing, just talking. Their conversations always end with a bit of what-if and "We need to stay in touch." During their time together at Chicago State U., their popularity and that of their teammates soared around campus after they won the school's first-ever NCAA Regional Track and Field Championship as freshmen. The championship will be remembered for years.

10

INVITATION TO CHILL

*J*amaican-born Maurice (Moe) Banks was fun-loving and gregarious as a youngster. He had a warm heart and a kind spirit and did well in school. He enjoyed sports with an affinity for soccer but loved running track. After his parents divorced when he was only 13, Moe and three other siblings lived with his mother. However, he had difficulty adjusting in his father's absence, and he struggled to focus in school. His interest in soccer drifted, but running track on the Jamaican under-17 club was the last thread that kept him afloat. However, his social choices were what his mother called the wrong crowd, and they pulled hard on those loose threads. Unfortunately, minus his father's consistent teaching and discipline, Moe began spending more time hanging out with his new friends, slowly diminishing his passion for running track. Eventually, his choices were too much for his mother to stand as Moe began to have brushes with the law. His London-born mother, Monnie Anderson, a former track star for the Jamaican National Team, was busy trying to provide for her family as a fashion designer and was at the end of her rope. She did her best to guide Moe, but with three other children to care for, she quickly lost the battle to reign in her son.

In a desperate attempt to keep her child out of Jamaica's jails, and out of options, Monnie reached out to her mother, Beulah Jenkins, who lived in America on the South Side of Chicago. Monnie asked her mother for her help to save her wayward son. Monnie also had three brothers living in Chicago, so she prayed they would accept her pleas to help their mother and check on Moe occasionally to help keep him on the straight.

The move to Chicago was a blessing that Moe didn't see coming. After his initial reluctance to live with his grandmother, the attention from Moe's uncles, who kept an eye on him and played an active role in their nephew's life, was tremendous. The uncle's insistence on doing well in school and participation in a track program was the tonic that kept Moe out of trouble as he adjusted to his new environment.

After an outstanding track season during his senior year at DuSable High School, Moe's exploits as a sprinter caught the attention of college track coaches. He had multiple offers to consider but decided to prolong his decision until after the KeShawn Coleman signing day event. Not long after the school ceremony, where KeShawn announced his intentions to attend Chicago State University, Moe accepted a scholarship to join his fellow DuSable mega-star at Chicago State University.

TODAY, Moe and his wife, Gladys, live in the Mona Hills area of Kingston, Jamaica, where they raise their two middle-school kids, Zion and Sherry. The quiet and peaceful middle-class neighborhood is the polar opposite of the hectic street life Moe knew as a youngster. His kids spend time in a mostly safe and secure community with a top-rated school system.

Moe valued KeShawn's unique friendship and the cherished memories of their times together in Chicago. There was never a question or doubt about doing a favor for his friend if the situation warranted it. The journey they shared on the track and, more than they probably should have, off the track brought back priceless and painful memories. The track accident that stalled KeShawn's career was the most painful memory one can imagine. After the accident, KeShawn was never the same dynamic and explosive runner he was before his knee injury.

Moe recalled that sad day when he watched the great KeShawn, walking with a slight limp that rehabilitation treatments could not resolve, return to the track. "The King" tried his best to regain his old form, but his signature acceleration to run down opponents was absent. Sadly, his legs would no longer respond to his commands, leaving him looking older and slower. The bitter reality of his fading skills was evident when freshmen runners, who in the past would not even be able to carry his gym bag and were elated just to be on the same track as "The King," began out running him. It became common for them to outrace KeShawn in practice consistently. The jolt of reality just ate away at KeShawn. The slow erosion of his pride and self-esteem was painful, and his once charming personality began to slowly sour. The great KeShawn Coleman had become a shell of his former self. His exploits had been reduced to an afterthought.

Moe, who was busy trying to make a life in Jamaica, got word through the proverbial grapevine that KeShawn was experiencing some troubles and was struggling with depression, anger, and regret. Moe often wondered why he and his buddy didn't communicate more often, but now he understood this may have been why. Surprisingly, one day, out of the blue, Moe received a phone call from an operator assistant; it was KeShawn on the line.

Moe's deep Jamaican voice answered, "Ya Mon, this Key?" a name Moe tagged KeShawn when they were in college. The two pals continued, relishing each minute of the unexpected but welcomed phone call. An overly excited Moe kept thinking, "This can't be real," but at the same time, he thought this might be an excellent time to invite KeShawn to visit him on the island. Perhaps Jamaica could be the antidote to resurrect his friend's life.

"Say what, visit Jamaica. Man, I've always wanted to visit

Jamaica, so, yeah, let's do this," replied Key, the man in hiding from his true feelings. In the middle of the excitement, Moe quickly reminded KeShawn about the process of visiting outside the States. "You know, Mon, you have to get a passport and shit, so do your thing and check out what you have to do to get here. Let me know what's up as soon as you know your travel dates." Moe laughed and continued, "I've got some vacation time I need to use, so just let me know; I'll be here for you, Mon. My house is your house."

THE REDWARE PEOPLE are believed to be the first inhabitants of Jamaica. But it was the Arawak, also called Tainos, an Indian tribe from South America, who named the island Xaymaca, which meant "land of wood and water."

When Columbus, believed to be the first European to reach Jamaica, landed in 1494 and claimed discovery in the name of Spain, the Arawak were already inhabitants of the island.

Jamaica was colonized by the Spanish in 1494 and was named Santiago. In 1865, the British defeated the Spaniards and renamed the island Jamaica the parish of St. James.

Jamaica is a tropical island known for its rich and diverse culture. It was shaped by its location and forged by the slave trade and the lucrative agriculture industries of sugarcane, bananas, and coffee. Jamaica is the third-largest island of the Greater Antilles in the Caribbean and continues to be a Commonwealth realm, with the British monarch as King of Jamaica and head of state.

11

PREPARATION BEFORE PARTICIPATION

The phone conversation with Moe was exhilarating and excited KeShawn. The warmth and generosity he felt during the call inspired him to dislodge his constantly worn frown. Preparing for a trip out of the country would require KeShawn to surface from his shell and interact with others, something he had abandoned months ago. So, he reasoned that the little steps he takes now to improve his disposition will go a long way to help him make giant steps in the future.

After a phone call to the Chicago Passport Agency, KeShawn learned that the processing time for a new passport could take between four and six weeks. Initially, the news frustrated him, but then he realized the wait time could benefit him and allow him to take care of some crucial business before leaving.

The first thing on his agenda was to apply for a passport, something KeShawn needed to do as quickly as possible. The application process had a few key steps that must be followed, and if not, could lead to untimely delays, which KeShawn wanted to avoid. The passport agency instructions were clear: Bring to the Passport Agency Office a driver's license, a color passport photo, a completed DS-II application form, and, of course, cash or check payment.

To occupy his time while seated in the Passport Agency reception area, KeShawn curiously looked around the room and found an interesting mix of people who, thankfully, were minding their own business. Except there was one kid no older than eight or nine who kept staring at him out of curiosity or fascination. As he tried ignoring the kid, KeShawn thought customer service ticket number three couldn't get called quickly enough. The good news, however, that comforted him was that nobody in the room, including the kid, was privy to his travel plans. As his eyes wandered about the room, KeShawn spotted a Chicago Defender newspaper discarded in the trash basket. The paper looked pretty good despite the half-completed crossword puzzle, and it was void of spilled coffee or chewing gum. KeShawn quickly glanced over the headlines before looking at the sports section. Nothing noteworthy stood out in either section besides the same partisan politics and the City Council's rejection of the White Sox's funding request for their badly needed ballpark renovation project. But just as KeShawn was about to return the paper to the trash, something caught his eye in the Want Ads section. Someone had indicated an interest in a short-term apartment rental and posted an ad. Because he was in the early stages of his plan to travel out of the country, KeShawn had never considered what to do with his apartment or car. But the thought of renting or subletting his apartment now had his attention and intrigued him. After ripping the Want Ad rental request from the newspaper, KeShawn heard the receptionist say, "Final call for ticket number three."

While he drove home after successfully submitting the Passport application, KeShawn became so deep into thought about the possibility of renting out his apartment that he ran a stop sign two blocks from his apartment. "Dam, a stunned KeShawn said out loud for no one in particular to hear. That was too scary. I could have killed someone or worse, been killed myself."

He knew he would return to Chicago, but KeShawn didn't

know precisely how long he would be away. He didn't want the apartment to sit idle if he was gone for a month or more. So, after calling the number listed on the Want Ad, Lady Luck smiled at him. The Want Ad request was not for an immediate rental but five to six weeks from today.

KeShawn explained the details about his apartments and what would be required of the prospective renter. He shared with the wannabe renter the idea of renting his apartment on a short-term sublease agreement when he said, "Because the utilities are included in the rent, all that would be required would be timely rent payments." The idea of a sublease initially surprised the renter, but he became increasingly interested as he processed the information KeShawn shared. The idea was to rent a furnished apartment only minutes from the City Center. This was perfect, he thought. However, minor details had to be resolved before the deal could be cemented. First, KeShawn needed the consent of his landlord to sublease his apartment, and second, he needed a contract that covered the lease terms.

Sitting in his favorite oversized chair, KeShawn remembered someone he knew from college who worked at the Chicago Public Library. But, he wondered if she was still there, and if so, would she be willing to assist him with his rental paperwork? So, the following day, he took a chance and drove to the Madison Street library. When he got there, and much to his surprise, he saw the former Chicago State University student, Kathy Whitmore, sitting behind a glass-covered desk. KeShawn's and Kathy's paths crossed several times at Chicago State, mainly when she was an undergraduate tutor assigned to helping athletes who made the "unsatisfactory grade report" study hall list. She works full-time as a Reference Librarian while completing her graduate degree in Sports Psychology at the University of Chicago.

When Kathy saw this tall man approaching her desk, she lowered her glasses, which were attached to a pearl-beaded chain lanyard, a birthday gift from her grandmother years past. She immediately recognized the recognizable KeShawn Coleman from their time at Chicago State.

After exchanging a few pleasantries and doing a brief catch-up, Kathy asked, "So, Mr. Coleman, what brings you to the Chicago Public Library today?" KeShawn, hesitant to explain his intentions, kept his request short and basic and replied, "I'm looking for information about contracts for apartment lease and sublease agreements." Curious at the request but not wanting to be unethical in inquiring further, Kathy obliged the former Chicago State star athlete and did a quick document search.

Kathy returned, bearing multiple copies of lease contract forms, displaying the skills of a seasoned Librarian. She told KeShawn, "I think these might be what you want. Why don't you look them over while I help someone else."

Impressed by Kathy's quick work, KeShawn looked over the documents she provided and found precisely a Sublease Agreement Form he was looking for. When Kathy returned, KeShawn asked if he could have a copy made of the form, and if so, was there a copy fee for the service? Kathy smiled and said, "I can make you a copy. There is a nominal fee, but it's my pleasure to waive it for you." Blushing and grateful for her assistance, KeShawn thanked Kathy and, as a courtesy, promised to stop by again, if nothing more than to say hello.

Armed with the information he sought that spelled out the terms and conditions of the sublease, KeShawn moved his plan forward and contacted the landlord to explain his intentions. On the strength of his good standing as a tenant, the landlord approved KeShawn's short-term sublease request.

But to make it clear, the landlord reiterated to KeShawn that he is ultimately responsible for the monthly rent and not the subtenant, then cautioned KeShawn when he said, "Choose your subtenant carefully."

Feeling encouraged as each step of his plan came to fruition, KeShawn showed signs of emerging from his self-imposed exile.

His next step was to connect with his brother, Freddie, whom he had put on ice while he drifted aimlessly after leaving Chicago State.

Freddie was overcome and joyful when, out of the blue, he received a phone call from his estranged brother. After the glee subsided, they agreed to meet for lunch at the famous 'Jimmy's Burgers' on Cottage Grove Avenue in Bronzeville. While he waited outside the restaurant for Freddie to arrive, KeShawn was repeatedly greeted and waved at by the passersby who fondly remembered him from his legendary time at DuSable. The recognition boosted his fragile ego and made him feel good about his renewed emergence. As the brothers approached each other outside the restaurant, without saying a word, they shared a long embrace that had an emotional feeling extending back to Alabama, and it was priceless.

As they took their seats in a booth, a view of the streets gave them a reason to smile. Freddie said, "Just so we're clear, lunch is on me," KeShawn could only laugh as his brother finally beat him at something. In between bites of the delicious burger, KeShawn, although not quite ready to spill his guts about how the accident on the track had taken an emotional toll on his life, shared his pending Jamaica travel plans.

Sparing Freddie the details, KeShawn did acknowledge an epiphany he had that his life was about to change. "I don't know who, what, when, where, or how, but I feel a change in my life is coming." Looking astonished, Freddie asked, "What gives you that impression? How can you be so sure? What's changed?"

KeShawn laughed and said, "You know how when we were kids growing up on the farm, we thought God talked to us?" Agreeing, the wide-eyed Freddie listened intently as KeShawn continued. "Well, I believe God is talking to me right now. He reminded me that just because I fell doesn't mean I can't pick myself up, physically and mentally." Freddie, unnerved and overcome with emotion, used his napkin to wipe the trickling tears from his eyes, put the napkin aside, and, while seated, shook his big brother's hand. Freddie told his brother, "I can't begin to tell you how happy I am to hear you say that. The family has been worried sick about you." He continued, "If it's alright, can I share what you told me?" "Sure," KeShawn replied. "I'm good with that."

"I do have a small favor to ask of you, well, two favors," a smiling KeShawn said. Freddie returned the smile and said, "Anything but a race," which gave them both a hearty laugh. "I got lucky and found a renter for my apartment. He's a former football acquaintance from DuSable who was looking for a short-term furnished apartment to rent," explained KeShawn. "Wow, that's great," said Freddie. "Yeah, the short-term month-to-month sublease agreement just fell into my lap, but it's not for another five weeks, so the timing couldn't have been better," replied KeShawn.

He then asked Freddie for the two favors. "I don't want to leave my car parked on the streets at the apartment for an unknown amount of time, so would it be okay if I left it at your house?" Before Freddie could answer, KeShawn continued, "Would you also drive by the apartment occasionally? You can use my car if you want, just to see what you see." "Yes, and yes," replied Freddie.

"I don't mind at all keeping an eye on things. Anything for you, brother, and you know this," Freddie said. As KeShawn handed him a set of apartment and car keys, KeShawn explained, "You won't need to go in or anything, but just in case there's an emergency or something, you can have access." KeShawn continued, "I'm not sure what my time frame in Jamaica will be, but after a few weeks, Moe will probably be glad to get rid of my butt, and I'll be ready to get back to Chicago my damn self." Then KeShawn told Freddie, "Thank you, and tell Papa, Mom, and Althea I truly love them, and I'll be sure to connect with the family when I get back." The brothers slapped hands, embraced, and fought back tears as they walked away. After taking a few steps, KeShawn turned and called back to Freddie and said, "Oh yeah, I'll call you from Jamaica once I get a feel for what's going on. Love you, man!" Freddie pointed a finger at KeShawn and nodded in understanding his brother.

The anticipation escalated as the weeks passed, and KeShawn got increasingly excited about his voyage of rediscovery. He could only hope that God grants him the strength and courage to change the things he can. He knows the voyage may not be smooth, and there may even be storms, but if he can take one step forward, he can inch closer to removing the shackles that have imprisoned him for months.

Four weeks into the document waiting game, full of anticipation, KeShawn showed signs of nervousness and became fidgety. The slow wait on his passport created an unwanted anxiety and tested his patience. Consumed by questions, he wondered how soon the documents would be ready. What do I do in the meantime? His sublease agreement has been signed, and the tenant was expecting to get the keys in less than a week. Doing his best to remain calm, KeShawn began sorting through ideas about what and how much to pack. How long am I going to be in Jamaica? A week, a month, maybe longer, he fussed. The passport was expected to arrive in less than two weeks, but KeShawn's impatience continued to stress him. He thought the passport was late, but that wasn't the case. There was no delay. The passport process was taking its typical timeline. But that didn't stop KeShawn from becoming edgy. After making calls to the Passport Agency almost every other day, KeShawn was now harboring paranoid thoughts. He wondered if his credit was still in good standing or if the system was deliberately trying to keep him from traveling out of the country. After putting items from his apartment into the trunk of his car, KeShawn spotted the postman across the street. To appear relaxed, KeShawn walked over and calmly asked if there was any mail for him. The postman laughed and said, "I know you've been waiting for something. Here you go." A quick flip through the handful of junk mail revealed the envelope from the Passport Agency. The long-awaited process was finally over; KeShawn Coleman now possessed a United States travel passport.

The Yellow Taxicab arrived at KeShawn's apartment earlier than expected. After blowing his horn several times, the impatient cab driver, while still looking at the apartment address through his rolled-down window, slowly began to pull away from the curb when suddenly KeShawn emerged carrying two suitcases and a carry-on bag strapped across his body. As KeShawn approached the cab, the driver looked up and scowled before recognizing his passenger. "KeShawn, KeShawn Coleman, damn, man, what's happening? My name is Skeeter, Skeeter Evans. You might not remember me, but I was at DuSable when you were killing it." KeShawn could only smile as he offered Skeeter a handshake.

During the ride to Chicago's O'Hare International Airport, Skeeter talked about the days at DuSable while also trying to explain that his three-year cab driving gig was temporary until he got on his feet. KeShawn was listening but not fully engaged; his mind was somewhere over the Caribbean Sea. After arriving at the terminal, Skeeter helped unload the bags and carried them to the ticket counter. In return for his help, KeShawn dropped Skeeter a generous tip and extended a handshake before wishing him good luck getting on his feet.

Carrying his passport in one hand and a roundtrip ticket in the other, KeShawn strolled through the terminal looking like a man on a mission as he checked in at gate 14. The boarding agent reminded the waiting passengers that the flight was full and all carry-on luggage must fit underneath the seat or be stored in the overhead compartment. The good news about this trip was that KeShawn didn't bring any extra baggage. He accepted his good friend's R & R invitation and only brought love in his heart and an open mind.

As the 6-foot-5-inch former star athlete gracefully settled into his legroom-friendly aisle seat as passenger 57 on the United Airlines Boeing 787 non-stop flight bound for Kingston, Jamaica, he finally exhaled as he fastened his seat belt. KeShawn was delighted to get away and looked forward to relaxing, re-energizing, and reconnecting with his good friend, Moe. He thought, what better way to let go of the past and embrace the future? Little did KeShawn know how this R&R trip would unfold. Events home and abroad that would alter a world he thought he knew and turn it upside down and 360 degrees.

12

WELCOME TO JAMAICA

When he landed at Kingston International Airport, KeShawn's anticipation of seeing his old friend overwhelmed him. His attempt to contain his excitement caused him to succumb to lightheadedness.

After reaching the baggage claim area and feeling uneasy, he anxiously looked around for a place to sit. While seated, KeShawn tried to compose himself, but the unfamiliar surroundings only added to his anxiety. So he thought, "If I can just put some water on my face, I should be good to go." As he looked around, he spotted a barely visible sign that read 'Men's Restroom.'

Walking purposefully, KeShawn reached the restroom, but only after navigating around travelers rushing to pick up their luggage. They must have thought KeShawn was invisible because bumping into him seemed normal. Using a water faucet that started and stopped on its own accord was unnerving, but KeShawn, determined to get himself under control, could splash enough water on his face to find a bit of relief. He turned from the faucet and found an air blower that refused to put out air. Luckily, mounted side-by-side were two paper towel dispensers. However, one was empty, and the other was reluctant to release the paper towel.

The more KeShawn pulled from the stubborn dispenser, the less paper towel he got. So, in a huff and carrying multiple pieces of paper towel extracted from the temperamental machine, KeShawn dried his face.

Then, he swished the used paper towel into an overflowing trash container using a basketball-shooting motion. Finally, KeShawn felt composed and was ready to face whatever awaited him in Jamaica.

He returned to the baggage claim carousel, where most of the luggage had already disappeared into the hands of flight 787 passengers. Only six pieces of luggage remained in the circling carousel. KeShawn, holding tight to his carry-on draped across his body, took a deep breath, followed by a sigh, identified his luggage, grabbed his two bags, and headed outside the terminal to look for his friend.

Unsure in this new land but still calm, KeShawn spotted someone who resembled Moe, and as they walked closer to each other, vast grins as wide as the Caribbean Sea creased their faces. They screamed and embraced each other in a bear hug that on-lookers found startling but understandable. After wiping away the emotional tears of joy and giving high-five hand slaps, KeShawn stepped back in disbelief to get another look at his friend. Moe, sporting a nicely fitting red, black, and yellow cap on top of his long dreads, couldn't contain his joy at the moment's reality. Despite the passage of time, and if it weren't for his change in hair-style, Moe still resembled the lead runner on the Chicago State championship 4x440 relay team. Still in disbelief that he was standing in front of his friend, KeShawn took another deep breath and inhaled the fresh air of this island called Jamaica.

While Moe, who could still not remove his ear-to-ear smile, looked KeShawn up and down, he couldn't help but notice his unmistakable broad shoulders and distinguished-looking full facial beard. KeShawn's limp from his track injury was barely noticeable, and he still looked like the big man on campus he was. Simultane-ously, they bellowed out, 'What is time?'

The drive from the airport to Moe's house was filled with chatter and laughter, and before long, they were unloading luggage from the car. Moe and his wife Gladys had prepared their home and guest bedroom to accommodate Key's stay, but Moe had failed to mention to Gladys just how tall KeShawn was, which raised her concerns about the bed size. Key assured them that all would be well, and he was thrilled and appreciative to be a guest in their home.

After a few days of getting acclimated to island life, listening to reggae music, and smoking a little ganja, Key and Moe were in total Jamaican chill mode. The following morning, Gladys prepared her favorite but not-so-typical American breakfast. After washing their hands for the third time, Moe explained the history of the meal, which consisted of ackee and saltfish, fried plantain and dumplings, roasted breadfruit, boiled dumplings, and yam. The delicious breakfast was consumed in a matter of minutes. After patting his stomach, KeShawn pushed back from the table, smiled, and confessed after a brief laugh, "That was a great breakfast, but kind of different from what I usually eat in Chicago."

The tattered and well-used backyard lounge sofa served as a perfect place to kick back and enjoy an after-breakfast conversation. Though he's thoroughly happy spending time chiding his friend, Moe couldn't help but reminisce about the good old days and how they shared an unbreakable bond in Chicago. The thought of Key living on the island permanently and re-establishing their friendship constantly ran through Moe's mind.

On cue, Gladys brought cups of herbal tea from the kitchen that smelled delicious but was still too hot to sip. She also got a copy of the daily Jamaican Observer newspaper and wanted to share something that caught her attention. She came across a Montego Bay job fair announcement, so she took liberties and used a yellow highlighter that had seen better days to mark the date.

While living in Jamaica, Moe had never considered moving his family from Kingston to Montego Bay, so why would he be interested in attending the job fair? What was Gladys thinking? Even the "that sounds nice" needle wasn't registering enough to budge his interest. He was content and quite comfortable living in his tight-knit Mona Heights community.

But after he took a few sips of tea and shuffled back and forth in bewilderment, Moe looked over at Gladys with a smile, and she winked. An ulterior motive was in play. Listed on the job fair advertisement was one particular position that caught Moe's attention, a job that he thought might raise an eyebrow from Key. Moe was hopeful that KeShawn's journeyman experience as a carpenter and his technical certification just might elicit interest or, at best, a curiosity in the position. Moe also fathomed that if KeShawn showed any interest, the job recruiters would be all over him, just like in his basketball recruitment days.

The tickler here, and this was a giant tickler. If the recruiters offered KeShawn a job by chance, how receptive would he be about moving to Jamaica? Now, where was Moe taking this hair-brain thought? Perhaps his overzealous imagination to rekindle his friendship was nothing more than wishful thinking.

As he explored angles to support his subtle plan, Moe suggested to KeShawn that they take a day and drive over to Montego Bay. Along the way, Moe would casually take the longer scenic route through the resort town of Ocho Rios. On the surface, the plan didn't appear too suspicious. However, the vacation time he set aside was nearing an end, and Moe needed to fast-forward his plan to ensure they got to the job fair while he still had time off.

Gladys and Moe discussed his plan and his dwindling vacation time. Gladys quickly reminded her husband about his company's extended vacation time policy. The policy also stated that employees with three or more years of continuous full-time employment could borrow from the following year's vacation time allotment. "This is great," Moe said to Gladys. He added, "I can add time and extend this year's vacation time. I did not know this."

Since Moe was eligible to take advantage of this unique policy provision, he needed to act quickly. The provision stipulated that a notice to borrow time must be submitted within 48 hours of the expiring vacation time. So, besides a sense of urgency and the clock ticking, Moe had to draw up his vacation request before driving to Montego Bay.

Moe called his supervisor on the morning of the deadline and verbally requested that his vacation be extended by one week. Concerned that he might be needed on site to oversee a major renovation project, Moe assured his supervisor that he would submit in advance a plan of action that his work unit would follow to address the renovation project during his absence. Due mainly to his outstanding leadership as site supervisor at the Kingston Armory HVAC Unit, Moe was given some latitude. Based on the phone conversation, the work supervisor approved his extended vacation time request only if he submitted his request in writing.

The extra vacation days he has had to be used strategically if Moe wanted to influence his friend. He was determined to fill the time using every available resource to influence KeShawn's thoughts about living in Jamaica. He was convinced that taking the scenic Montego Bay route through Ocho Rios could overwhelm KeShawn by showing him the beauty of the white-sand beaches that lie just off the Caribbean.

Despite a reminder from Gladys to get the family car serviced before making the trip, Moe, his eyebrows raised, assured his wife their Morris Oxford sedan was up for the challenge. At the same time, he dismissed the notion of taking the bus as this would dampen his scheme for KeShawn. But after shaking his head, Moe acquiesced, went to the garage to satisfy his wife, and performed a quick oil check. While there, he pulled a tire pressure gauge from the bottom of his glove box and checked the inflation level of each tire, including the spare. The garage check was detailed enough to satisfy Moe and gave him confidence that his car could handle the two-and-a-half-hour road trip. Just adding gas would be the last thing to do.

KeShawn shared the embarrassment of not having a resume. But Gladys let him off the hook when she asked, "Did you know you would need a resume when you left Chicago?" A smiling

KeShawn replied, "No, I guess a resume never crossed my mind; getting my travel documents was the only thing I was focused on." Gladys replied, "But I think it's important that you bring a resume to the job fair. You never know what may happen." She suggested, "Because Moe has a job-related assignment to complete, I'll have time to help you put a resume together." KeShawn, humbled by Gladys' generosity, accepted her offer. So methodically, Glady captured KeShawn's employment experiences, skills, and qualifications. "All possibilities are open to you when you submit a resume. But you can guess what will happen if you don't," a laughing Gladys said to KeShawn.

The trip up to and through Ocho Rios, then over to Montego Bay, added almost an hour of extra drive time, but Moe was unconcerned. His extended vacation freed him from the worry of abandoning his island-inducing plan to Montego Bay. The scenic views and the people they would meet along the way would expose Key to more island hospitality and Jamaican love.

The beautiful but long drive to Montego Bay was enough time for Moe and Key to have a realistic conversation about the "what-if" possibilities: jobs, family, and the feasibility of permanently moving to Jamaica if everything was everything.

Moe was optimistic but wondered if his sales pitches sparked an interest from KeShawn. But Key, at this point, was uncertain about almost everything. His silence didn't dismiss the possibilities, but he didn't give a ringing endorsement either. The omission left Moe wondering what he could do next to influence his friend.

As the car approached the parking area in Montego Bay, a large green and yellow sign welcomed them to the "Montego Bay Airport Jobs Fair." Consumed in thought and his mind working overtime, Moe imagined two scenarios that might tip the scales in his favor: finding KeShawn a job or finding him a female friend.

Dressed neatly in their business casual attire, Key and Moe slowly walked by the rows of job fair tables. They stopped several times at different tables and casually picked up job-related information but decided not to engage the table host in conversation.

Continuing their stroll, they glanced at two Montego Bay Jamaica Airport recruiters seated at a corner table underneath a green and white canopy. Moe gave KeShawn an elbow nudge and said, "Those must be the job recruiters mentioned in the Jamaica newspaper job fair advertisement Gladys talked about." As Moe and KeShawn walked closer, the two recruiters could be seen sipping what looked to be some type of fruit smoothie drink. They were overheard talking about the big football match later in the week in Kingston.

A third representative was having technical difficulties operating a stubborn carousel slide projector. Company flyers, brochures, a bowl of candy, and logo pens were spread out on their table. The two men from Kingston took notice but kept up their stroll when Moe's attention was diverted to another table that displayed something of interest to him: the airport's proposed multi-million-dollar HVAC renovation model.

One of the two airport table recruiters, a young man who looked to be in his mid-20s, appeared more engaging than his senior-looking partner. He stood and waved his hand to beckon KeShawn to return to his table.

While looking at the HVAC renovation model, Moe turned and glanced over his tinted sunglasses and noticed KeShawn conversing with the young airport recruiter. Shortly afterward, KeShawn had removed his sunglasses and pulled from his leather cross-body satchel the two-page resume he and Gladys had hastily put together. A surprised Moe had to bite his lip to keep from saying something. He thought, "Is it possible that Key is interested in a job in Jamaica?"

The interaction at the recruiter's table started to take on a life of its own. After he gave the resume a cursory look, the recruiter asked his partner to look at it. The senior recruiter and KeShawn acknowledged each other, gave nods, and smiled. The recruiter then asked KeShawn how he was on time.

KeShawn, casually going along, minding his business, was now seated and taking questions from the two Montego Bay Airport job recruiters. The senior recruiter led the conversation and said to KeShawn, "We like your resume, so we want to review a few job-related details if you don't mind." He began by sharing company and job-specific information such as job benefits, growth, and career opportunities, information usually reserved until later in the hiring process. Not wanting to interrupt the conversation but curious about what was happening, Moe looked to his left as if distracted. He walked to his right toward the table where the two people discussed career opportunities.

The recruiter shared that the company urgently needed to fill a vacant journeyman carpenter position as soon as possible. The position had primary job-specific requirements: reading building plans, measuring building materials, installing cabinetry and flooring, and framing windows and doors. The salary for the position is commensurate and directed at someone having a skilled background as a journeyman carpenter — someone certified and experienced, someone like KeShawn, for example. As he leaned over, KeShawn whispered to Moe, "Man, I can do this job. It's right up my alley."

KeShawn indicated his interest in the position and agreed to submit the completed application and resume. Before they shook hands to leave, the recruiter invited KeShawn and Moe to help themselves to some candy in the bowl. Then, the young recruiter asked Moe if there was something he was interested in. Muffling a laugh, Moe replied, "No, not at this time, but you never know." As they departed, the senior recruiter told KeShawn, "You can expect to hear from HR in about a week or less regarding a background check and references."

Not long after leaving the job fair area, while still at the Pier, Moe suggested they stop and have lunch. He wasn't sure of the location, but he recalled a restaurant offering an excellent seafood menu. "There it is," snorted Moe. Although they didn't have table reservations, the two men were escorted to a booth at the open-air Waterfront Seafood Restaurant. The restaurant offered spectacular views of the Caribbean Sea, enhancing the atmosphere of a great lunch. Moe smiled broadly as KeShawn looked out in amazement.

Unbeknownst to them, a pair of eyes followed them as they walked across the room to a view table. KeShawn said to Moe, "I feel someone is watching us."

The tall, debonair-looking man from Chicago, wearing a nicely trimmed facial beard, had caught the attention of someone else having lunch. His awareness antennas were fully galvanized and on full alert. KeShawn, determined to find out if his intuition was correct, casually scanned the restaurant, intending to find where this attention was coming from. His mindset turned from curiosity to caution when suddenly, across the room, seated alone at a table that opened up to a nice view of the Caribbean, he met another set of eyes. Those eyes then quickly glanced down in an attempt to avoid discovery. Occupied looking at the lunch menu, Moe ignored KeShawn's restaurant surveillance.

Alone, in a restaurant during a busy lunch hour, an attractive-looking woman, casually dressed and with no visible signs that she was spoken for, sat. The soft sea air blew gentle breezes from the Caribbean that caused her medium-length hair to shade just enough of her face to make her look mysterious. But it was her big hazel eyes that were captivating.

KeShawn's casual gaze had turned into a full-blown stare. He had found the person who belonged to those eyes. Meanwhile, Moe repeatedly asked Key for a meal preference, but KeShawn was preoccupied as his attention was transfixed elsewhere.

Left alone to answer the thoughts racing through his mind, KeShawn wondered, who was this person having lunch all by her lonesome? Was she spoken for? Maybe she worked nearby and was on her lunch break." He couldn't take his eyes off her, which was disconcerting. Finally, her head raised, their eyes met in a gawk. And as she smiled, she gave a slight nod for being recognized. KeShawn then made a move. He adjusted his shirt collar and walked across the room to introduce himself.

Moe finally looked up from the menu and asked, "Where are

you going?" However, KeShawn was already across the room, extending a greeting. "I take it you're not from the island," the woman said. KeShawn, blushing and laughing, replied, "Was it my shoes that gave me away?" And they both laughed like they'd known each other for years. Moe walked over carrying the menus and said to Key, "Ya Mon, are we having lunch?" And the three of them laughed aloud. Jokingly, Moe said, "Since you two know each other so well, why don't we have lunch together?" And more laughter ensued.

Moe anticipated Gladys's anxiety about the job fair and when she could expect them home. So he excused himself to call Gladys to give her the day's details and a time frame for their return to Kingston. But, more importantly, Moe couldn't wait to share the exciting news about Key's interaction with his newly found friend. Before leaving to make his phone call, Mo turned to the table and muttered to Key in his Jamaican accent, "Be careful, Mon," before laughing.

In a soft voice, she introduced herself as Dorothy Livingston. "Occasionally, when I'm not working, I'll come to the pier and have lunch at this beautiful restaurant. The food is just so incredible," Dorothy said matter-of-factly. Little did KeShawn know that the work she mentioned was at the beach resort in Ocho Rios, where he and Mo had stopped earlier after leaving Kingston.

As they sat across from each other in the open-air restaurant, the breeze from the Caribbean continued to blow in their direction and served as the perfect backdrop for a pleasant conversation. Initially, the conversation between KeShawn and Dorothy was limited to small talk and jokes about shoe references. But then Dorothy, sensing an emotional vulnerability, shifted the conversation and asked questions about the job fair. More importantly, she wanted to know what brought KeShawn to Jamaica. What were his plans here, and did he have family back in the States?

In the company of his new acquaintance, KeShawn felt calm and at ease and was more amenable to conversation. He sat up and straightened his back and, in an earnest look, responded to

Dorothy's questions in an honesty he hadn't anticipated. He shared fond memories of his childhood in Alabama and his father's decision to relocate the family North to Chicago.

But when KeShawn began talking about his college days, where an accident on the track derailed his promising career, which subsequently led him down a path of anger, depression, and self-destruction, he had to take a long pause as he realized that he was opening up for the first time.

His words about his rage and distress spilled out raw and unfiltered, revealing an honesty that caught him and Dorothy off guard. Dorothy let KeShawn continue when she realized that his honesty, like hers, was straightforward. She knew from personal experience that honesty about a challenging experience can sometimes be painful, primarily when spoken from the heart.

Growing up as a child of divorced biracial and bicultural parents, Dorothy was acutely aware of her honesty that exposed painful memories. But at the same time, it allowed those painful memories to breathe in the open air and rush in relief and healing.

Dorothy respected that KeShawn felt comfortable enough around her to unburden his pain in only their first meeting. By doing so, he unknowingly built a thread of trust within her. KeShawn knew that if he were anything but sincere and came across as pretentious or self-serving, Dorothy would see right through the facade and dismiss him as a flake.

He figured he had nothing to lose and everything to gain, even if it was just her friendship. The freedom to finally be truthful and honest with himself and unlock those haunting memories stored in his mind gave him the clarity he'd sought for a long time.

Taking a moment to catch his breath, KeShawn realized he had said a mouthful to someone he just met and felt slightly embarrassed. He offered an apology that Dorothy refused to accept. She quietly but confidently said, "Don't let your rise and fall define who you are. Instead, let what you do after you get up from your fall be your legacy." Dorothy, placing her hand on KeShawn's, continued when she said, "After all, isn't that part of your reasoning for coming to the island? To find relief and freedom and return to being the man your friends and family in the States truly love."

KeShawn remained speechless as he absorbed Dorothy's words like water on a sponge. He then gripped her hand and explained that Moe and his family were his only friends on the island, but he had room in his heart for someone else and would like to get to know her better.

The sincerity of KeShawn's honesty tugged at her heartstrings, and Dorothy realized she was not ready for the spark she felt to ignite. So she checked her watch and said to KeShawn, "It was a pleasure, but I need to run some errands." This was code for "Yes, I want to see you again, but you must show me how determined you are about seeing me."

KeShawn tried to conceal his excitement, which caused his words to get ahead of his thoughts. He breathed deeply before asking Dorothy if he could see her again. She paused her reply and nervously searched her purse for sunglasses that sat precariously on her hair. She then agreed to KeShawn's request and wrote her phone number on a 'Waterfront Restaurant' napkin, which KeShawn treasured like gold. Their goodbye was awkward. Dorothy was unsure whether to offer a handshake or give a friendly embrace. KeShawn, on the other hand, already smitten, didn't hesitate and drew Dorothy close and, in a slight embrace, kissed her on the cheek.

Feeling re-energized and lighter on his feet, KeShawn put his hand on his palpitating heart and watched Dorothy disappear into the open spaces of the Pier 1 shopping center.

Moe's extended vacation days were like a breath of fresh air. They allowed him to continue his respite from his daily work grind, enjoy the company of his good friend Key, and spend additional time alongside his family.

Upon returning to work, Moe knew management would expect him to provide updates and progress reports regarding the new renovation project. In addition, he faced the unenviable task of sorting and prioritizing the slew of work orders that remained idle when he was away and needed his attention. Moe assured his supervisor that his extended vacation wouldn't negatively impact the renovation project's completion timeline. However, despite the project's urgency, Moe was thrilled to have his good friend's company in Jamaica. He wouldn't change one thing, as he thought aloud, "Being there for my friend when he needed support—well, isn't that what friends are for?"

13

CAN'T GO HOME

Despite Moe's insistence and pleas from his kids, who had grown fond of KeShawn's playful ways, KeShawn decided it was time to move out of Moe's house. So he offered this explanation, "Moe, it's time. You're returning to work, plus I don't want to wear out my welcome; I might have to come back here one day." As he laughed, KeShawn went on. Because of you and your family's hospitality, I was able to unlock and release from my mind some very dark issues that were very troubling." Turning, KeShawn looked at Gladys and continued when he said, "I'm in a perfect place now, so I'm looking forward to what the future might bring, and I have the both of you to thank. So, from the bottom of my heart, I appreciate your kindness and generosity; they meant a lot to me."

As promised, KeShawn needed to contact his brother, Freddie, and inform him about the pending opportunity in Jamaica. KeShawn was also aware that Freddie was busy doing his family life and his job at the college, so it wouldn't be fair to burden him with another favor, even though Freddie would probably say yes to anything his brother asked of him.

However, after meeting by chance a wonderful woman,

someone he wanted to spend more time getting to know, and the strong possibility of getting the job at the airport, KeShawn faced a dilemma. The recruiter clarified that the airport urgently sought to fill the vacant journeyman's position as soon as possible. This difficulty caused KeShawn to wonder. What if returning to Chicago makes him miss out on this opportunity? Would there be more opportunities in his line of work? What about Dorothy? Would she be willing to wait for him? Despite the questions, KeShawn knew he needed to handle his business back home. He couldn't rely on others to do for him. After all, he had a semblance of a life in Chicago, plus his family was anxiously awaiting his return.

KeShawn was confident that Jamaica was where he wanted to be, but possibly losing Dorothy troubled him. So he sequenced how quickly he could get things done in Chicago before returning to Jamaica: meet the landlord about his apartment obligations, sell his car, close his bank accounts, and especially carve out time to visit his family. While he enjoyed what was supposed to be his last dinner as a guest in Moe's home, KeShawn informed Moe and Dorothy of his need to return to Chicago to handle his business affairs. At first, Moe was startled to hear, 'Return to Chicago.' But after hearing the rest of the story, he understood completely. To put his plan of action in motion, KeShawn, after pulling Freddie's phone number from his satchel, asked Moe if he could use their telephone to call long distance. Moe stood up from his chair and motioned to KeShawn to use the phone in the den where he could sit and enjoy some privacy.

To get a quick apartment update and find out if he would be available to pick him up from Chicago O'Hare International Airport, KeShawn dialed Freddie's home number. The voice on the other end of KeShawn's long-distance phone call sounded alarming. "KeShawn, man, I'm so glad you called," said an exasperated Freddie. "There was a fire at your apartment building last Friday night. The news from Freddie caused KeShawn to drop the phone momentarily. KeShawn asked Freddie, "What happened?" Rushing his words, Freddie tried to describe what he knew about the fire, "I wasn't there, but from what I understand, one of the elderly tenants, in his haste to get to the grocery store, forgot to turn off his stove top gas burner, and a breeze from a partially opened kitchen window waved the curtains ever so slightly, but just enough for them to catch fire from the stovetop."

Loud enough to cause Moe and Gladys to come rushing into the den in a panic, KeShawn let out a piercing scream, "What?" Freddie went on, "Yeah, man, it was bad. Fire trucks were everywhere, and firemen were carrying people out of the building left and right." After a deep sigh, Freddie continued analyzing, "It was awful, KeShawn. I don't think the firemen were able to save the building." KeShawn echoed his earlier shock statement and yelled into the phone, "What?" as his hand rested on his lowered head. Moe and Gladys, standing in the den next to KeShawn, looked at each other, deeply concerned about what they just heard and the sadness on KeShawn's face. "What's going on, Key? Is everything alright?" bellowed Moe.

KeShawn put his giant paw over the receiver and said to Moe, " There was a fire at my apartment building in Chicago, and the entire building was destroyed."

The shock of the devastating news rendered Moe speechless. In disbelief, his mouth remained open, but the words were silenced. He only replied, "What?" While Gladys gasped in utter shock, she immediately felt a sense of profound sorrow for KeShawn. After the brief pause, KeShawn returned to the call and asked Freddie, "Is there anything being asked of the tenants?" Freddie answered, "Right now, the word on the street is that the insurance people are investigating, and tenants who had insurance might be entitled to some type of compensation." Then Freddie asked, "Tell me you had insurance?" In which KeShawn replied, "Do you remember what Papa told us? Whether you rent or buy, make sure you have insurance coverage because you never know, so it's better to be safe than sorry."

Breathing a sigh of relief, Freddie replied, "Thank goodness." Speaking in a low tone of shock and disbelief, KeShawn continued his reply and said to Freddie, "I had a rental insurance policy, but the paperwork, I'm sure, was probably destroyed in the fire. However, the good news is that I know the insurance company's name." Freddie offered his help when he said," I'll keep on top of this as best I can from this end. I'll get some information from some tenants I know that attend the college." Then Freddie added, "I briefly talked to a man who said he was the landlord. So I asked him why the sprinkler system didn't help contain the fire." Waiting to hear the answer, Freddie continued. "He told me because of inadequate or outdated water lines, the sprinkler system, which had been flagged for code violations, failed to respond. The landlord also mentioned that a sprinkler system renovation project was in the works but was caught up in some labor dispute." Still shaking his head in disbelief, KeShawn said to his brother, "Thanks, Freddie, for staying on top of this, but, Damn! That's the last thing I would have expected to hear."

Then, after a big sigh and still reeling from the news, KeShawn shared, "I guess I can't come home right now." As he continued, he said, "I need to follow up on some things here in Jamaica, but I will update you in a few days about what's happening. I must process this information before talking to the insurance people." Then he added, "No worries, I'll figure out how I want to handle things and let you know." Freddie had nothing but empathy for his brother, who was just starting to climb back from the dark place he had retreated to. Freddie tried to offer encouragement to keep KeShawn's spirits upbeat, "Don't worry, brother, you just stay up, and together, we can figure out how best to move forward from this." Before hanging up, KeShawn replied, "Sounds good. I'll talk to you soon. Love you, man, and thank you for looking out."

14

FINDING LOVE

It was only fitting that KeShawn shared the devastating news about his Chicago apartment with Dorothy; after all, she was the one around whom KeShawn wanted to rebuild his life. Upon hearing the news, Dorothy was just as heartbroken as KeShawn and politely asked if she could do anything to help. But at the same time, she wondered how KeShawn was going to react. She wasn't in panic mode, but her thoughts of concern confused her. Would KeShawn leave the island to attend to his affairs? And if so, how long would it take before he returned, if at all? Before their friendship went any further, Dorothy figured this would be a good time to temper her feelings as a precaution and to protect herself from the possibility that KeShawn might leave and never return.

KeShawn had only spoken to Dorothy once since the news of his Chicago apartment fire. But, despite the immediate attention to his business affairs in Chicago, she occupied his mind constantly. At the insistence of Moe, KeShawn remained a guest at his house in Kingston, where he spent the past three days conversing with Huntington Bank regarding his checking and savings accounts. KeShawn and Freddie communicated often about their family, the sale of his car, and his attempt to reconcile fair compensation for his apartment loss. However, negotiations stalled as the claims agent representing Liberty Mutual Insurance insisted that additional information from the fire department was necessary before they could complete their investigation.

Unsubstantiated rumors circulated that the fire may not have been an accident, and Liberty Mutual wanted to exhaust all plausible leads that could affect their tenant compensation.

While handling his long-distance affairs, KeShawn found time to follow up on a condominium lease he had his eyes on in a neighborhood just outside Montego Bay. The condo's lease availability was why KeShawn wanted to end his stay as a guest of Moe and Gladys. He figured he had enough money to invest in a three-month lease, which would give him ample time to assess not only the Montego Bay Airport job possibility but any other job that might come his way. More importantly, an extended stay in Montego Bay would allow him time to continue developing his budding relationship.

KeShawn and Dorothy finally had a lengthy and meaningful phone conversation. They spent much of the time talking about the apartment fire and the headaches it had caused him. However, the tone in Dorothy's responses, although sympathetic, was much more calculated. The uncertainty of KeShawn's Chicago status gave her cause to be a little more reserved. Dorothy desperately wanted the relationship to continue, but the uncertainty of KeShawn's affairs in Chicago made her uncomfortable, so she chose to guard her emotions. Putting herself in an emotional compromise and taking a fall a short time later would not be in her best interest. Sensing Dorothy's standoff-ish posture, KeShawn revealed his plan to move out of Moe's house and rent a condominium in Montego Bay. The news of this revelation was much more comforting to Dorothy, and the tone and excitement in her voice quickly returned. She was feeling good and eager to help KeShawn look for a condo. She even offered to drive to Kingston to pick him up from Moe's house.

Dorothy's encouragement, familiarity, and knowledge of the

Montego Bay area helped to ease KeShawn's concerns. He secured a three-month condominium lease at the property he initially identified. Much to his liking, the condo was located just outside Montego Bay, accessible to the City Center and multiple bus lines.

More good news awaited KeShawn when a letter from Liberty Mutual Insurance Company, sent to Moe's Kingston address, informed him that his rental insurance claim had been resolved. And that he could expect a compensation check within the next ten to fifteen business days. A short time later, another letter addressed to KeShawn was sent to Moe's home address. The Montego Bay Jamaica Airport letter informed KeShawn that his name had been elevated to the shortlist for a full-time probationary journeyman position at the MBJ Airport.

One letter was bittersweet, and the other was very timely. KeShawn shared the good news from the letters and asked Dorothy to take him car shopping. The money KeShawn brought from Chicago had begun to dwindle, but the compensation news from his insurance claim and the possibility of a job offer brightened his day immensely. Confident that his financial situation would take a positive turn, KeShawn rolled the dice and used his last savings to buy a pre-owned Morris Oxford, a car similar to Moe's that he found appealing.

It was not just the job prospect that motivated KeShawn to buy a car and take on a condo lease; he desperately wanted his relationship with Dorothy to move beyond exploratory. He was ready to push all his chips into the center of the table to win her love.

On most nights, KeShawn and Dorothy talked and exchanged laughs well into the evening. Even though he apologized for the lengthy conversations that kept her up late, his guilty indulgence was well received. Dorothy found KeShawn's extended conversations entertaining as well as enlightening. She thoroughly enjoyed getting to know more about her new friend from Chicago. KeShawn insisted they move beyond phone calls and find time to see each other regularly. Using a bit of humor, KeShawn suggested that if they couldn't see each other every day, then twice on

Sundays would make up the time. Despite her work schedule, Dorothy, just as eager to share her life with KeShawn, happily agreed to his request.

Waiting for confirmation on his job status, KeShawn, swept off his feet, would meet Dorothy on her bus ride to work and after work. He even surprised her by meeting her for lunch in Ocho Rios. KeShawn, restored spirits, had finally found a love and happiness that had eluded him for far too long. Dorothy was equally enthralled as their relationship continued to blossom. She had wholly revamped her life and made KeShawn a priority. She regularly mentions KeShawn to her co-workers and tells them how great an athlete he was in Chicago.

Even though Dorothy was initially reluctant to spend the night at his place, she now spends weekends at the condo. Following multiple weekend visits, Dorothy has her own set of condo keys. The relationship was officially on the fast track.

Dorothy's intuition told her that KeShawn was guilty of neglecting to see his best friend, Moe. Since the day he moved out of Moe's house in Kingston to live in Montego Bay, KeShawn's energy has been directed at Dorothy. She insisted he make time to visit Moe and Gladys. Dorothy told KeShawn, "I'm not going anywhere, plus it's important that you maintain a strong relationship in the company of your good friends." She laughed, "Isn't Moe the reason you're here dating me? So please take time to go see them." KeShawn agreed, and in the days ahead, he and Moe connected. KeShawn asks if he could take him and Gladys to dinner. But Gladys insisted KeShawn come to the house for dinner because her kids wanted to see him again.

So, after confirming dinner arrangements at Moe's, KeShawn thanked Dorothy for reminding him how special Moe and Gladys are to him. The drive to Kingston was not hard, but to give himself plenty of time to avoid any traffic congestion, KeShawn left Montego Bay around Noon. The 175-mile trip along the A1 highway was expected to take roughly two and a half hours. The thought of such a lengthy drive caused KeShawn to laugh. He thought about the many times he and Moe made four-hour road trips from Chicago to Detroit, sometimes at night. KeShawn muttered to himself, "Man, those were some crazy times. I can't believe how foolish we were." But this drive was different. This was about going to see his friend Moe. KeShawn then quickly turned his attention back to driving as his eyes glanced at road signs that told him he was near his destination.

The bottle of Josh Cellars Cabernet, bought in Montego Bay, was KeShawn's attempt to make amends for his absence. KeShawn arrived at Moe's house late that afternoon and was joyously greeted at the front door by Moe's young kids, who were home from school. While Gladys finished dinner, KeShawn and Moe enjoyed talking as the kids kicked the football back and forth.

Gladys had prepared a lovely dinner of Jerk Chicken, brown stew chicken, rice and peas, and sweet potato pudding. Moe took the honors and poured everyone a glass of non-alcoholic ginger beer. After dinner, the kids helped clean the dishes, then occupied KeShawn again before Gladys escorted them to bed.

Finally, alone, Moe and KeShawn retreated to the den to finish the last of the wine and play catch-up. KeShawn revealed to Moe that he expected word any day now about the job at MBJ Airport as a full-time probationary employee. He also lets Moe in on his secret. He told Moe that he and Dorothy were spending more and more time together. A laughing Moe replied, "Ya Mon, you think I don't know?" The two slapped hands, and Moe continued, "I knew something was up. You don't have time for your boy, huh? It had better be a woman," as he laughed out loud." Then KeShawn quickly reminded Moe, after a chuckle, that he and Gladys are the blame/reason for his new life, a life made possible by the love and kindness they showed him when he arrived from Chicago.

Looking around to ensure the coast was clear, KeShawn gave Moe the scoop about his relationship with Dorothy when he said, "Man, this is crazy. I think she put a spell on me because every time I put my arms around her, I get a fever." KeShawn continued. "I think I've fallen in love, and it's the best thing that's happened to me in a long time." In response, Moe lowered his head, laughed, and agreed not to reveal all the details to Gladys. He said, "Key, what a lovely way to burn." Before adding, "I must admit, you seem happy, Mon, so just keep on.

It wasn't long before Key started showing up at Moe's house in the company of his lovely companion. Now, it was KeShawn and Dorothy making the occasional weekend drive to visit Moe and Gladys. KeShawn and Dorothy's relationship moved fast, was open for public viewing, and displayed no signs of slowing down. At a glance, everyone seemed happy.

While they sat in the company of others, KeShawn and Dorothy spontaneously shared kisses. Gladys, ever intuitive, saw the interaction and sensed there was more to the story. She casually looked over at Moe and said to him, "Do you see what I see?" But Moe, who had prior intel, smiled at his wife and simply replied, "Wow!"

During one of their Saturday double-date night dinners at Cru's rooftop terrace Bar & Kitchen in Kingston, which gave views of the City. Amidst the chatter, KeShawn informed Moe and Gladys that his Montego Bay Jamaica Airport probation period had ended. Fearing the worst possible outcome, the table became deafening silent.

KeShawn could not contain the serious look on his face. Finally, he broke the silence by laughing and telling his friends, "I am now permanently employed full-time as the assistant maintenance supervisor at MBJ-Airport." Cheers and high-fives erupted, and a kiss from Dorothy cemented the announcement. After the glee calmed down, KeShawn continued sharing the day's news, saying, "I have more good news. Dorothy and I are getting married." Mo, feigning surprise, said to Gladys while she wiped tears from her eyes, "That is so shocking; I didn't see that coming at all." Then he laughed, embraced his good friend, and whispered in his ear, "It all started over lunch."

15

THE FAMILY IN JAMAICA

After his marriage to the lovely Dorothy, a Jamaican national, KeShawn could use the combination of his employment at MBJ-Airport and Dorothy's citizenship status to apply for permanent residency. The Jamaican protocol requires all permanent residency applicants to submit fingerprint clearance, employment verification, and birth certificate verification. After a five-week wait, KeShawn, no stranger to waiting for documents, was granted Jamaican permanent residency, thus making him a Jamaican citizen. He now maintains dual citizenship in the USA and Jamaica.

KeShawn, Dorothy, and their three children, Jabari, Ania, and Xavier, enjoy their lives in a quiet, middle-class Montego Bay mixed community of blue-collar workers, professionals, and retirees. The three-bedroom house near the end of a cul-de-sac was quiet except for an occasional taxi, which emitted noise pollution from a muffler that needed repair. When Moe and his family drive over from Kingston for a visit, you can count on an abundance of smiles, laughter, good food, and lots of teasing. Moe quickly reflected on the day Key and Dorothy first met and the challenges KeShawn faced from some of the local Jamaicans who had their eyes on Dorothy.

This was the epitome of Moe's vision, which started when KeShawn first set foot on the island: friends and family living together and enjoying each other's company. But what lurked on the horizon, no one could have imagined.

KeShawn's children, Jabari, Ania, and Xavier, were bright, intelligent, and heavily invested in sports. KeShawn boasted that their athletic genes were his gift, while Dorothy relished that the kids got their smarts from her. The emphasis on academic achievement was not lost in the Coleman house, and Mom readily served as that reminder.

Jabari, the oldest, a senior at Cornwell High School for Boys, was an outstanding sprinter who, in addition to running the long sprints of the 100, 200, and 400 meters, ran for three years on the Jamaican Jr and National Track teams and was highly sought after by college coaches. It was not uncommon for Jabari to receive multiple scholarship offers on any given day. The onslaught of college scholarship offers forced Jabari to create a system that categorizes and prioritizes the offers into a yes, no, or maybe pile. This was done in part as a way to weed out the pretentious from the serious offers. His system also allowed Jabari and his family to take a realistic view of what mattered most to him. The focus was narrowed to include geographical location, coaching staff, and academics. Jabari's matrix criteria ultimately churned out Texas A&M, Florida International, and the University of Oregon as his top choices. Florida International made the finalist list more to please his mom, whose bias favored a school closer to Jamaica, thus making the final choice challenging but exciting.

Ania was a junior running the sprints at Montego Bay High School for Girls. In addition to running track, she developed a passion for animals and has given considerable thought to becoming a veterinarian after college. She showed promise early on in the sprints, but the coaching staff knew that her future success depended on improving her technique. Title IX played a critical role in promoting sports and educational equity. Mandated by law, colleges scramble to offer equal women's and men's sports. This new law made talented women athletes easy targets for scholarship opportunities. The time was ripe for girls and women looking for a college opportunity to take a consequential approach to their athletic development, as college recruiters were scouring the country on the lookout for talented female athletes. Ania was in the crosshairs of college recruiters who were ready to offer her a scholarship if she continued to improve. Meanwhile, Xavier was a gangling freshman who resembled a baby gazelle, all arms and legs, while he grew like a weed yearly. In the fall, he played on the junior varsity soccer team to help him improve his footwork and coordination.

But basketball remained his passion. In his obsession, Xavier fantasized daily about playing point guard. But for now, he played center on the JV team. Although he displayed good instincts for rebounding and blocking shots, his lack of strength and confidence to play inside amongst the big boys led him to drift and play outside.

Dorothy was proud of her children, and although she worked weekdays, she found time on weekends and some evenings to watch them compete in games and meets.

Riding the bus to work allowed Dorothy time to socialize with her friends, think, and reflect beyond the worries of driving her car.

This particular morning started like many other workday mornings. The Jamaica Regional Bus was driven by a friendly, bearded middle-aged man, neatly dressed in a blue Kangol Tropics Cap that sat atop his long dreads. His gold-colored polo shirt prominently displayed the company logo, while the creases in his beige khaki pants were so sharp they might cut your finger. As the driver settled into his seat, the grip on the oversized steering wheel exposed fingertips protruding from his LambSkin driving gloves. Using the palm of his left hand to generate a sweeping circular motion, he turned the bus out of the Montego Bay Substation at

6:00 AM sharp and departed for the hour-and-a-half drive with Dorothy and friends happily aboard.

The 65-mile scenic coastal journey to Ocho Rios includes favorite tourist attraction stops at Club Mobay, St. Ann's Bay, and Dunns River Falls & Park. However, the youthful and elderly passengers aboard have grown accustomed to the time-consuming stops and didn't seem to mind. They were content to pass the time by sharing family stories, catching up on the latest gossip, or staring aimlessly out the window.

For the past seven years, Dorothy Coleman, wife to KeShawn and mother to high schoolers Jabari, Ania, and Xavier, started her work shift as an office clerical for Sandals Oci Beach Resort in the exclusive beach resort town of Ocho Rios. Only within the past few months did Dorothy begin to critically question if the morning bus ride would be her last. The daily back-and-forth commute had worn on her, especially considering the planned highway road construction. The newly funded North Coast Highway Development Project, spearheaded by the government's investment of $125 Billion to expand the existing roadway network into a four-lane highway, was a welcome inconvenience by civic leaders. However, despite the route and its scenic views being comparable in some ways to the Pacific Coast Highway in the U.S., the project's estimated completion timeline of three to four years would have doubled the travel time from Montego Bay to the Ocho Rios Resort.

The thought of a three-hour commute did not sit well and weighed heavily on Dorothy's mind. If she were to continue working, a job closer to home would be a much better alternative and relief from the stress concerning her. The resort's management knew of Dorothy's travel concerns, so losing her to a resort company closer to her home might be a problem for them.

Considering that time was of the essence, the resort's management prioritized retaining Dorothy. Upon her arrival at work, the morning receptionist followed management's directive and escorted Dorothy to a meeting in the administrative office.

Dorothy followed the staffer to the director's office, puzzled as they walked through the maze of offices and boutiques. Dorothy wondered why there was an emergency meeting so early in the morning. Was there a problem? Maybe someone had injured themselves?

After the obligatory greeting, Dorothy sat in the guest chair near an open-air window. The Resort director got to the point and said to Dorothy, "We would like to offer you a well-deserved promotion and pay raise to Staff Supervisor." She continued and shared a few specifics. "The position oversees daily operational activities and has supervisory responsibilities." Unaware and surprised by the offer, her first in a salaried position, Dorothy was left speechless. Leaning forward in the leather guest chair, Dorothy replied. "Thank you for the promotion, but before I answer, can I discuss the offer with my husband?

The unintended consequences of the highway development project negatively impacted small businesses, residents living along the road, and those commuting from Montego Bay. The mere thought of losing her travel partners and the longer commute times added stress and anxiety to Dorothy's life. Her friends on the commute and their family stories meant a lot to her. That connectivity brought her a sense of shared value, so the absence of that connection could profoundly impact her mental health.

Dorothy attempted to conceal her true feelings of discomfort while around her family, but KeShawn took note. His wife's usual jovial personality and quick wit were noticeably absent and gave way to a quiet and somber demeanor. For Dorothy, the occasions she wanted to open up and talk about her nagging concerns seemed to take a back seat to other family issues. She thought to herself, "If I don't talk about my concerns and get them out in the open, how am I ever going to resolve my anxiety issues?"

It was customary in the Coleman household for the dining table to serve as the focal meeting point for discussions, good and bad. So Dorothy thought, with no games on TV and no track or basketball practices to attend, she would finally get everybody back to the dining table after dinner and have a discussion. Dorothy, after preparing a healthy rice, seafood, and yams dinner, was looking forward to finally being able to address her concerns. KeShawn instructed Jabari, Ania, and Xavier to clear the dishes. It was Xavier's turn to wash the dishes while Jabari and Ania played "Guess how many fingers" to see who dried the dishes; the loser of the finger game had the honor of sweeping the kitchen floor.

KeShawn sat at the head of the table with his arms folded, waiting for the kitchen details to be completed. He called everyone back to the dining room as his elbows rested on the table. Xavier sat opposite him at the other end, while Ania and Dorothy sat across from Jabari. Assuming that the call-to-the-table discussion would be about his scholarship offer, Jabari, unable to control his exciting news, blurted out, "The college I'm choosing will be the University of Oregon." A scream of excitement from Ania and Xavier followed, but not the enthusiasm Jabari expected from his parents. Instead, they looked at him in silence. Finally, KeShawn extended his overly excited son a high-five and a fist bump. Dorothy continued her silence but deep in thought. She loves her family dearly, but this was supposed to be her time to be heard. She also thought that Jabai ignored her request for him to select a school closer to home. Dorothy finally relented and gave Jabari a congratulatory hug. Rubbing his hands together, Xavier only wanted to know when he would get an Oregon cap and T-shirt. Still bubbling over his choice of colleges, Jabari remained unaware of any other reason as to why they were summoned to the dining table. Dorothy remained quiet while the kids talked and giggled over Jabari's college decision. Not aware of their mother's concerns, KeShawn excused his children from the table as he gave Dorothy a resolute look.

Sensing Dorothy's frustration, KeShawn wrapped his hands around hers, as he's done on my occasions, and said, "Honey, I love the kids, but I think you and I should talk alone." Dorothy just smiled and said, "Thank you." Then, she began to unleash the issues that troubled her as they sat at the table. Her emotions were on the verge of getting the best of her when she pointed out the new job promotion, her friends on the bus commute, the impending road construction delays, the children's education, and the cumulative effect those issues had on her health.

Emphatically, Dorothy said to her husband, "The kid's college education is my biggest concern, and no decision I make will jeopardize that goal. Remember our promise: a college education takes priority over anything else." KeShawn listened intently, then reassured Dorothy that the kids would attend college." But he issued a half-hearted attempt at humor when he said, "But what they do in college will ultimately be up to them." Dorothy replied, "KeShawn, I'm not joking." KeShawn then offered, "I know our kids, and they will be fine, and as Jabari was so quick to remind us, he's going to college, so that's one down." He continued, "The other two? Well, I have a plan." As he gently squeezed Dorothy's hand, KeShawn said, "I promise to do everything possible and use my connections here and in the States to get Ania and Xavier the help they need to develop their talents to the fullest. And if that happens, the scholarship offers will come in bunches." Dorothy looked exasperated, trying to keep her head from lowering in further, but KeShawn had more to add: "Maybe that sounds like a big if, but I'm confident we can make this happen. "Hey, it's in their genes, baby," he chuckled. Dorothy was not so sure but didn't question KeShawn about his plans. KeShawn said to Dorothy, "I don't want you stressing anymore. Leaving your job in Ocho Rios will be best for you." He continued, "My job at MBJ is secure, plus I've been told I'm in line for a possible promotion within the coming year." Dorothy raised her head after getting KeShawn's blessing to leave her job. He told her, "We'll be in a good place when the promotion happens. Plus, without your health, nothing else matters. You are my priority, and the kids are our priority; the rest will follow."

KeShawn often used his experiences when he spoke to his teenagers — reminding them about the importance of being honest with themselves. He said to them, "Honesty was not a tricky proposition. But sometimes, your honesty will get cloudy and even questioned in the face of adversity or peer pressure." He went on as only KeShawn could. "A dishonest person might find initial success, leading to short-term gains. But somewhere down the line, success will be challenged by authenticity. False promises and fake smiles are fool's gold; all that glitters is not gold. So don't fall for the trap," KeShawn continued by saying. "We all have choices when we make our decisions. So be smart, decisive, honest, and trust yourself. If you do those things, you needn't worry about results or the noise that conceals your dreams. All will be well."

Absorbing their father's words of wisdom, the children understood that what their father did and the decisions he made were in their best interest. KeShawn's development plan for Ania paid off. Training alongside the Jamaican National Track team during her senior year in high school, Ania performed at an elite level in the short sprints, earning her a track scholarship to Texas A&M University in College Station, Texas. The thrill she felt to follow in Jabari's athletic footsteps was overwhelming. More importantly, Ania was accepted into A&M's College of Veterinary Medicine & Biomedical Sciences (VMBS), which would augment her plans to pursue a graduate degree before beginning a career as a veterinarian.

However, the plan KeShawn envisioned for Xavier was a bit more complex, and convincing Dorothy of his brilliant idea would take some doing. The plan required Xavier to move to Chicago to finish his final two years of high school. Offering smooches and hugs, KeShawn desperately tried to sway Dorothy from her entrenched, reluctant position of 'no way that's happening.' He finally convinced Dorothy to fly to Chicago with him and Xavier during spring break to visit his brother, Freddie, and learn more about this (foolish) idea.

16

UNCLE FREDDIE

Freddie (JuneBug) Coleman, younger brother of KeShawn, was 12 years into his marriage with the former Claudia Morales. They raised their family in Oak Park, Illinois, a pleasant suburb along Chicago's Western border, only 10 miles by Metra Rail Transit from downtown Chicago. A graduate of Chicago State University, Freddie taught history at the two-year City College Malcolm X-Campus. Since their childhood in Alabama, Freddie admired and looked up to his big brother.

Although he didn't possess the extraordinary athletic ability of his brother, not many did; Freddie followed KeShawn's career fervently and even reaped residual benefits as his brother while attending Chicago State U.

During a long-distance phone conversation, KeShawn wanted Freddie to explain what he knew about the coach at the Prep school, which he had heard so much about. Freddie shared what little he knew using information from the word that was spoken on the street. The South Side's new Prep Academy and the basketball program's potential for success were getting positive reviews.

Freddie's wife, Claudia, who worked in Human Resources at the administrative office of Chicago Public Schools, maintained a casual friendship with one of the Prep Academy counselors, so arranging a time to visit campus would not be a problem.

Freddie continued to gather information about the Prep Academy coach from constituents in and around the city. He shared his intel when he said, "From all accounts, Coach Parker is considered a fundamentalist by profession and a decent and caring individual by nature." Freddie went on. "Coach Charles (Charlie) Parker is better known for using a disciplined and structured approach to developing his players. However, the city still waits for him to deliver a championship." As he continued, Freddie said, "Nevertheless, one of the big attractions to his program is that each year, most of his graduating seniors earn college scholarships from D-I to D-III schools."

Freddie's information intrigued KeShawn and inspired him to move his plan forward. KeShawn was convinced that few coaches in Jamaica could help Xavier reach his full basketball potential.

Despite the years away from Chicago, KeShawn was still revered as a legendary athlete. Upon arriving at O'Hare International Airport, he was immediately recognized by a few airport employees who greeted him with star status as he passed through the terminal. Dorothy and Xavier were surprised at the recognition that KeShawn received. After all these years, they had no idea how popular a figure KeShawn remained. Following smiles and handshakes, the family went to the baggage claim area, where an unknown person picked up KeShawn from behind and bounced him up and down.

Looking startled at the scene, Xavier started to move to assist his dad. But, after the screaming and hugging subsided, KeShawn introduced his brother to Dorothy, whom he immediately embraced and kissed on the cheek. Then he introduced Xavier, who stood almost a foot taller than his Uncle. Still stunned after witnessing the wild greeting, Xavier looked at his uncle with a wide grin, offered him a firm handshake, and then slapped a high-five. "Xavier, this is my not-so-little brother, your uncle Freddie," explained a joyful

KeShawn, who, besides occasional phone conversations, hadn't seen his brother in years.

After retrieving their luggage from the crowded baggage claim carousel, Freddie loaded the family into his spacious Buick Electra. He drove toward downtown Chicago before driving West to his suburban home in Oak Park.

Freddie purposefully avoided the freeway to give the family a look at the towering city landscape. After arriving in Oak Park, Freddie's wife, Claudia, was the first person to greet the travelers from Jamaica. She welcomed them inside, where she had prepared a light pre-dinner lunch. While the family settled and munched on the timely meal, KeShawn explained to Freddie his urgency to visit the school as soon as possible. KeShawn was all in on the plan for his son and didn't want to waste any time finding out if he was making the right move. Claudia followed Freddie's request the next morning and called the school.

Meanwhile, Freddie updated his brother on the status of their elderly parents, Papa James and Momma Essie. "You know both of them are having memory issues, but other than that, they are doing as well as expected. Freddie went on, Momma is using a wheel-chair, and Papa has to use a cane when he moves about." KeShawn then asked, "Are they okay? I mean, do they need help?" Freddie replied, "At first, I was okay knowing that the aging process is inevitable, but now I'm getting concerned. Maybe we should consider finding them a place like assisted living."

The look of concern after hearing what Freddie just said to him caused KeShawn to worry about Althea. He asked, "How is Althea, and what does she think?" Freddie replied, "She's holding up pretty good but is just as concerned as I am. She's been looking at potential assisted living facilities on the South Side." KeShawn replied, "If you don't mind, I need to see them and Althea as soon as possible." Freddie eagerly replied, "Of course, but don't worry, you know Althea, she's strong. Because she was Papa's baby girl, it's hard for her to see them aging like this. Between her busy teaching schedule and mine, we make time each week to stop by and check on them as much as possible."

It wasn't long after a tasteful morning breakfast that included scrambled eggs, turkey sausage, raisin bread toast, fruit, juice, and coffee that Claudia called her friend, Jody Hunter, at the Carter G. Woodson Prep Academy. "Hey Jody, how are you?" Claudia asked. Jody replied in her usual upbeat tone, "Claudia, good to hear your voice. I'm doing fine." After exchanging pleasantries, they talked about their families, and Claudia asked Jody about getting her famous peach cobbler recipe. After they laughed, Jody asked, "Is there anything I can help you with besides the pie recipe?" Claudia replied, "As a matter of fact, there is. "My husband, Freddie, would like to schedule an appointment at the school to meet Coach Parker. His brother KeShawn and nephew Xavier are in town visiting and wanted to schedule a time to come on campus." Then Jody asked, "That wouldn't be KeShawn Coleman, would it?." Claudia said, "Yes, he is my husband's brother." Super excited, Jody said, "Oh my word! I remember KeShawn, he's a legend here in Chicago, and he was so handsome." Jody continued, I have a class schedule of all the teachers, so let me check." After a brief pause, Jody informed Claudia that Coach Parker would end his teaching schedule at noon on Friday. Claudia asked, "Can you put the Colemans down for 1:00 P.M. on Friday? This should give the coach time to have lunch or return phone calls before our meeting." Jody laughed, and as she wrote down the appointment time, she said to Claudia, "I see you haven't forgotten how things work." After hearing Jody's comment, Claudia smiled and said, "Some things you don't forget." As she confirmed the appointment, Jody said, "You're all set for Friday, and don't forget to ask your husband to stop by my office. I want to say hello to KeShawn." While catching herself, Jody said, "I meant to say I look forward to meeting your family." Unable to control her laughter, Claudia replied before ending the call, "I know what you meant, but thank you very much, and I will ask Freddie and KeShawn to stop by to say hello."

On Friday, two days after the phone call to the school, a light rain began to fall. As usual, the unpredictable Chicago weather reared its head. This added nuance only made KeShawn a little more anxious. He was adamant about being early to the meeting rather than late, so he gently reminded his brother to factor in the weather for his leave time. As the men prepared to leave, Dorothy kissed her husband, hugged Xavier, and reminded KeShawn to come straight home after the meeting with all the details. Freddie kissed his wife and promised to come right back. Freddie, KeShawn, and Xavier were ready to make the 20-minute drive, but the drive might take a little longer due to weather issues. Heading towards the door, Freddie suddenly stopped and patted his pockets, "Oh boy," he murmured, "Claudia," Freddie shouted, "Have you seen my keys?" KeShawn could only chuckle while Xavier turned to take a courtesy look at the table near the front door. Claudia exhaled, and with her hands on her hips, she said to her husband, "Not again, dear. You and your darn keys. Have you checked the bedroom or the jacket you wore to the airport?" In less than 60 seconds of frantically looking, Freddie came smiling from the bedroom and tossed his keys in the air, and as he caught them, he said, "We're good, let's roll, and out the door they went.

The drive to the Carter G. Woodson Prep Academy to meet the coach, who many in the community have been impressed by, went smoothly, and weather was not a factor. The drive also allowed Xavier to look at the surroundings as Freddie took the residential street route. They arrived at the school in plenty of time only to find the visitor parking area full. After circling the parking lot, Freddie spotted a car leaving, so he put his car in reverse and backed into the spot, which impressed Xavier. They were greeted immediately by campus security, a friendly man who looked like he had maintained a fitness club membership. In a deep baritone voice, he gave Freddie directions to the administration office, followed by a directive, "Be sure to sign in and get a visitor pass once you get to the administrative office. Otherwise, you won't be allowed on campus." Following those explicit orders, the visitors made their intentions known and signed in at the reception counter, where they were issued campus visitor passes.

Before heading to the gymnasium office to meet with Coach Parker, Freddie asked the student escort to take them by the desk of Claudia's friend, Jody Hunter. Jody's desk sat empty, only her eyeglasses on the keyboard and a sweater slung across the back of her chair, indicating she may be still on campus. Freddie told KeShawn, "That's too bad. Claudia wanted us to meet Jody. Maybe we can stop back after the meeting." The group then continued their walk to the gymnasium. The student escort, a boy's basketball team member, glanced over at the tall Xavier and wondered curiously about the nature of his visit to meet the coach.

The campus visitors finally reached the gymnasium office on the second floor of the three-story school building. Freddie quietly knocked before he peaked inside the office. What he saw were multiple unoccupied desks. Freddie thought to himself, maybe the coach forgot about the meeting. Meanwhile, Xavier stood in the hallway and gawked at a wall that displayed team photos from previous seasons. Suddenly, Xavier found himself conversing with a man 30 years his senior. "Hey, young man, how are you? I'm Coach Parker. Won't you come in?" Caught off guard, Xavier replied in his Jamaican accent, "No problem, Sir." As he ducked to avoid hitting his head, Xavier entered the office and sat between his Dad and Uncle.

Freddie proceeded to make the introductions, and before he could finish, Coach Parker stood and, with great admiration, reached out to shake the hand of KeShawn. Coach Parker then explained to Xavier that he had admired his dad since high school. "Did you know your dad is still a legend here, son?" A beaming Xavier looked at his Uncle and smiled proudly.

The conversation continued when Freddie explained to Coach Parker that KeShawn and Xavier live in Jamaica but were visiting family in Chicago during Xavier's spring break recess. In a somewhat weak attempt to keep Dorothy's reluctance in mind, KeShawn interjected and said to Coach Parker, "My wife and I were considering sending our son, Xavier, to a school in the States where he could further develop his basketball skills." Coach Parker looked at Xavier and asked, "How tall are you, son?" Xavier replied, "When the school last measured me, I was 6' 7", but I was told I could grow more." Xavier's honest answer was followed by light-hearted laughter from the men in the office.

KeShawn, "If you are sincere about moving,"… KeShawn quickly interrupted and said, "We're not moving, but he, pointing to his son, might be moving," and they laughed again. "Carter G. Woodson Prep Academy can offer a great learning environment for your son, and as a coach, developing players is what I do, offered Coach Parker." He continued, "I get enjoyment from player development on this level. Helping these young men reach their potential is equivalent to learning to walk before running. Parker continued, "But I must admit, if Xavier were to enroll here, he would be my first international student, so there's a challenge in that aspect alone." Coach Parker went on in his assessment. "We're talking about a cultural change and homesickness from leaving your family and friends behind. Plus, there's me working your tail off. But more importantly, we're talking about the Chicago winters." Everyone erupted into profound laughter except Xavier, who looked on, clueless about how true that last statement from Coach Parker was.

"Yes, most definitely, we can't forget about the Chicago "Hawk," said Freddie. "It's no joke." Coach Parker added, "I can't make any guarantees, but I know that if you come here, I promise you will be a better player and, more importantly, a better man by the time you leave."

Parker then excused himself to go into the gym to look for one of his players. While Parker was away, KeShawn, curious about how Xavier felt about the information he just heard, quickly looked at his son's body language before asking his thoughts. Although the back-and-forth information that Xavier heard seemed overwhelming, he said to his dad, "I'm not sure, but I think it will be good for me here." Then KeShawn looked at Freddie, and they both nodded in agreement. KeShawn turned back to Xavier smiling and said to his son, "I think this will be the right place for you." Still unsure or convinced about anything, Xavier just sat, absorbing and processing the many questions running through his mind.

Coach Parker returned to the office with one of his players and said to Xavier, "If you decide to come here, this will be your guy. Meet Willie Mitchell. Willie has been around me for a few years, and I trust him, so I trust him with you. He can show you around and tell you how we do things here at Carter G. Woodson."

After shaking hands, Willie and Xavier walked into the gym to look around. Parker and the Colemans briefly touched on a few of the next steps regarding transferring, transcripts, and physical exams. Parker said to them, "I'm going to have you meet one of our school academic advisors before you leave. The advisor can get you more accurate information regarding transfer requirements, enrollment procedures, and medical requirements, including vaccinations."

Pleased that their meeting with Coach Parker went well, the Colemans left the campus much more optimistic than when they arrived. Just before he turned the car away from campus, Freddie brought the car to a halt. "I remembered something. We forgot to stop by to see Jody. Wow! I hope she doesn't think we blew her off."

On the ride back home, Freddie again chose to take the longer, slower route. He wanted to show KeShawn the changes in the old neighborhood and drive by the campus of Chicago State U. KeShawn shook his head in amazement and replied to Freddie, "I can't believe how much things have changed." Freddie then turned on Colbert Street, and to KeShawn's amazement, the corner liquor store was still there. KeShawn noted, "The men standing around might look different, but passing that brown paper bag back and forth still resembled the same behavior, much like the guys back in the day." Freddie replied, "Some things change, and some just stay the same."

Excited to talk to his mom about his day, Xavier bounced up the steps of Freddie's Oak Park home, two at a time. As they entered the house, Dorothy breathed easier, as her expression was more relieved that they were home safely than of frustration that they had been gone most of the day. She then asked, "Where have you all been? We were starting to worry."

Claudia, who had just finished preparing dinner, instructed everyone to wash their hands and come to the table. She had prepared one of Freddie's favorite dinners: baked salmon, chicken, mashed potatoes, asparagus, a tossed green salad, cornbread, and a bottle of Chateau Cabernet. At the table, everyone joined hands and bowed their heads, and in a moment of silence, Freddie said grace. After the amen, the clinking of utensils against plates and happy chatter followed by laughter ensued.

As KeShawn pushed back from the table, he raised his second glass of wine and offered a toast to Claudia and Freddie for their hospitality. Dorothy, also pleased, said to Claudia, "That was a terrific dinner. Thank you so much." KeShawn, feeling no pain, raised another glass in appreciation for dinner. "Xavier, tell your Auntie thank you," instructed Dorothy.

After the delicious and well-timed meal, it was time for a team effort to clear the table and wash the dishes. Afterward, the family descended to the living room to hear all about the day's events at the school.

KeShawn and Freddie took turns sharing their impressions, first about the school and then about Coach Parker. KeShawn looked fondly at Dorothy and said to her, "I was impressed. I was. The coach came across as an honest and passionate man." Sitting nearby, Freddie nodded in approval of KeShawn's comment. KeShawn continued, "Coach Parker told us about his development plan to help Xavier reach his basketball potential. I am confident Coach Parker and his team will keep a tight rein on Xavier on and off the court." KeShawn continued, "Coach knows his business and has a respected history of developing his players, so I trust him." KeShawn went on to add, "But aside from the coach. A giant relief for all of us is that Freddie and Claudia are opening their home to Xavier. They will look after him like he's their son. And that is huge and puts my mind at ease." Freddie interjected and said, "Absolutely," while hugging Xavier around the neck.

Full of emotions, Dorothy used a Kleenex handed to her by Claudia to dab the tears from her eyes. While she squeezed KeShawn's hand, she told him how much she loved him and trusted his judgment. She confessed that her baby was growing up and needed to find his path. "I want you to call me daily, and I expect you to obey your Aunt and Uncle," Dorothy instructed her son. The puzzled look Xavier returned was priceless. He replied, "Mom, we've got time; I'm flying home with you, remember?" School doesn't start here until next fall," and everyone laughed hysterically.

17

COACH CHARLES "CHARLIE" PARKER

Coach Charlie Parker, a military veteran, was born in Horry County, South Carolina, during the latter part of the Depression era. After his first marriage ended in divorce, he married his second wife, attorney Trina Crawford, in Cleveland, Ohio. Parker is the father of two boys, CJ and Alton, who neither played competitive sports. He spent decades as a civil rights advocate in Cleveland and Detroit, where he was instrumental in organizing the Detroit March for Equality in downtown Detroit. He remained actively involved as an advocate for human rights and social change in Chicago. Parker's discipline and structured coaching style, emphasizing academic achievement and love for his players, has followed him wherever he has coached. He is appreciated by his players and admired by his peers. His impact on basketball and football, the people he worked alongside, and his unwavering commitment to his players' success were commendable and deserved recognition.

An outstanding student-athlete in high school, Parker was recruited to play football at the University of Illinois in Champaign, Illinois. Still, an unforgettable experience derailed his opportunity to shine at a major university. After his scholarship was revoked due to questionable circumstances, he moved away from that painful chapter.

Parker had the fortitude to turn that unpleasant experience into years of joy and accomplishment after transferring to Tennessee State University, an HBCU University in Nashville, Tennessee, where he played football, basketball, and baseball. As a senior quarterback, his team went undefeated, earning him first-team Division II All-American honors. In addition, he earned All-American honors as a forward in basketball, where his team lost in overtime during the finals of the national championship game. Parker graduated from Tennessee State Magna cum laude.

HE WAS INITIALLY RECRUITED out of high school by the University of Illinois on a football scholarship. As a 19-year-old freshman, Parker was one of three African-American players on the football team. His relationship with the football program turned sour when, during pre-season practice, he made claims that his teammates subjected him to racial taunts and racial prejudice, which caused him to feel uncomfortable, unappreciated, and unwanted.

As a young freshman, 756 miles away from home, Parker had no campus liaison willing or available to hear his complaints. So Parker relied on the football coach to bring the situation under control. After listening to both sides of the argument, the coach refused to believe Parker's allegations and accused him of taking light-hearted humor out of context. He sided with the white football players and blamed Parker for overreacting and making unfounded accusations that disrupted his team's chemistry.

A week later, when Parker tried to use his cafeteria meal card, he was told it was invalid and must be surrendered immediately, or he would face disciplinary action. Absent common courtesy, Parker's football scholarship was also canceled without notification, and all rights previously afforded him as a scholarship student-athlete were deemed null and void.

Furious, Parker attempted to appeal the decision but was told he must either pay the tuition and fees or withdraw from the college. Parker insisted that his case be heard, but the athletic department was unwilling to come to his defense or offer him advice. However, when Parker found himself in the Student Union, desperately seeking information, he encountered a freshman distributing free student publications. She kindly shared insights about the importance of knowing how to interpret information in the College Catalog and Student Handbook and how to benefit from the multitude of free campus resources and services.

The young student knew nothing about Parker's situation, but considering all the drama that he faced, Parker welcomed her kindness and sunny disposition. The feeling was like sunshine shining through the twin clouds of doom and gloom. She introduced herself as a third-year College of Urban Planning & Public Affairs student, Ruth McBride. Ruth loved pets, painting, and walks in the park. As a student advocate, Ruth was assigned to help first-year students navigate their way around campus. Parker, at ease for the first time since setting foot on campus, thanked Ruth for her kindness and willingness to share the student-related material. While seated on a sofa in the geometrically designed Student Union, Parker carefully examined each booklet, page by page, looking for information that could help him.

Parker found detailed information in the college catalog and the student handbook that addressed his concerns, such as student discipline procedures and due process, code of conduct, graduation requirements, and grievance procedures. Although he was unaware of the effectiveness of the Grievance Procedures, Parker hoped the process would be unbiased and fair. He followed the grievance procedure guidelines to the letter, leaving no detail unturned. Parker completed the multi-page paperwork and submitted the required information within the prescribed timeline.

While his grievance hearing application moved forward, a meeting was scheduled before the University Student Grievance Committee (USGC). While he waited, Parker wondered if the treatment he received from the football coach would be any different from the grievance committee.

Sitting alone in front of eight students and one faculty representative, none of whom looked like him, Parker received instructions on how the grievance process worked. If the initial ruling was not in his favor, he could schedule a meeting with the Dean of Students on a second appeal, but only if the football coach supported a second appeal.

During the USGC meeting, which felt more like an interrogation without representation, Parker was not questioned but grilled about the allegations in his grievance application. After the one-hour meeting concluded, Parker was asked to sit outside the interrogation room. Parker was invited back inside in less time than it took to get a cup of coffee. Grievance committee deliberations typically take 24 hours or more to decide a student's fate. But, in this case, 30 minutes was allotted to Parker's complaint.

While standing before the all-white student grievance committee, comprised of five males and three females, Parker realized his fate at the University of Illinois was in their hands. The committee rendered a life-altering decision and denied Parker's appeal. The committee based its decision on the circumstantial evidence Parker presented, such as the lack of corroborating witnesses and lack of support from athletic department staff.

The appeal, dead on arrival, was never allowed to reach the executive level. Parker, with no recourse and no support from the athletic department, withdrew from the University of Illinois and later enrolled at Tennessee State University.

18

FIRST COACHING JOB

After graduating from college, Parker's professional life began to take shape.

He started coaching AAU basketball in Cleveland to stay connected to the game he loved. Soon after, high school athletic directors around Cleveland noticed the discipline and structure in Parker's AAU team's style of play and wanted to know more. East High School on Cleveland's east side, experiencing social and behavioral problems, contacted Parker and offered him a teaching and coaching position.

Parker's strong desire to coach superseded the warnings about taking the coaching position. He saw the position as an opportunity, not the challenge many of his closest friends thought it would be. Before long, this troubled school and Parker's brand of basketball started to mesh. The team's relentless offense and suffocating defense proved too much for the league's traditional powers. Parker's team was taking names and kicking butt.

Players from the community deemed incorrigible or uncoachable adopted the new philosophy and changed their attitudes about school, class attendance, and grooming habits.

Their success on the court supplemented the team's adaptation to buying into the new cultural shift. The success on the court soon translated to the classroom, and teachers were amazed at the transformation. This was the first step in Coach Parker's pillars of success plan: establishing credibility in the school.

He wanted to turn these young men into students before he turned them into basketball players. Parker initiated study hall and tutorial time and used team meetings to reinforce his commitment to learning.

It was common practice for his players to read aloud during team meetings. They would research and read world and local news stories of interest mentioned in the daily newspaper. Those players who frowned on these tactics or didn't buy into this transformation were allowed to quit. Well aware that there would be resistance to his coaching methods, Parker had no problem embracing those who chose to stay and reap the benefits.

Faculty soon took notice of the change and became more engaged with the student-athletes, showing a willingness to be patient and positive in their teaching style. The players, in return, dismissed their negative anti-school attitude and began to give teachers in the classroom the respect they deserved. Players subsequently found enjoyment in learning. Suddenly, the student body began to follow the lead of the basketball and football teams and initiated school pride activities. The school's transformation from underachieving to achieving in just over three years was shocking and unexpected. It made school administrators, district administrators, and especially families in the community take great pride in the cultural change.

Parker's team didn't win a championship during his tenure, but athletes went from dropping out of school to graduating, and some went to two — and four-year colleges.

What Parker was able to do at this troubled school was phenomenal and did not go unnoticed. Soon, the Detroit Public Schools came calling. One particular school on the Lower East Side of Detroit was experiencing social and behavioral problems very similar to those in Cleveland.

Many in the Detroit community blamed the school's situation on underfunding and an apathetic administration indifferent to helping students achieve a quality education. During one intense school board meeting, tempers flared, and residents, tired of the procrastinating lip service, demanded that something be done.

They blamed the board for sitting on their hands while doing nothing to address the school's rapidly declining attendance and graduation rates. The school's community was fed up and demanded change, starting with the school principal, who had alienated the community and demonstrated an ineffective leadership style that must be replaced. They wanted a collaborative leader who could create a positive learning environment. Someone who believed in student-supported teachers and was solid but fair in their convictions.

Despite their deep love for teaching and willingness to not abandon the students, the school's faculty were not equipped or supported enough to handle the behavioral issues that besieged the school. The environment for learning was crippled and thus stifled those who wanted to learn. The ongoing behavioral problems at the troubled East Side school had reached a tipping point, and something drastic needed to be done.

19

GOING ON TO DETROIT

Dr. John Hilliardson, a distinguished Speech Communications Professor at Wayne State University and a seven-year member of the Detroit School Board, attempted to quell the burning inferno. During a recent board meeting, Hilliardson made a surprising recommendation. He was familiar with Charles Parker, his leadership and coaching methods, and the success he achieved in Cleveland. Hilliardson was convinced that Parker was the man who could work magic here in Detroit. He insisted the board take a critical look into hiring Parker.

A month later, Dr. Hilliardson, on behalf of the school board, contacted Parker in Ohio and told him of the board's interest in hiring him for a teaching/coaching position in the Detroit Public School System. Parker knew a little about the Detroit Public League, showed interest in the position, and responded, but wanted to know more. In a phone call, Parker was told how the process worked. He had to complete and submit an employment application and three letters of recommendation. He also had to submit a copy of his college transcripts, teaching certification, and fingerprint clearance card. In addition to a criminal background check, the board wanted Parker to submit to a medical exam. Dr. Hilliardson explained to Parker that he would be brought in for interviews once the preliminary information was completed. Under the impression he was applying for a coaching/teaching position and not a job at the Pentagon, Parker agreed to the demands without protest but was void of his usual enthusiasm.

Satisfied with Parker's credentials, the board scheduled the interviews that included the high school's principal, his assistants, and selected faculty members. The lengthy back-and-forth interview process spanned multiple days. It wasn't until the end of the third day, after the final reference checks were completed, that a decision was made which included the endorsement of the Detroit Public School Board, the Detroit Paradise Valley High School (PVHS), located on Dubois Street between Chene and Waterloo, in the predominantly Black community on Detroit's Lower East Side, extended to Parker an offer to become the school's next basketball and football coach. The coaching offer also included a full-time, benefit-funded teaching position.

Despite facing long odds, pushback from disgruntled white coaches, and a furious and outraged community who wanted a new school principal, not a basketball coach, Parker remained the preferred candidate.

To show their anger and disgust, the community protested vehemently, marching and shouting obscenities outside the campus administration office.

They wanted to know how a coach from out of town, who knew nothing about their community, could come in and magically solve the school's many problems. Parker, however, was undaunted. As he professed when hired in Cleveland, he looked at the dire situation as an opportunity, not a challenge. He agreed to the school board terms and accepted the position, thus becoming the first Black high school coach in Detroit Public Schools.

An assembly to introduce and welcome Parker as the new head coach of the boys' basketball and football teams at the troubled

Paradise Valley High School was met with indifference. More staff attended the assembly than students, but Parker was not discouraged by the lukewarm reception and lack of enthusiasm from the students.

A straight-up and honest man, Parker brought to Detroit a sharp wit and distinctive discipline and structure. He applied this formula to his teams when coaching AAU basketball and successfully implemented it in Cleveland.

Slowly, Parker began to initiate a cultural change to build his philosophical foundation, which included his foundational pillars of education, teamwork, responsibility, and accountability.

After the initial team meeting, to get his message across, Parker approached one of the players considered the most gifted on the team, who was also known to be one of the most undisciplined players. Parker believed that if his methods were going to be successful, he must first reach the player most respected by the others. "It starts by building a relationship, showing them that you care," Parker emphasized to his assistants. After leaving the lengthy meeting, the team leader felt good, especially after hearing the coach's message about his four pillars of success, which stressed education, teamwork, responsibility, and accountability. Over time, that same message resonated with the rest of the talented squad. Parker's demand that class work, the cornerstone of his transformational action plan, took priority over playing and was non-negotiable. And the lack of attention to classwork or reported behavioral issues would have grave consequences.

In prior years, the athletes at PVHS gave lip service to academic achievement. Playing sports had been their priority, and everything else could wait. In the absence of discipline and structure, the teams at PVHS, although talented, underachieved. At the onset, Parker received resistance to his plan, but he was not deterred. Because of his track record, it was just a matter of time before the cultural shift took effect. However, the task was more appealing and expedited when the team's better players were willing to adhere to Parker's demands. The few remaining holdouts soon fell in line, and thus,

Parker's plan was in motion. One advantage in Parker's favor was the abundance of talent at Paradise Valley High School and the surrounding community. So, if a player insisted on bucking his system, he would soon find himself on the outside looking in.

During Parker's first year on campus, and for the first time in the school's history, students who participated in sports were viewed as student-athletes and not student-troublemakers or troubled jocks. The new culture conversion spread renewed pride within the school, spearheaded by teachers who promoted and willfully engaged their students in extra-curricular school activities.

The once skeptical community, which quickly diminished Parker, took notice of the changes at PV High School and began to take an active role in endorsing and supporting games and attending school-sponsored events.

Led by Parker and the success of his sports program, this once undisciplined school in the heart of the so-called ghetto, affectionately called "Black Bottom," was able to transform its culture and create a respectful and positive learning environment along with a burgeoning sports dynasty.

This lower East side area of Detroit, abundant in gifted athletes, was quite the opposite of what Parker had in Cleveland. The athletes here just needed someone to show them he cared, someone with the ability and tenacity to challenge and hold them accountable. By instilling a measure of discipline and structure, accompanied by love, Parker, like he had done before, was the right man for the job.

It wasn't long before Detroit's Paradise Valley High School (PVHS) began to dominate the city's public school sports leagues. To maximize the community's wealth of talent, Parker and his assistants collaborated with a staff of community volunteers to establish a development pipeline program that targeted feeder schools and youth programs throughout the surrounding neighborhoods. The program was entitled Student Preparation and Success Program 4 Kids (SPSP4K).

Parker's team at PVHS consistently produced All-City, All-

State, and professional-caliber athletes from every sport, winning an unprecedented eight consecutive City basketball and seven consecutive football championships. The track team, comprised chiefly of basketball and football players, enjoyed equal championship success. But an undercurrent was swelling, starting with the talk that something must be done to slow down this championship juggernaut.

Although PVHS was the talk of the city and the state, decades-old racial restrictions prohibited Detroit Public School basketball teams from participating in state championships. Unable to dethrone PVHS's run of City championships, frustrated coaches and officials from around the league conspired and mounted a plan to sabotage PVHS.

Secretly, athletic directors met to discuss a plot to weaken PVHS. They designed and implemented a plan that included making unsubstantiated academic eligibility claims. The ADs, at the bequest of their coaches, took their complaints to the state legislature.

After a year of meetings and investigations that rocked the Detroit School, no eligibility improprieties were substantiated. But that didn't stop the Republican-led State Legislature from implementing part two of the sabotage plans.

Despite an outcry from Detroit politicians, the recommendation was implemented to redraw and create new school district enrollment boundaries.

The new boundaries had the sole intent of diverting students from the South Detroit school's enrollment pool. The measure was intended to put the clamps on PVHS effectively. Although State officials denied the allegations, it didn't stop the community from being outraged. They were powerless to stop what many residents believed to be the racially motivated stripping of the school's talent pool. Even though school district politicians challenged the measure in court, the newly drawn school district lines that forced students to enroll in schools further away from their homes remained in place. The power of the political system prevailed, and the challenge was unsuccessful. After the court's decision, PVHS saw the evaporation of talented athletes and promising students. Subsequently weakened, PVHS and Miracle Parker, as some had called him, were done in by their success. As a result, the reign of terror his teams brought down on the Detroit Public Schools ended.

20

CHICAGO ON THE HORIZON

The Chicago City Council consisted of 50 members who served as Aldermen and Alderwomen. Each member represented one of the city's 50 Wards. The Bronzeville neighborhood in Chicago's 3rd Ward was one of five diverse neighborhoods in the 3rd Ward.

Nobody anticipated the vast population explosion in the South Side community of Bronzeville, where more than 3,000 high school students were forced to travel long distances to attend schools outside their neighborhoods. As a result, the City Council's decision to move a plan forward to build the Carter G. Woodson Prep Academy was reinforced. The unanticipated growth boom on Chicago's near south side was the final straw that made the plan, with the blessings of the Chicago Board of Education (CBE), easier for the City Council to digest.

Even though the projected budget was $40 million over the original estimate, support from the City Council was enough for the Bronzeville Community Action Council (CAC) and the CBE to approve by vote the building of the new Charter School at an estimated cost of $160 million. Funding for the neighborhood's new

1,500-diverse-student school project included $60 million from State Funding and an approved $20 million from a special tax district to buy the land from the Chicago Housing Authority (CHA).

Despite the approvals, there was strong opposition against building the school. Housing advocates and a large segment of residents from the 3rd Ward expressed anger and disappointment at the plan, arguing that the school shouldn't be built on land promised for public housing and that the new school could undermine the historically Black schools in the area. However, in response to the criticism, CHA said. "We are still determined to build the subsidized housing units made in an earlier promise to the community, just not on this parcel of land."

Therefore, despite the angst, the school project had the blessing of prominent Black members of the CAC, who were growing tired of the second-class educational issues plaguing many inner-city schools.

The community wanted a school that prioritized learning. They wanted a private school curriculum and a public school open-door policy, but not at the expense of interscholastic sports competitions. The CAC allocated time and resources to promote the vision and uniqueness of a school that prepared students to embrace their place in a diverse 21st century by offering science, technology, engineering, and math curriculum and a competitive interscholastic athletic program.

The promise of hope was for Carter G. Woodson to become a school that graduated students who could address the cycle of high unemployment, crime, and hopelessness. The community had experienced a disproportionate number of ill-prepared student-athletes whose failure to graduate because of low grade-point averages or having their promising athletic careers cut short because of incompetent coaching was alarming and unacceptable.

Parents were vocal during the CAC meetings; they wanted the best of both worlds. They wanted Carter G. Woodson to be a model for what students can achieve if given the right tools and leadership, and just as importantly, they wanted competent athletic coaches.

Momentum was building for this learning and sports competition model, and excitement from parents and students throughout the 3rd Ward generated interest. However, a familiar concern surfaced during the CAC's weekly meetings that got their attention. The priority of hiring a competent, knowledgeable, and compassionate team of administrators, faculty, and coaches had to be on the agenda. Building the school from the ground up was a rare opportunity to implement all the components for success. Therefore, the school board could not afford to drop the ball on this opportunity. If the board failed to address the hiring priorities, the 21st-century ambitions spouted in meetings and forums would be doomed from the start, and the naysayers would proudly boast, "I told you so."

Attendance at the weekly CAC forums continued to garner attention as participation increased. The open discussion of concerns, idea sharing, and making recommendations sparked the attention. During one particular evening forum, where emotions ran high, and tempers flickered, nobody paid much attention to the inconspicuous middle-aged, European-dressed man sitting in the back of the room. But, it was apparent he was not from the community.

However, his tweed sports coat and horn-rimmed glasses did not camouflage his note-taking.

When the agenda item for hiring a basketball coach was opened for discussion and recommendations, the name of a long-standing community resident and former coach surfaced as an overwhelming favorite. The ringing endorsement from the forum's moderator sealed the nomination for Harvey Small, the partisan group's preference. However, the recommendation was not without pushback. There was a flurry from a hostile crowd faction who opposed the nomination. It was brought up that if Harvey's well-known personal issues came to light, he probably wouldn't be able to stand the scrutiny of the school board or the CBE. So, in a tone of resignation from his outraged followers, Harvey's name was begrudgingly dropped from consideration.

As the hour passed and the energy in the crowded room faded, the discussions became cantankerous. Suddenly, a dark-haired woman wearing a twill pants suit, who had been quiet all evening, raised her hand to be recognized. As she stood, patiently waiting for the handheld microphone to make its way around the room to reach her, the low murmur from attendees in the room intensified. In a soft but purposeful voice, just above a whisper, which forced everyone in the room to silence their voices, she said, "I would like to make a recommendation." Immediately, one of the vocals in attendance wanted to dismiss her before she could continue and blurted out, "What does she know?" "She's not from around here." In a quick rebuttal to the outburst, another voice was heard, this time coming from the back of the room from the man in the tweed coat. "Let her speak," he said. The crowded forum stirred as they turned to look at the person whose voice they heard. Puzzled at who they saw, their hushed whispers grew louder as the energy in the room returned. The crowd curiously wondered who he was and what he knew about their concerns.

Delicately holding the hand-held mic in her hands, the mystery woman spoke. "Thank you," she said before continuing. "My name is Ruth McBride, and I live in Oak Park. I recommend Mr. Charles Parker for the basketball coaching position," she offered before sitting down.

In an attempt to restore order in the room, the burly-looking moderator banged his oversized gavel several times on the table to get the attention of the stirring crowd. Like many in the room, the moderator was curious about Ruth's recommendation. He asked, "How do you know Charles Parker?" Is there anyone else here who knows Charles Parker?" Before she could continue, the gentleman in the back of the room raised his hand to be heard: "Sir, is there something you would like to add?" In a respectful tone, he introduced himself, "My name is Paul Shultz, and I am here representing a group of businessmen known as the Friends of Chicago.

Has anyone heard of the Friends?" The moderator interrupted Shultz before he could finish and asked, "Did you say Friends of Chicago?" "If so, then yes, I have heard of them as well as the projects the Friends of Chicago have been involved in, including the millions of dollars committed to building the very school we are discussing tonight."

Shultz replied, "That's good," before continuing. "The Friends are well acquainted with Charles Parker," which was followed by a gasp and more rumblings from the crowd. In another attempt to bring the room back to order, the moderator gave two pronounced bangs of the gavel on the table and asked the crowd to settle down before asking Schultz to continue. "Thank you," Shultz said to the moderator before continuing. "I have attended several forums, and each time, I have reported back to 'The Friends' and shared your concerns. Trust me, they are sympathetic to your interest, and like you, they want what's best for the school." As the room listened intently, Schultz said, "The organization is confident that Mr. Parker is the person you seek. He is an educator first, an excellent coach, and a heck of a human being."

After the back-and-forth Q&A with Shultz, someone directed a question to Ms. McBride. "Do you work for the Friends of Chicago?" She stood and, without hesitating or stammering or the benefit of the microphone, replied, "No, I do not work for the organization, but let me explain how I came to know Charles Parker. "I met Charles Parker years ago while attending the University of Illinois. At the time, I was a student, and by chance, we met when he was seeking campus information." Ruth explained, "I will spare you some details, but Charles made a lasting impression on me many years ago. I believed that if Charles were given an opportunity, he would be successful in whatever he chose to pursue." The forum was now ever more interested in knowing more as Ruth continued. "Charles left the University under, let's say, unusual circumstances, but I was so intrigued by that one brief encounter that I followed his career, which I might add has been nothing short of miraculous." Before she sat down, Ruth added, "I stand by my recommendation, and I am confident you won't be disappointed." She then took her seat. The room was dead silent for about fifteen seconds after she finished speaking. The moderator, stunned by the silence, thanked Ruth for sharing her experience and, hearing no further comments, adjourned the meeting.

21

TO GO OR NOT TO GO

The Friends of Chicago asked their liaison, Paul Shultz, to contact their colleague, the Superintendent of Chicago Schools, Dr. Kent Huntsman. Kent was a hard-working veteran Chicago administrator of twenty-plus years and possessed a wide range of connections and a well-known reputation for getting things done. The Friends and Kent shared long-standing memberships at the prestigious Chicago Golf & Country Club as well as membership at the Chicago Yacht Club. The Friends requested that Shultz converse with Kent and encourage him to use his influence to intervene on their behalf. Charles (Charlie) Parker was their target. It was communicated to Kent that the Friends were making a polite inquiry into the availability of Charlie Parker coming to Chicago.

Having exchanged favors in the past, Kent looked at the request as a reciprocal favor to the influential group. Kent knew from experience that when 'The Friends' ask about something, they expect to get what they ask for. In this case, the ask seemed urgent. Kent immediately contacted his colleague in Detroit, Dr. Ray Pringle, Superintendent of Detroit Public Schools. Like Kent in Chicago, Pringle was a member of a Yacht Club, Detroit's Bay View. Kent and

Pringle's Yacht Club memberships bring them together once a year as competitors when their respective Yacht Clubs take turns hosting the Shelly Hansen Sailing World Regatta Series. This year, the Motor City and the Detroit Yacht Club hosted the three-day racing event on the freshwaters of Lake St.Clair. Although not considered one of the Five Great Lakes, Lake St. Clair, situated six miles northeast of downtown Detroit, is considered part of the Five Great Lakes as it is connected, along with the Detroit River to Lake Huron on the North and Lake Erie on the South.

The sailing competition assembled the finest local and national sailors from around the globe. Last year, just off the shores of Lake Michigan, which many consider one of the best racing venues in the world, the Windy City and the Chicago Yacht Club hosted the three-day racing competition.

During his phone call to Pringle, Kent explained the urgency of his request, and that an answer other than yes would not go over well in Chicago.

Shortly after his informative conversation with Kent, Pringle contacted Charlie Parker. Pringle wanted to gauge Parker's interest in relocating from Detroit to coach high school basketball in Chicago. So after pleasantries were exchanged, Pringle asked Parker if he would be interested in relocating to Chicago to become head basketball coach at a newly built Prep Academy on Chicago's South Side. Pringle explained that the coaching position package included full-time teaching along with health and medical benefits. Although the offer sounded enticing, Charlie showed no interest in relocating and didn't bite on the question. Parker felt the only way he would be willing to uproot his family from Detroit was for a college or university coaching position. Dr. Pringle explained to Charlie, "I appreciate your honesty, but I don't think you understand what I'm asking. Therefore, I will give you a few days to rethink your response seriously. I'll get back to you before the week is out." Parker was miffed at Pringle's remark about rethinking his response. He thought he made himself clear. He wasn't interested in relocating to Chicago.

Kent was not pleased when told of Parker's reluctance to accept the coaching/teaching offer. So, he took a different, more direct approach with his colleague in Detroit. Kent reiterated to Pringle the urgency of the situation and that the powers in Chicago were not in the business of having their offers rejected. Kent wanted Pringle to understand the request's magnitude and ensure Parker understood the ramifications of his response. The tone in which Kent spoke suggested to Pringle that a no answer from Parker was not an option. Kent told Pringle, "Dispense with the niceties of asking and tell Parker that whatever it takes, we expect him in Chicago for the start of the fall semester."

When Superintendent Pringle made his second call to Parker, he got right to the point and clarified that remaining in Detroit was not an option. Pringle didn't like being scolded by his colleague in Chicago, so his tone to Parker was totally different from that of his first call. The relocation clarification and subsequent consequences were made abundantly clear.

Consequently, Charlie agreed to come to Chicago. There was, however, one minor detail Parker wanted addressed. Exercising what little remaining leverage he had, Charlie requested to the superintendent that arrangements be made for his home in Detroit to be sold at fair market value and to purchase a new home in Chicago in a community of his choosing. The superintendent responded to Parker's request when he asked, "Is there anything else?" Charlie replied, "No, not at this time." After a brief pause and whispers in the background, the superintendent responded to Parker and said, "Done deal. Someone from my office will be in touch." Then, the conversation abruptly ended.

22

WELCOME COACH PARKER

Parker was preceded to Chicago by his reputation. He was formally introduced as the new basketball coach at Carter G. Woodson Prep Academy during a press conference in the school auditorium. In attendance at the press conference were community leaders, two city council members, members of the basketball team, TV and Tribune sports writers, and Paul Shultz, the representative of the "Friends of Chicago."

During an interview, a veteran Chicago sports writer asked Parker to share key points about his mission and success plan. Parker promises to do what he does well, no matter the task, great or small. Parker explained to the journalist, "This is not my first rodeo. I have been entrusted many times to build programs nationwide from scratch, most of the time. In this case, I was not given a contract. For now, all I have received is a handshake agreement from some people who will remain anonymous. They made me no promises or funding for assistant coaches." Parker continued, "That's when you realize the only expectations you have to meet are your own. Fans are fickle! They love you when you're winning and hate you when you're losing. So, all you can do is the best you can do while you can."

Implementing his success plan began in the classroom but extended into the community. "There's a great big world out there, and learning about that world is part of my plan, "Parker quipped."

He continued, "Before the players become good players, they must first become good students and good people." The reporter was all ears as the veteran coach shared his well-traveled coaching philosophy.

"Players have to care for one another, care about the school, and care about the neighborhoods they come from. When they do that, then they will be ready to learn how to play basketball the right way, my way."

On the first day of practice, Parker introduced his team to his coaching style using his trademark coaching pillars of structure and discipline. The players went through a series of foot drills, ball drills, and rebounding drills, which were then followed by the never-ending defensive drills, sprints, and, lastly, laps around the court. "Don't be last, Parker barked." Then, after four grueling hours of practice and before he sent his exhausted players home, who now looked at him like crazed men, he made one last comment: "Take care of your homework."

It's been three years since Parker's arrival, and although the graduation rate was high, and the team played hard on the court, very few of them have received Division I basketball scholarships. Members in the community, especially those who opposed Parker's hiring in the first place, were rumbling and mumbling as nearby South Side schools continued to dominate Carter G. Woodson. They were stirring the pot, asking questions about when or if Parker would produce a championship team.

Finally, after some arm twisting and conversations with Paul Shultz, Parker brought in two well-respected assistants from Detroit Paradise Valley High School. Those new hires proved pivotal to Parker, as one of the new hires happened to be Claudia Coleman's cousin.

23

THE WINGS OF A PHENOM

Autumn leaves were turning shades of brown and gold, and humid summer temperatures gave way to cooler evenings. The third day of September was the first day of school, and students at the Carter G. Woodson Prep Academy were busy taking care of their "first day of school" business activities. Some took their photo IDs and secured parking decals, while others negotiated to get hall locker assignments near their friends.

When Xavier looked around, it was apparent to him that most of the Woodson Prep students on this first day of school were dressed in their "opening day dress attire," which was not that surprising since there was only one "first day of school," so you dressed to impress.

While the freshman class participated in mandatory orientation and advice-related breakout sessions, the upper-class students, especially those who thought they knew everything about the school, were busy serving as guides and hosts.

Before heading over to team meetings, varsity athletes, some wearing their letterman jackets, mingled near the cafeteria's entrance, looking to catch the attention of someone (girls, most likely) who might require their assistance.

The boys' and junior varsity basketball teams assembled in the gymnasium bleachers, talking and comparing first-day notes while they waited for the first of many team meetings. Coach Charles Charlie Parker addressed the group using his usual high-spirited, business-like approach. He reminded the team to make time to discuss their academic progress with school counselors and verify that they were enrolled in the appropriate number of semester credits that were transferable to four-year colleges.

Parker also used the meeting to remind and encourage (demand) his players to participate in a fall sport. It was a customary requirement and part of his basketball culture at Carter G. Woodson for those trying out for winter semester basketball to participate in year-round sports. Players could play football or run cross-country in the fall or run track, play baseball, golf, or tennis during the spring. But doing neither when not playing basketball was not an available option.

On many nights when the moon lit the sky, Xavier could be found sitting alone in his bedroom, looking out into the night. The sounds and sights of the night, including the speeding Chicago L train, simply amazed him. He often wondered how the L-train traveling that fast could make the corner turn and not come off the rail. This nighttime fascination took him away from the recurring thoughts that occupied his mind about his mom and dad in Jamaica and the friends he left behind. He wondered if they missed him as much as he missed them.

Living in a town where his dad remains a legend and his famous Uncle teaches at Chicago City College was a concern for Xavier. He felt like people who knew his dad and uncle constantly watched his every move. The invisible target on his back generated unfair questions that seemed to follow him wherever he went. Questions such as, "Will he be as good as his father? I have doubts he will be good. He's from Jamaica." Those were just some of the constant noise that surrounded him every day.

As a promise to his brother, Freddie and his wife, Claudia, made their Chicago home Xavier's home. They treated him like the family he was. Xavier had his bedroom and free access to the refrigerator, something he relished and took advantage of early and often.

During the basketball season, Xavier's most prominent and loudest supporters were Freddie, Claudia, and two of their three children, Jake and Zeke. The oldest, Vanessa, didn't spend much time at the family home except for an occasional weekend visit. She attends Northern Illinois University and plans to continue her graduate studies before pursuing a law degree from the University of Chicago Law School.

Jake and Zeke attend Oak Park/River Forest High School, where Jake is a football team captain. Zeke, the youngest, enjoys basketball but seems naturally gifted in baseball. When the family attends Xavier's games, they often arrive early to congregate and mingle with other parents before and after the games. Usually, while they waited on Xavier after the game, Zeke managed to get involved in three-on-three basketball games by challenging kids from other waiting families.

Claudia meticulously kept a scrapbook of Xavier's exploits, like she did for her two boys. She collected all general news and sports articles about Xavier's school and basketball activities. She has taken it upon herself to send articles about Xavier back to Dorothy and KeShawn in Jamaica.

Xavier Coleman, the kid from Jamaica and son of Chicago legend KeShawn Coleman, and under the tutelage of coach Parker, had transformed phenomenally. His development and rise to stardom began during his junior year at Carter G. Woodson Prep Academy. As KeShawn envisioned, Coach Parker's coaching program accelerated Xavier's skill development. He was no longer the gangly kid playing out of position. His motor skills and coordination were now in harmony, which allowed him to display a skill set that had not been seen around Chicago in quite some time.

Xavier also possessed an attractive charisma and a smile that could light up a room. But when it came time to play ball, he was as fierce and competitive as anyone, and that was his edge. Xavier was internally motivated and driven by a desire to play in the NBA and be the best in the NBA.

Parker saw and coached talented athletes during his legendary career, especially at Paradise Valley High School in Detroit. But he openly admitted that Xavier had all the tools to become the best he had ever coached. Over two years, this prodigy's development allowed him to dominate and terrorize the Chicago high school basketball scene like none before him.

24

GAME TIME

Thanks to Coach Parker, Xavier's brotherly relationship with teammate Willie Mitchell was special and by design. Xavier's love and support from his high school teammates, known around Chicago as the Knights, helped accelerate his meteoric rise to stardom that took off like that of a shooting star. Throughout their senior championship season, Xavier and the Knights, following the lead of their legendary hall-of-fame coach, beat back every challenge and finished the regular season with an impressive and unblemished record of 26-0.

As expected, the rugged and competitive Chicago Public High School League, which consisted of all-star caliber players on every team, prepared the Knights for their championship run. They were pushed and challenged weekly, withstanding close road games at Harlan, DuSable, and Simeon. The Knights were a well-coached team that took advantage of its opponents using teamwork, discipline, precision, and poise. They never panicked, and tense moments never seemed to phase them.

It has been four years since Parker arrived at Carter G. Woodson Prep Academy. Despite the academic success his previous team enjoyed, he has this year's team on the cusp of playing in the long-awaited and much-anticipated state championship game.

The Knights played flawlessly and quickly breezed through Regional and Sectional rounds before anyone could put up much of a fight. In the finals, however, playing to a lively overflow crowd of 16,300 screaming fans at the State Farm Center, home of the University of Illinois Fighting Illini, the Knights may have met their match. DuSable High School, winner of multiple championships and has banners hanging in its gymnasium to ensure everyone knew, had just beaten Harlan in the semi-finals and was confident and determined to cap its season as state champions.

The Knight's motivation to win the game was Coach Parker. They wanted the coach to win his first Chicago State Championship. So, with Willie at the point, Xavier dominating on the inside, and Derek going to work from the perimeter, the battle-tested Knights stayed strong despite the challenge coming from DuSable.

The two teams traded body blows all evening in the back-and-forth thriller as each team tried to impose their will. The Knights, however, ended up being the last team standing when Xavier came out of nowhere to block a potential game-tying layup attempt as the buzzer sounded. By defeating perennial powerhouse DuSable High School in a thrilling nail-biter 81-79, Carter G. Woodson became the first-ever prep academy to win the Illinois High School Association State Class 4A boys basketball championship.

State journalists described the game as a well-played barn-burner, as both teams went at each other the entire evening. Some journalists would later describe Parker's team as one of the greatest high school teams the state had ever witnessed. The entire senior class of players earned college scholarships, and three of the starters played professionally in various sports.

Derek "Silk" Chambers, a Junior on the title team, scored a sensational 36 points in the finals. After his All-American sophomore year, Derek turned pro and had a 12-year career in the NBA, playing with the Denver Nuggets and Detroit Pistons. He made four All-Star game appearances and won an NBA championship.

Kirby "Magic" Martinez, a smooth-fielding baseball shortstop, played with the Seattle Mariners organization for ten years and made two All-Star game appearances.

Captain point guard Willie "El Tigre" Mitchell, Xavier's closest friend, was a starting guard at Denver University and earned a doctorate from the University of Colorado. He was a professor at the University of Denver and a Board Member of Xavier's Non-Profit Foundation.

Left-handed and unorthodox shooting James "Spider" Connors," played and graduated from Howard University and went on to become president at North Carolina's Shaw University, the oldest Historical Black College (HBCU) in the South.

Darnell "DMV" Marcus-Vance played college ball at Metro State University before attending Morehouse Law School in Atlanta. He partnered with his Morehouse Law School roommate and Frat brother to form a Civil Rights law firm in suburban Union City, Georgia.

Aaron "Kool-Aid" Jenkins played wide receiver at Northwestern University and six years of pro ball with the Chicago Bears. Allegations of accounting mismanagement within his nonprofit foundation tarnished his reputation but did not keep him from joining the Chicago Sheriff's Department.

After being taught the game's fundamentals from Coach Parker's structured, disciplined style and his sage lessons on navigating life, Xavier graduated as a two-time high school All-American. He was ranked by major prep publications as the second-best player in the country, rocketing him into the national spotlight. But his journey would unknowingly be impacted by some unlikely forces and ultimately be defined by the country's highest court of law.

25

TIME TO GO

I t was the summer of 1967, and Chicago was about to explode. Residents in the Windy City had become increasingly agitated with the social injustice and increased police brutality. Racial tensions were boiling, but the spark that lit the powder keg was the police shooting of three unarmed Black Men at one of the nightclubs on Chicago's South side.

The city erupted, and into the night, groups of people vented their frustration by burning and looting any and everything in sight; it was ultimate chaos and bedlam. Even though the city was burning, there was no time for distress; it was time for Xavier and Willie to leave and head to college. Xavier was heavily recruited, but Louisiana State University (LSU) became Xavier's school of choice. However, Coach Parker insisted, "If you want Xavier, you must also take Willie in a package deal."

An attempt to enroll at the Baton Rouge campus, where Xavier and Willie would become the first Black athletes to play basketball in the Southeastern Conference (SEC), did not go as planned due to the long-reaching influence of veteran University of Tennessee coach Randolph Ruppert, plus the fact that LSU coaches changed plans and wanted Xavier and Wilie to attend a Junior College. This sudden about-face did not go over well, especially after the university promised Coach Parker that Xavier would be enrolled at the University.

Ruppert's well-documented stance on segregation and integration and LSU's insistence that Xavier attend a JC of their choosing was all the excuse Coach Parker needed. Parker acted as quickly as possible to get his guys out of Louisiana. He consulted with several two-year college coaches to find a last-minute option even though fall semester classes at most schools had already begun.

Although classes had already started, the multi-diverse student population of Long Beach City College, located 25 miles south of Los Angeles and nine miles from the coastal beach, was the campus that welcomed the newcomers from Chicago.

Wearing clothes that resembled Chicago's nightlife, the boys from the city, wearing their silk tees, gabardine shirts, and alligator shoes, would soon find out that college students on the West Coast preferred a different wardrobe vibe.

A sophomore member of the basketball team, Vernon Akquia, greeted his new teammates and made an immediate and stark assessment when he said, "You guys look like pimps." While everyone laughed, Vernon added, "But, no worries, just wait until you get your dry cleaning bill." The fellas all laughed and slapped high-fives. Vernon's suspicion was correct, and within days, tee shirts, jeans, and sneakers had replaced the street-life look.

Vernon was not only a great soothsayer but also a great basketball player. He possessed an uncanny hook shot that even Xavier had difficulty defending. He was also an outstanding artist. He entertained the team by drawing pictures ranging from characters to abstracts to the realities of the times. The trio's friendship was genuine and would last for decades.

Fortune smiled at Xavier once again. One year removed from high school, he became the JC leader in scoring and rebounding, averaging 28 points and 22 rebounds per game. At age 18, those impressive numbers earned him unanimous first-team All-American honors.

26

THE OLYMPIC GAMES OF MEXICO CITY

The Olympic Games are the world's ultimate global, multisport athletic competition. The world of nations comes together to compete, and the Olympics serves as a stage where athletes showcase their talents, dedication, and hard work. The Olympics foster international friendship and unity, but for three weeks, athletes gather to do battle for the love of country and sport.

THE HISTORY of the Olympic Games goes back almost 3,000 years to the Peloponnese in ancient Greece, where sports contests took place every four years. The first modern Olympics were held in Athens, Greece in 1896.

However, the Olympics became an international event after 1924, when the VIII Games were held in Paris.

In 1968, Mexico City became the first Latin American city to host the Olympic Games, beating out Detroit and Lyon for the honor.

THE 1968 SUMMER Olympics were more than just a sporting event. They were a stage for political and social upheaval and outstanding athletic performances.

On the strength of his remarkable freshman-year performance, Xavier received an invitation from the U.S. Olympic Committee to attend the Olympic trials in Albuquerque, New Mexico. There were no guarantees he would make the final cut, but Olympic coaches wanted to see firsthand how Xavier's junior college talent measured against Division I players.

All 50 invited players assembled in Albuquerque and received an orientation, physical examination, and a detailed briefing on what the coaches expected in building an Olympic-caliber team. The seven-day tryouts consisted of meetings, drills, and scrimmages, as players were evaluated and released daily.

The final roster, including alternates, will be determined by the end of the week. Xavier's performance during the first scrimmage was nothing short of sensational. He astounded the coaches, who had never seen him play in person until now. Xavier was as good as advertised, and his remarkable skills and talents justified the coach's decision to notify him in advance that he had made the Olympic team, amazingly after only one day of scrimmaging.

As fate would have it, this was the first year that USA Basketball allowed junior college and non-senior athletes to participate in the Olympic trials. However, one glitch had to be addressed: all participants had to produce a valid birth certificate verifying their American citizenship.

As a foreign-born player, Xavier had to get clearance from the International Olympic Committee (IOC) to become eligible to participate as an American.

The formality was quickly addressed when county records verified that Xavier was deemed a U.S. Citizen even though he was born in Jamaica. His father, KeShawn, a natural U.S. citizen, maintained dual citizenship, thus making Xavier eligible.

Few events in an athlete's career can beat the Olympic experience, a moment like no other. For Xavier, all the history and colorful pageantry associated with being an Olympian, the Games of the XIX Olympiad, commonly called Mexico 1968, was a humbling experience.

The sobering thought of representing USA basketball in front of millions of viewers was not a dream Xavier had given much thought to while growing up. Considering the origins of his journey, making the Olympic team was monumental, but all Xavier wanted to do was play against the best. So, the magnitude of being an Olympian remained out of his conceptual mindset.

However, this moment of reflection soon gave way to the realities of the times. It was 1968, and the world outside the fieldhouse walls was experiencing a radical social and cultural revolution. It was, in fact, a ball of confusion.

Distinguished University of Nevada Las Vegas African American History Professor Dr. Arthur Byrdsong viewed the Olympic games as a platform to address the inequities perpetrated against, notably, Black Americans. He organized the Human Rights Project Plan (HRPP) movement in response. Momentum for the movement moved swiftly as it gathered support from student-athletes on campuses nationwide. Collaboratively, students brainstormed to develop effective strategies and methods to protest their discontent with the United States. The protest methods included any potential victories for a country that failed to acknowledge their basic human rights.

AFTER MEETING FOR WEEKS, *the HRPP settled on three demands: "Restore Kareem Mustafa's heavyweight championship title, which was stripped from him when he refused induction into the military.*

Remove Forest Shuster as head of the U.S. Olympic Committee (he was considered by many as a white supremacist), and Disinvite apartheid states South Africa and Rhodesia.

THE MEXICO CITY Olympic games were the most politically charged Olympics since the 1936 games in Berlin. Ten days before the Games were to open, students protesting the Mexican government's use of funds for the Olympics rather than for social programs were surrounded in the "Plaza of Three" by the Mexican army and, unprovoked, were fired upon. More than 200 protesters were killed, and thousands more were injured.

During the medal ceremony for the men's 200-meter run, American medal winners Tim Jordan and Frank Carlson stood on the podium in their sweat clothes, a tribute to their African American heritage and a protest of the living conditions of Black Americans in the United States. In a symbolic gesture, they removed their shoes, bowed their heads, and raised a black-gloved fist during the playing of the national anthem.

Officials from the IOC and the U.S. Olympic Committee were stunned and outraged at the expression. When they addressed the media, the USOC vehemently opposed such a display and considered the demonstration counterproductive to the spirit of the Olympics.

The IOC demanded the USOC deal with what they called an embarrassment. So, staggering from IOC pressure and hurt feelings, the USOC agreed that swift and decisive action had to be taken. Then, in a knee-jerk reaction devoid of due process, the USOC punished the two American medal winners by banishing them from the Olympic Village. The punitive action to ban the two Olympians, which many thought was racially motivated, did not go over well with the HRPP organizers. Local police were summoned and surrounded the Olympians while they packed their bags before escorting them from the village to the airport. HRPP organizers immediately turned their attention to planning more demonstrative demonstrations.

Over 5,500 athletes representing 112 countries attended the Games of Mexico. East and West Germany competed for the first time as separate nations, and drug testing and female gender verifications were conducted for the first time. These Mexico City Olympic games were far different from the typical Games.

Under constant duress from HRPP and its leadership, a young Xavier started to experience mixed feelings about participating. He became torn and uneasy from the unyielding pressure to join the protest movement and boycott the games. He was reminded of the discrimination that took place in Chicago and Black communities throughout America. The HRPP organizers asked Xavier, "If you don't take a stand now, when will you take a stand?"

Aware of the mounting pressure being applied to its athletes, Team USA brought in the great Jesse Owens, winner of four Gold medals during the 1936 Olympics: 100 meters, long jump, 200 meters, and 4x100 relay; indeed, a truly remarkable achievement. On behalf of Team USA, Owens spoke explicitly to the basketball team and tried to convince them that boycotting the Games was not the best solution and could have long-lasting repercussions.

He asked, "How would you have felt if you had to run before Hitler? If I can do that without protesting, so can you. He continued his speech by saying, "If you boycott, you will never be able to get a job." That's when USA guard Silas Ford replied, "No disrespect, Jesse, but what the hell, I can't get a job now."

Despite Owens's emotional speech and the pleading of Team USA leadership, the boycott continued to gain momentum, splintering the basketball team. Over half the team favored boycotting, while others were unsure how to express discontent. In another desperate attempt to stem the tide, the Olympic committee contacted Xavier's father, KeShawn Coleman. He and his wife Dorothy had just landed in Mexico City after a 3-hour and 20-minute flight from Jamaica.

While his parents settled after their flight, Xavier continued to grapple with an inward struggle between the truth of the Human Rights Project Plan and the chance of a lifetime to do the thing he loved the most: play basketball, but this time on the world's biggest stage, the Olympic Games.

After explaining to the Olympic Committee that they needed more time to process all the information, the Colemans retreated to the Olympic Village, where they planned to talk to their son and, if necessary, to any of his disgruntled teammates. Because of his encounters with discrimination and segregation in Chicago, KeShawn favored the boycott, while Dorothy was more sympathetic and preferred finding another form of protest.

The skeptical media viewed the team of unknowns relying on a 19-year-old junior college player to win the gold medal as the underdog and out of the question to think they could win any of the three medals.

The Olympic Committee was keenly aware that if Xavier and others agreed to the boycott, there wouldn't be enough time to assemble a new team and get them up to speed, virtually ensuring the USA's gold medal-winning streak would end.

In response to one of KeShawn's suggestions, the Olympic Committee agreed to fly in from Chicago Xavier's respected high school basketball coach, Charlie Parker. The hope was that Parker could talk some sense into the team and quell the growing boycott sentiment.

Upon his arrival, Parker addressed the Black athletes in a closed-door meeting. He asked them to think long and hard about the greater good of playing instead of what might happen if they chose not to play. He explained, "You represent a country, not a race." Coach Parker agreed and was sympathetic to the boycott movement on many issues but didn't feel now was the time or place for this fight. He said to the group. "Right now, it's us, the USA, against the world. So let's send another type of message by kicking some ass and bringing home as many gold medals as possible."

After Coach Parker delivered his passionate speech, many of

Xavier's teammates favored playing instead of boycotting. Coach Parker pulled Xavier aside and relayed a direct message from the Olympic Committee, who said to Parker, "Xavier is our guy. He's America's savior; we can defeat Russia and anybody else and win this thing with him." The message Parker conveyed rang loud and clear and was the tipping point that put Xavier's growing political ideology on hold and his focus back on playing basketball for now.

Confident and free from indecisiveness, Xavier was hyped and no longer vacillated about the boycott issue. Despite the challenge of reigniting the team's chemistry, Xavier was confident he could bridge the concerning gap and get his teammates back on track to focus on the one goal they all came here with to win the gold medal.

After an early morning practice consisting mainly of team-building exercises and a film session, Xavier wanted to take advantage of the small downtime window to have lunch with his parents, Uncle Freddie, Coach Parker, and friends Willie Mitchell and Vernon Akquia. So he hurried over to the Olympic Village. However, there was a moment of anxiety at the Olympic Village entrance, where all entries must show their official Olympic badge ID or guest ID to access the Village. When Xavier, who usually wears his badge around his neck, couldn't produce his badge, an argument with the gatekeeper ensued, and a few choice words were exchanged.

While trying to convince the gatekeeper that he was a USA athlete, a female athlete from France tapped him on the shoulder and said, "I believe this belongs to you. I was walking behind you when I saw your badge fall out of your backpack." Calmness was restored, and what was once lost was now found thanks to the alert athlete from France. A stern look at the gatekeeper was followed by a sigh of relief from Xavier. Xavier thanked the French athlete, extended her a handshake, and, to show his appreciation, invited her to join him and his family and friends for lunch.

As the Colemans soaked in the aura of being in the Olympic Village, they became excited when they saw Xavier walking their way. Dorothy thought, "This is great. I'm having lunch with my son in the Olympic Village in Mexico City." But as Xavier drew closer, Dorothy nudged her husband and whispered, "Do you know who that nice-looking woman is walking next to Xavier?" Before he could answer, the twosome was upon them, so KeShawn and the men at the table, in a customary display of manners, stood and waited to be introduced. But the look on Xavier's face was telling. He apologized for not knowing the young woman's name and asked her to introduce herself.

Sophie obliged with laughter. In a French accent, while extending her hand in Dorothy's direction, she replied, "Bonjour, my name is Sophie (So-Fee)Turner Dumas; I am here representing France in the women's Heptathlon. I found Whatsisname's ID badge. I mean to say Xavier Coleman's ID badge." Everyone laughed at the play on words, which served as the perfect icebreaker.

Excited and curious to know more, Dorothy patted the cushion in the chair next to her and asked Sophie to take a seat. While KeShawn, Willie, Vernon, and Coach Parker talked to Xavier about the team's practice and the chances of getting a medal, Dorothy listened to Sophie, who, in small talk, discussed her family in Paris and her excitement about participating in the Olympics.

Dorothy, feeling comforted, opened up to Sophie and shared knowledge about her parents, which only one or two of her close knew about. "My mother was born in France and moved to Jamaica to teach." Catching Sophie by surprise, Dorothy continued, "After marrying, she continued teaching the French language in Kingston at the-Alliance Française de la Jamaïque, a non-profit organization that promoted the French language and the preparation for earning French diplomas and certificates."

Dorothy said, "Sadly, my parents divorced during my first year of high school, but although they are not together, they remain civil most of the time."

Glancing over at Xavier, Sophie shared information about her family, "My mom is French, and my dad, an avid basketball fan, was born in Kalamazoo, Michigan, but moved to Montreal, Quebec, Canada as a young child. They now live in the Chaillot quarter, a quiet section of the 16th arrondissement in Western Paris."

As a scholarship junior at UCLA, Sophie competed in the Heptathlon. She hoped to give a good two-day performance but admitted that she needed to do well in the final event, the 1500-meter race, if she expected to medal. Willie, who overheard Sophie mention her final event, asked if she was nervous. Sophie replied, "Honestly, I am. However, it's a good nervousness, not a nervousness of fear." Sophie added, "Competing for your country in the Olympics against so many world-class athletes was mind-blowing compared to competing in college. But I'm prepared, so I don't worry. I can't wait to get started."

As the lunch table continued their conversations, oblivious to their surroundings, someone from afar caught Xavier's eye. A tall-looking athlete wearing broad shoulders, a USA sweatsuit, and a shiny gold medallion dangling from his neck walked their way. Six other stern-looking men, also wearing sweatsuits, followed him. "Hannibal Simpson," yelled Xavier, "Ya Mon." Xavier and Hannibal were frequent lunch partners who had no problem trying to see who could eat the most food in the Village. "Big fella, come over and let me introduce you to my family and friends." After an embrace, Xavier slapped hands and introduced his fellow Olympian and lunch partner to everyone sitting at the table. This time, Xavier made sure he didn't forget or mispronounce the name of his French savior.

The pleasantries aside, Hannibal turned serious and began to express his feelings about the boycott and said, rather emphatically, "There's been a lot of talk about boycotting and who should do what and when, but I've made up my mind." As he looked at Xavier, Hannibal went on, "I will represent the USA, period, and my focus is to destroy the Russian heavyweight and anyone else standing in my way of getting a gold medal."

Listening to the words coming from Simpson's mouth was music to Coach Parker's ears as he smiled and nodded to acknowledge the boxer's words. As his voice of determination settled, KeShawn and the fellas at the table fist-bumped Hannibal. Sensing he had taken up enough of their lunchtime, Hannibal bowed his head toward the women and saluted the guys. Big Hannibal Simpson then pointed a finger at Xavier and said, "See you on the podium," then excused himself and walked away as his trailing entourage followed.

The afternoon was fading fast, but before heading back for a team meeting, Xavier thanked everyone for spending lunch time together. He embraced his mom and dad and slapped hands with his boys, who asked while laughing, "Where's our hug?" After laughing at their gesture, Xavier, having his pride restored and his sense of humor in tack, asked Sophie if she had time to walk back and retrace the steps of the lost ID badge. Keeping the humorous situation going, Sophie rubbed her chin, and after a slight hesitation, she smiled and replied, "Sure, I have time."

Because of an apprehensive USA media, still bitter about why America's top senior All-Americans chose not to participate, they sowed seeds of doubt to alert journalists around the globe about USA basketball's chances of winning a medal. Despite their valid reasons, the US media still harbored ill feelings toward the senior All-Americans. They called their decisions not to play nothing more than a boycott and, therefore, should be considered un-American. As a result, USA basketball entered the Olympics in an unfamiliar underdog position to the favored Soviet Union and solid Yugoslavian and Brazilian teams.

The chorus of worldwide journalists who had joined the US media in fanning the flames of doubt labeled America's Olympic team the B-Team, a team that can't possibly bring home a gold medal. However, the message of Team USA's demise seemed greatly exaggerated.

After summer training and a series of successful exhibition games against NBA teams, Team USA was unfazed and undaunted despite the ongoing gloom-and-doom rhetoric spewing from the media. The team understood that the unconventional path they've traveled, the challenges they've overcome, and the bond they've built have far more meaning, and no outside noise, no matter how loud it gets, can shake their resolve or alter their focus. Instead, the team used Carpe diem (seize the day) as a rallying cry. The team also used the mounds of negativity to fuel their insatiable appetite to shake up the world. Team USA would enjoy nothing better than taking home the gold and, once and for all, silencing all the skeptics, critics, and haters.

Team USA opened pool play and made quick work of a gritty Spain before spanking them 81-46. Then, an overmatched Senegal was walloped 93-36 as Xavier smoothly and efficiently scored 16 points. Before taking on Yugoslavia, one of the gold medal favorites, the pesky Philippines, despite a good showing, swallowed the bitter pill of defeat, 96-75.

Confident or overconfident? Before an anxious sold-out crowd of over 22,000 fans, Team USA found themselves down 10 points early to Yugoslavia. Many in the press row and thousands at home wondered if this was the game where the unknowns, meeting a seasoned opponent, finally meet their match. Trailing by five at halftime, only a few knew what was discussed during the break as Silas Ford came out of the locker room on fire. His shots in the second half thrilled the crowd and helped the USA overcome the deficit to stun the Yugoslavians. Ford's 17 second-half points led USA to a comfortable 73-58 victory. Team USA, intent to get back on track, put a not-so-stellar performance behind them and took their frustrations out on poor Panama by steamrolling them 95-60, as Xavier dominated from the start, scoring 27 points, 15 rebounds, and seven blocked shots.

Italy was next to feel the sting of the now crowd favorite USA, biting the dust 100-61 as the young 19-year-old Xavier continued his domination, scoring 26 points and collecting 12 rebounds. After two relatively easy victories, Team USA, despite Ford sitting out to rest a tender shoulder aggravated in the Panama game, underestimated a determined and scrappy Puerto Rico team.

Puerto Rico employed a strategy to junk up the game and bottle up Xavier, using double — and triple-team coverage. However, despite the scare, Team USA survived and advanced, clinging to a 61-56 victory, as Xavier found enough wiggle room to score 21 points.

In the pivotal semi-final game, the U.S. jumped all over a seasoned Brazil, a team many thought would give the U.S. trouble. But, Brazil could not overcome an early double-digit deficit, which quickly dismissed any notions they had of an upset, as Team USA won going away, 75-63.

Following the semi-final victory over the experienced Brazilian team, the U.S. was one victory away from completing their improbable Olympic mission. Fans and supporters were riding the wave of excitement in anticipation of the championship game against the Russians. But something unexpected happened: Yugoslavia stunned the Russians in an intense semi-final game that came down to the last second to escape victoriously 63-62. The upset served as a cruel reminder of the dangers that lie in waiting along the bumpy road to gold.

Enjoying an unblemished 8-0 Team USA was prepared and eager to put the finishing touches on its Olympic journey. Although they easily beat Yugoslavia earlier in the Games, the coaches had to impress upon the team not to overlook the highly motivated and cocky Yugoslavians in the title game.

The media, however, remained unfazed. They couldn't seem to shed their coat of doubt about the undefeated Americans and declared the red-hot, 7-1 Yugoslavian team as the favorite to win gold. They cited the fact that Yugoslavia had just defeated the Game's favorite Russians and was anxious to avenge an earlier loss to the U.S.

Palacio de los Deportes arena was packed as over 22,370 fans found their way into the sold-out arena, including Xavier's inner circle of family and friends and millions more watching worldwide. The gold medal game was the highlight of the Olympic Games. Who would prevail, the unknowns, as they were cast, or the veteran-laden Yugoslavians who were quoted as saying, "We intend to put the young Americans to bed?"

The much-anticipated game was tight and tense from the opening tip; however, a high-arching corner jump shot from Silas Ford at the horn allowed the U.S. to take a slim but momentum-building three-point lead at the half. The halftime talk among the media centered on the Yugoslavian's successful strategy of making the game ugly, which slowed the game's pace to their liking. However, much to the delight of US supporters, the U.S. opened the second half with great energy and enthusiasm. Xavier began the half aggressively and was not worried about the foul trouble that plagued him in the first half. He attacked the glass with a vengeance while blocking shots from both sides of the lane, and the fans loved it. Yugoslavia could not get to the rim because of Xavier's domination in the painted area.

Using crisp ball movement and an inside-out strategy, the U.S.'s half-court motion offense resembled poetry in motion. The rotating perimeter defense and ball denial on the post-entry pass was a thing of beauty that effectively confused and stifled the Yugoslavians. Xavier's relentless work on the glass triggered a blistering fast break pace, allowing the offense to stay in downhill attack mode.

The Yugoslavians, seemingly caught off guard and unable to stop the attack, had no answers for Xavier, who, along with Silas and Mohamed Caldwell, were rolling. Over the next three minutes, the U.S. went on a 13-0 run to stun the Yugoslavians and the crowd. They took a commanding 49-29 lead and coasted home with an impressive 65-50 victory. Team USA completed these improbable Olympic games sporting a perfect 9-0 record and, in doing so, secured the USA's seventh consecutive Olympic basketball gold medal, as USA fans were beside themselves.

"What a game, what a performance, they put it on them," were some of the comments from the cheerful crowd.

When Xavier received his medal and flowers, the standing crowd applauded wildly and chanted his name repeatedly, prompting his teammates to urge the 19-year-old to acknowledge their cheers. In doing so, he was brought to tears while waving to the fans.

The surge of national and international TV and newsprint media who competed to get an interview with Xavier was overwhelming. However, through the media crowd, he found a news team from the U.S. to conduct an interview. Xavier was overheard saying to the interviewer, who singled out his sensational championship game, "I was just proud that I was able to meet the challenge and bring my game (21 points) to the biggest stage when it mattered most."

Still feeling the energy from the fans, Xavier took a deep breath to savor the moment before he continued, "The Olympics are special and an incredible experience, one that I never even dreamed about." Finally, he said, "Just magical. I am very honored to have had the opportunity to play and represent. The whole Olympic experience was just awesome."

After his interview, Xavier turned and smiled at the adoring fans still chanting, USA, USA, when he saw his parents and friends waving jubilantly in excitement as they walked his way. Although super-elated to embrace his family, Xavier scanned the growing crowd of well-wishers, intent on finding Sophie. But first, the outstretched arms of KeShawn greeted his son by slapping a hard handshake followed by and a huge embrace. Xavier tapped his dad in the chest as he grinned ear-to-ear, then turned, kissed, and embraced his mom, who was shedding tears of happiness for her son. In a love-filled gesture, Xavier placed his newly earned shiny gold medal around his mother's neck before giving her another embrace.

Despite all the cheering and chants, Xavier suddenly heard someone calling his name. After turning 180 degrees to find the voice that called out to him, he turned around and found Sophie standing before him. So excited to see her, Xavier instinctively hugged and lifted Sophie off her feet and kissed her. Surprised at first but overjoyed and loving the euphoria of the moment, Sophie wrapped her arms around Xavier's neck and happily returned the emotional kiss.

Although the victory in the basketball gold medal game was hard-fought and well-deserved, in the bigger picture, it was just a backdrop to a country virtually buried in a social revolution. The war in Vietnam, along with mounting deaths and casualties, seemed endless and raged on. There were the assassinations of President John F. Kennedy, Robert Kennedy, and Dr. Martin Luther King, Jr. While anti-war protests and demonstrations took center stage on practically every college campus across America, civil unrest in the streets remained a daily occurrence.

African Americans, fed-up, frustrated, and discontent with America's racial, social, and economic inequalities, feverishly took to the streets in protest and were reverently joined in the cause by white and brown Americans.

In contrast, other groups of protestors took to the streets to bring attention to what they considered an unjust war. America was burning from the inside, and people were fearful. These were the turbulent times that will be forever etched into the mind when Mexico 1968 is mentioned.

Xavier's remarkable Olympic experience as a 19-year-old college freshman solidified his fantastic talent and was a launching pad for future success. He became the youngest player to make the USA Olympic basketball team and accomplished some awe-inspiring personal achievements.

The total points he scored set a USA record that stood for years, and his incredible field goal accuracy of 71.9 percent also set a U.S. Olympic shooting percentage record.

While these individual accomplishments were impressive, Xavier remained mindful as he shared with his dad, "I am so blessed, but I am equally thankful to have had this opportunity." He said, "Even though the Olympics gave me a bigger platform to showcase my talents, I wanted to represent America despite her shortcomings." As KeShawn nodded in sympathetic agreement, Xavier said, "I especially wanted to represent my community and make them proud of our accomplishments." As he put his arm around his father's shoulder, Xavier explained, "My Olympic experience was made possible by the vision you had for me back in Jamaica when I was just learning how to play." KeShawn rubbed his son's head and allowed him to continue. "If you had not sent me to live with Uncle Freddie in Chicago and introduced me to Coach Parker, who knows what my path might have been. This is why I truly believe that God is watching over me."

27

THE BETRAYAL

DuPont University, located in Chicago's Lincoln Park neighborhood, bordered by Lake Michigan, is a private Catholic University in Chicago, Illinois. It takes its name from the 17th-century French Priest Saint William du Pont.

THIS DOWNTOWN UNIVERSITY made a verbal promise, like a gentleman's agreement, offering Charlie Parker the head basketball coaching position. Callously, the promise was cloaked in deceit and posturing from the onset. Parker believed he would be hired as the next basketball coach to replace the long-running coach Frank Pierce, who at mid-season told local radio sports station 670, The Score, about his retirement plans that would end his up-and-down tenure at DuPont effective at the end of the current season. Other regional affiliates, including CBS Sports, quickly picked up the story.

The caveat for Parker would be his ability to deliver Xavier Coleman to the University. This would be no easy task despite being Xavier's high school coach, especially knowing that UCLA is high on Xavier's preferred destination list.

Under this guise, DuPont University hit the jackpot when Olympic hero Xavier Coleman, who spent one All-American year of college at Long Beach City College and practically one signature away from joining a star-laden team at UCLA, shocked the country by agreeing to attend the small Division I, DuPont University in Chicago. But what few in the country knew was the understanding that Xavier's high school coach and mentor, the legendary and highly respected Charlie Parker, would be hired as soon as Frank Pierce completed his last year as coach.

When word leaked that Xavier, the Olympic hero and former Chicago High School phenom, was signing to play at DuPont University, the city joined the University in celebration to welcome him back home. DuPont went all out. They held a pep rally and invited city officials, celebrities, and local athletes to participate in the celebration of landing one of the best players on the planet. Xavier's signing had put the University on the map, and demand for home and away game tickets exceeded all expectations. Additional staff were interviewed and hired to handle the overwhelming demand for season tickets. The tired-looking fieldhouse was repainted, a new basketball floor was installed, and an aging sound system was upgraded. The signing by DuPont of Xavier Coleman was a game-changer and one of the biggest sports stories to hit Chicago in years.

Not long after Xavier's University press conference, DuPont's athletic department phone started ringing off the hook. Aware of Xavier's outstanding Olympic performance, players around the country showed great interest in joining him at DuPont and playing for legendary coach Charlie Parker.

Willie Mitchell, ecstatic to continue playing alongside his buddy and unite and play for his high school coach, turned down a full scholarship offer from Long Beach State University to sign a multi-year scholarship to come to DuPont. Vernon Akquia, a good brother and teammate at Long Beach City College, flipped his commitment to Marquette University, jumped at the opportunity to continue playing Division I basketball, accepted a scholarship offer, and joined his friends at DuPont.

DuPont's recruitment efforts intensified as they went out to sign the highly sought-after five-star prolific shooting guard, Shaffee Jefferson, from Edwardsville, Illinois. Bernard Russell, an All-State forward from Pontiac, Michigan, was their next target. They set their sights on Seiko Dunlop, All-State guard from Ferndale, Michigan, and big Otis Harden, 7'0" All-Region center from Toledo, Ohio. These recruits further proved the massive impact of Xavier's signing and Parker's pending hire.

Once coach Parker's official hiring was announced, more players were expected to commit. One particular recruit was Detroit high school All-American Lawrence Moore. The 6-foot-8-inch left-hander told his friends about his intentions to transfer from the University of Michigan and join the crew at DuPont.

The City of Chicago was still buzzing as the news spread that Carter G. Woodson Prep Academy coach Charlie Parker, a coaching legend, would become the next head coach at DuPont University, making him the first Black coach in Division I basketball history. However, after a closed-door meeting, the University Board of Directors withdrew their support for the hire. The University administration, forced to backpedal, issued an unexplained statement indicating that Parker would not be the next coach.

The Board was unanimous in their decision. They were uncomfortable and feared a political backlash if they hired a Black man for the position. The Board believed that the climate in the country was not ready for a Black head coach, and such a hire would alienate their constituents but, more importantly, their financial donors. Coach Parker, a proven coach and mentor to hundreds of players who had paid his dues, felt betrayed and used by the University just to sign Xavier to play basketball at DuPont University.

A Chicago Defender news columnist was not shy when he voiced his opinion about DuPont's lack of interest in hiring minority faculty. He described this latest debauchery as a classic double-cross where they "smile in your face while reaching into your pocket."

The sound in Xavier's voice reflected disappointment and anger as he spoke to his family in length in Jamaica, and like him, they were outraged and disappointed. KeShawn tried his best to mask the frustration when he asked a rhetorical question, "After all that coach Parker has done and meant to the City of Chicago, and basketball in general, why would the University renege on a promise?" Xavier, seething from knowing he was the pawn used in this game of deceit, was at a loss for words. He felt trapped in a sea of delusion and hypocrisy as he tried to navigate an unfair system that exploited the unsuspicious.

Once thought to be the highlight of his life, the Olympic gold medal now seemed like a curse, like a dangling gemstone used in a deceptive game whose meaning was distorted and its value questioned.

Still bothered and unable to focus on school, Xavier sought the counsel of Coach Parker in an attempt to diffuse his anguish and to share his thoughts about the University and the possibility of taking legal action.

Despite the personal hurt that Coach Parker felt, he took the high road in his conversation with KeShawn; after all, this was not his first time experiencing racism. He tries to quiet Xavier's anger by offering him words of wisdom and encouragement, reminding Xavier, "For whom god wishes to destroy, he first makes angry." Even though his words were sincere and meaningful, Coach Parker couldn't disguise his disappointment at a dream so close to fruition and admitted, "What happened was a bitter pill to swallow."

Despite repeated attempts to get DuPont athletic director, Butch Lewis, to answer questions about the hiring reversal, he declined to elaborate, citing the Board's privacy policy. Hiding behind a policy further angered journalists and followers of the program. No plausible explanation for their double-cross was forthcoming, so Xavier, Willie, Vernon, and recruit Shaffee Jefferson traveled off-campus to an undisclosed location, meeting with Thomas Richardson to vent their frustrations and explore all possible options. "Should we boycott?" Vernon asked.

A frustrated Xavier replied, "Now we know exactly why the Human Right Project Plan was so adamant in proposing the Olympic boycott; it's the same bull shit, Mon." As he raised his voice, Willie said, "There's no way the University should be allowed to keep feeding their bank accounts off the strength of your popularity." He continued his emotional rant when he said, "They make tons of money off you, and you won't get a dime." Vernon then added, "Plus, they screwed coach." Willie said, "That's why we came here, to play for coach and put the University on the sports map. Man, I tell you, this crap ain't right." Vernon jumped back in and said to Xavier, "You know what? Maybe you should just leave and go pro!"

That last comment struck a note and got the fellas to do some thinking. After doing some rudimentary library research, the trio of Xavier, Willie, and Vernon were disappointed to learn that professional basketball abides by the "four-year rule," which meant a player can't be drafted or sign a professional contract until his college class has graduated. Vernon replied, "You mean to tell me the NBA makes you wait until four years after graduating from high school to get into the league?" Willie added, "Then how can baseball players turn pro right out of high school?" Vernon, in a mixed tone of anger and seriousness, said, "I told you this shit ain't right." The group's anger escalated, and the temporary damper on the thought of turning pro was equally frustrating. Xavier recalled a lengthy conversation he had with Coach Parker. He said, "Coach told me that the National Collegiate Athletic Association (NCAA) and the National Basketball Association (NBA) feared the ripple effects if an underclassman were allowed to turn pro." Xavier continued, "My dad told me about what Wilson Chambers did." After his junior year at Kansas University, he left college and played one year as a Harlem Globetrotter." Vernon replied, "Deep!" Xavier said, "Ya Mon, that move was enough to satisfy the NBA's four-year rule."

Xavier explained his lengthy conversation by saying, "Coach told me that it was his understanding that the newly formed American Basketball Association (ABA) had a limited four-year rule exception. The only stipulation they required was that players prove financial hardship." Vernon quickly replied, "Shit, we don't have any money. That's the hardship right there." Xavier laughed but gave the reply some thought.

Because his parents were living out of the country and were unable to provide direct financial support, Xavier considered the possibility that his situation as an international student and that no other means of support might be enough to qualify him under the ABA limited hardship rule.

Cautious but excited about the possibilities, Xavier moved forward and asked Coach Parker to assist him in understanding the cumbersome ABA hardship application. Half-heartedly and with low expectations for approval, Xavier submitted the five-page document to the ABA Board of Governors. At the onset, the Board concluded that Xavier's hardship rationale was weak and stretched the rule outside the intended boundary.

However, after re-assessing their decision, the fledgling professional league, in need of star power, recognized they had a chance to get one of the best players in the country. They needed a savior, a high-profile player, to keep them afloat, attract others, and ultimately save themselves from dissolving. In a Board of Governors meeting, the league commissioner reconsidered and told the owners, "Hell, I'll take the risk; after all, we're talking about Xavier Coleman, a high-profile college All-American and an Olympic hero."

As fate would have it, this was Xavier's ticket of opportunity and a way to leave college basketball and DuPont University. It has always been Xavier's dream to play professionally. The possibility of leaving college early to join a newly formed professional league is becoming increasingly a reality. However, before deciding, Xavier needed to have an honest heart-to-heart family discussion about his pending decision to leave college. He desperately wanted their blessing on his decision to leave college before earning a degree, but he would understand if they balked. After all, a college education was something they both had stressed since he was a child.

His parents' reactions to his plans to leave college and turn pro were mixed.

No matter the situation or the disappointment in the betrayal of Coach Parker, his mom wanted him to stay in school and get his degree. She worried he would have no fall-back plan if he didn't have a college education. But KeShawn was all in. He told his son, "If you make the move to the pros, just bring the best of you every night. You've already proven you have the game, but now you'll get paid to do what you do. So, if the league lets you in, why not take advantage and be the best player in the world?"

Coach Parker was supportive of Xavier's desire to turn pro. But he offered a word of caution. He understood the new challenges that awaited his star pupil when he explained, "You're going into the men's league, and as a high-profile rookie, the vets are going to take exception and come after you." The coach said, "Also, ensure you get good legal representation; those contracts are tricky and full of fine print. If you need my help, you know I'm just a phone call away."

Xavier told his boys at DuPont that the deal was done and that he was turning pro. "Ya Mon, I'm signing a contract to play for the Denver Mountaineers of the ABA." Willie and Vernon were ecstatic and jubilant after hearing the news. They gave Xavier high-fives as they jostled and pushed one another. Together, Willie and Vernon offered, "We're so happy for you, man. Now go tear that shit up."

A laughing Xavier then said to Willie and Vernon, "The University was making money off of me, so now I'll make money off of me," He continued in retrospect. "It's unreal to think that me, Xavier James Coleman, the kid who just three years ago, trusted his father's vision, left his hometown in Jamaica, finished high school in Chicago, is now turning pro in Denver." Vernon said, "Man, when you think about it, that's too deep! All glory and respect to the Creator."

Much to the dismay and disappointment of the recruits and fans throughout Chicago, Xavier played only one season at DuPont. After leading the nation in scoring 32.1 points and 22.1 rebounds, which earned him first-team All-American honors in his sophomore college season, he decided to turn pro and put the blame squarely on the shoulders of DuPont University.

28

THE MILE HIGH DECEPTION

Founded in 1858 as a mining town, Denver, known for its breathtaking mile-high altitude, diverse population, and beautiful mountains and as the 19th Most Populated City in the United States, now claims Xavier Coleman as one of its own.

The American Basketball Association (ABA), a league in its infancy with no television contracts, needed attractions in its fight with the National Basketball Association (NBA) over star players. Days before he signed his contract, an ABA official told Xavier, "We didn't get the big fella, but we got you. So welcome to the ABA and Denver, Colorado, the mile-high city."

On the drive over from the airport to the Mountaineers arena, head coach Lonnie Fulton, now in his second season as Denver's coach, seemed overjoyed but tried to temper his enthusiasm, even though he knew the second-best player in the country was now a member of his team. He explained to Xavier that once word leaked that he was coming to Denver, season ticket sales increased, not just in Denver but around the entire league. Fulton then laughed as he caught himself. "I don't want to get ahead of myself. I just picked you up from the airport," a laughing Fulton said to Xavier.

Continuing his conversation, Fulton said, "But know this: you are the league's most prized commodity. They look at you as an attraction for others to follow. But you're also a member of the Denver Mountaineers, and our job is to win ball games." The young rookie listened closely, hanging on to every word his new coach delivered. But Xavier was unsure if coach Fulton knew anything about him as a player. As they neared the arena for the much-anticipated press conference and to meet his new teammates, Xavier informed his coach exactly what his mindset was when he told him. "I know the league, you as a coach, and the fans of Denver have expectations of me, and I get that, but in reality, the only expectations that matter are my own." He then shared, "Coach, I like to ball, and they brought me here to do just that. So, I guess I'm going to have to deliver." As they laughed and slapped hands, they were greeted in the arena parking lot by a group of excited photographers eager to take photos of Denver's first superstar.

Denver offered Xavier a three-year contract, estimated to be worth $500,000, which was one of the most significant contracts the new league had ever offered anyone, especially to a first-year player. But that didn't concern Xavier. He was determined to prove his worth and put to rest all the noise surrounding his decision to leave college early. What followed was unbelievable on all levels.

All Xavier needed was a platform to unveil his blossoming talents. As the season unfolded, night after night, Xavier showed up and showed out. However, despite Xavier's highlights, the team struggled to find its groove. Even though the team looked like they were making progress, the inconsistencies were enough to cause management to make a coaching change mid-way through the season. They replaced the well-liked and veteran coach Lonnie Fulton, the league's only Black coach when they hired a former basketball referee with limited head coaching experience at the professional level. The abrupt coaching decision didn't go over well with fans in Denver. They felt Fulton should have been given the remainder of the season to turn things around. Although disappointed in Denver's decision, the league's

Board of Governors took a hands-off approach and remained silent.

Despite the coaching shake-up and the fall-out that followed, Xavier kept his word and delivered on his promise. He put the league on notice, and then he set the league on fire. Xavier ended his professional rookie year as the league's leading scorer (30.0) and rebounder (20.0). He was chosen the Most Valuable Player of the All-Star Game, Rookie of the Year, and the league's Most Valuable Player. Those numbers were good enough to push Denver into its first playoff series. Although the young Denver team was eliminated in the first round, the six-game series saw an even better version of Xavier.

After completing his fantastic rookie season, Xavier unleashed the monster in him during Denver's first post-season playoffs, where he averaged 34 points and 17 rebounds. The die was cast, and the shape of things to come was set. The 6-foot-9 Xavier, who played neither forward nor center, exhibited an unbelievable style of basketball. Led by Xavier, the Mountaineers exploded into the national conversation, while locally, the basketball team supplanted the football Broncos as the primary sports talk in Denver. Xavier took professional basketball by storm and thrilled audiences throughout the league. Some executives even admitted that Xavier was a generational talent worth the price of admission and must be kept in the league at all costs.

After his fantastic rookie year, Denver management was so enthralled by having their newly discovered 20-year-old superstar and his impact on Denver that they offered to make him the highest-paid professional athlete in the world. The management team told Xavier, "We believe you are the best player in either league, and you deserve to be paid like the best athlete on the planet."

So, during the latter part of the summer, right before training camp was to start in what would have been his second professional season, the Mountaineers agreed to tear up Xavier's original $500,000 three-year contract and replace it with a lucrative and stunning $2.9 million six-year contract, making Xavier the highest-paid player in professional sports history. Xavier, who knew he would only get better, was surprised at the numbers and responded, "It's a lot of money for sure, but let's not get it twisted and label me as greedy. I didn't ask for a new contract; they offered it to me."

When the news of the unprecedented contract numbers reached the media, it shook the world of professional contracts to its very core. Veteran players across all the sports leagues were left questioning their agents about their contracts. High-profile college players who, before the contract announcement, were only half-heartedly considering leaving college early but now were showing renewed interest in coming into the ABA. Thanks to Xavier's high-wire act, the league promoted the contract as the type of generational wealth the ABA could offer prospective players with star ability.

Naturally, the sophisticated NBA, still stuck in tradition and control, took note and was furious with the new league. League executives throughout the NBA held closed-door meetings as they scrambled to find solutions to the threat at their doorstep. There was talk of offering bonus money to players for All-Star game appearances, but speaking of salary increases for all players was non-negotiable. The reluctance of the NBA to make significant salary adjustments was an eye-opener. They were caught off guard and unprepared to offer solutions to keep their players from jumping to a league that provided outrageous salaries and a creative, free-wheeling brand of basketball. The new ABA was no longer a joke. The league had gotten a firmer grip on the professional basketball market, partly thanks to Xavier's exploits. It could no longer be dismissed as a sideshow but was recognized as a viable business competitor.

During a phone conversation with his parents in Jamaica, Xavier tried to maintain calm about his new contract but understandably found himself unable to contain his excitement. He shared the news of his new contract, who before his phone call, relied on the news media to get bits and pieces of his new contract, but they were in the dark about the details.

Enthusiasm abounds. Xavier said to his mom, "Mom, wow. Can you believe it? I'm getting a big fat contract to do what I like: play basketball." He continued, "I want you all to know you won't ever have to worry about money again; I will make sure you and Pops are taken care of for the rest of your lives."

Xavier delivered, and the Mountaineers responded by offering a contract to make him a very wealthy 21-year-old man. Xavier's mom, Dorothy, expressed her happiness but couldn't say the same about her husband. She told her son, "You need to talk to your father. He has concerns."

As a child, Xavier's slow-developing motor skills kept him from keeping up with his schoolmates. He was different from other kids who were singled out as most likely to succeed in sports. Not only was he the target of jokes, but Xavier was teased unmercifully until a growth spurt suddenly made him taller than his classmates. But KeShawn, reared by hard-working and loving parents, had a premonition about Xavier and never gave up hope for his son.

He knew that Xavier would be special. He watched over him like a mother hen, taking him places for exposure and teaching him about hard work and self-sufficiency.

KeShawn and his son worked tirelessly, using simple drills and activities to improve Xavier's agility and hand-eye coordination. KeShawn was unapologetic and without remorse for giving his young son deference and paid no attention to those who whispered he favored Xavier more than Jabari and Ania, something KeShawn vehemently denied. But he knew that if Xavier were going to be successful in this world, he would need help developing a solid foundation of self-confidence and faith. And when combined with an unyielding determination, great things would come his way. When the time came to send Xavier to Chicago to find his wings, KeShawn knew he had given his best to prepare his son, and it would be just a matter of time before everything would come together. He was confident and trusted that Coach Parker would be the last ingredient to make everything come together at the time it was supposed to happen.

Still smiling, Dorothy handed the phone to her husband. "Hello, son. It's good to hear from you." Xavier replied, "Hey, Pops, likewise." KeShawn continued, "I heard on the news. Congratulations on the new contract. But I have some concerns that may or may not amount to anything, but hear me out."

KeShawn offered his son some cautionary advice, something he inherited from Papa James.

The tone in which he spoke to his son reflected a man who had experienced quite a bit in his life, yet he always maintained unconditional love for his family when talking to them. "My advice, and you've heard me say this to you and your brother and sister. Watch those who come bearing gifts." Xavier remained silent because he knew his dad was prepared to offer some wisdom. KeShawn continued, "As Papa would say, trust nobody and always verify. Don't get me wrong, son, I think the contract is great, and I'm happy for you. But let's take a minute and pump the brakes, especially when asked to take someone's spoken or written word."

KeShawn paused to make sure his son was absorbing his message. He then went on to remind Xavier about the failed promises made by DuPont University to coach Parker and his own experiences with the verbal agreement Chicago State made regarding his physical therapy rehabilitation plan. "Let me repeat, son, I'm happy for you, and believe me, based on your performances, you've earned that contract and some. However, I have to admit, I am skeptical and hope I'm wrong, but it's hard for me to trust them." Xavier was quiet but listened intently as if he were a kid again sitting in front of his dad, engrossed in listening to his many lessons.

Sitting across from her husband in their Jamaican living room, Dorothy silently wished he would go easy on Xavier. But she knew it was for the best that her son heard the message that nobody else could deliver. While his father's words of caution echoed in his mind, Xavier realized he was unaware of the contract's specific details; only the significant amount of $2.9 million stood out to him, not the fine print.

Before ending his conversation, KeShawn said, "Son, do me a favor and allow someone you trust to put eyes on the contract details, then have someone get eyes on them. You know what I'm saying, right?" While he vigorously rubbed his hand over his head, Xavier replied, "I hear you, Pops, loud and clear, and I appreciate your advice." Just before Xavier finished the phone call, he told his dad, "Pops, I'm on it, but no matter how this shakes out, I will survive. Tell mom I love her." Before replying, KeShawn wondered if he was too blunt, then replied, "Will do, son, and you stay strong and keep us informed. We love you."

The downstairs deli, strategically located between the florist, shoe cobbler, jeweler repair, and dry cleaning shops, offered a nice mix of cold and warm sandwiches. The owner, who knew Xavier by name and reputation, smiled and happily asked, "The usual, Mr. Coleman?" Returning the smile, Xavier replied, "You can call me Xavier. It's cool, and yes, the usual, but please include a slice of your fabulous cheesecake."

Like most professional athletes, Xavier was a novice when dissecting contracts, boasting only a rudimentary understanding of professional contract language. Basic questions like how much, for how long, and when I am getting paid were quickly answered on the first page of most contracts. However, the devil and the details were in plain sight on the following pages but written by design in what is commonly referred to as legalese.

His Pops' words were still ringing, so Xavier decided to clear his mind and sit down after lunch to try and make sense of the lengthy contract. The express elevator took him uninterrupted from the first-floor deli to his luxury high-rise apartment unit that overlooked downtown Denver. Next to his piano was a mixture of hanging plants and art paintings donated to him by Vernon. Even though Sophie makes periodic visits, Xavier's apartment reflects that of a bachelor. Like he's done a hundred times throughout the season, Xavier tossed his keys into a porcelain bowl made in the image of a half basketball and changed into his Mountaineers sweatsuit. Like his dad's fascination with music, Xavier's musical interest was a constant companion that followed him wherever he traveled. His selection while he ate lunch was a toss-up. Keep the Latin Jazz vibe of Mongo Santamaria, already on the turntable from the night before, or choose his favorite Miles and Coltrane album. Considering the importance of the task, Mongo was removed from the turntable. Holding the album in his hand, he paused momentarily to stare at the bustling downtown Denver traffic, deep in thought from his picturesque window.

The sound of falling ice cubes from the refrigerator's ice maker snapped him back from his trance. Lunch was waiting, and the contract reading was to follow. Using one of his many album cleaning cloths, Xavier erased the few smudges on the Miles Davis album, So What, featuring John Coltrane. The horns of Miles and Coltrane immediately soothed Xavier's wandering mind as he sat at the table and enjoyed his deli sandwich.

To set the reading mood, Xavier turned the music down low, then slowly pulled the $2.9 million contract from his desk drawer, followed by an unused Yellow Highlighter. Unsure of what he expected to find, Xavier collapsed his tall frame on his new Roman Ivory leather Barcalounger and propped his size 16 shoes on the leather Ottoman. Xavier, on a mission the great Sherlock Holmes would have been proud of, began to meticulously read over the contract pages line by line and in between, underlining anything that needed to be clarified or looked questionable.

His untrained eye thoroughly examined the contract pages before encountering confusing and ambiguous legal language. Using the highlighter that waited anxiously to be used, Xavier underlined each word and sentence that alarmed him. Most notable were the contract paragraphs that spelled out the terms, conditions, and payment obligations. The legalese in which the contract was written was bewildering and unclear, adding to the mystery of the contract's true intentions. Even after he re-read the payment and obligation paragraphs, the legal terminology and its true sense continued to baffle him and raised his level of suspicion.

Xavier shrilled when he tried to dissect the contract's dollar figures and compare them to his original contract. Even this novice sleuth knew something was amiss at the sight of the numbers.

Xavier became incensed for that reason, and as he rose from his Barcalounger, he flung the contract papers into the air in a rage. Fuming and angry, he stomped around the apartment, muttering in a damming tone, "Something just doesn't smell right with this contract." Xavier continued his muttering. "Why did I let my excitement about the numbers get the better of me? Shit, I knew I should have gotten a professional agent to help me understand this contract. But I trusted them, dammit."

Walking back to the window, trying to let off steam, Xavier once again peered out on a city that knew nothing about his contract situation. As he continued to fume and beat himself up, he even jiggled the window to find out if it would open. For a fleeting moment, what crossed his mind after feeling bamboozled and betrayed was the unthinkable—a way to end the nightmare. "I could end this charade right now and be done with the deception," he thought. Instead, the words from his father swiveled in his head. "Trust no one." That's when Xavier realized giving up was unacceptable and not a part of the Coleman DNA. He was a product of warriors and fighters. And when the going gets tough, as it has been for generations before him, you don't quit; you step up and fight for what you believe in. After a deep exhale, Xavier blinked his eyes several times, and calmness was restored in his mind. He stepped back from the window and regrouped. He had unfinished business that needed his attention. So, despite his misjudgment of the team owners, Xavier knew the fight had just begun.

Sadly, the outrageous dollar numbers that shook the sports world were only smoke and mirrors. Only $400,000 of the six-year playing terms of the contract would be paid as salary, not the reported $2.9 million.

Those were the low-down and dirty devil in the details that

only a trained contract professional would have detected, not a 21-year-old rising superstar.

Xavier was completely comfortable playing for his original $500,000 three-year rookie contract. However, out of the kindness of their heart and as a tribute to Xavier's outstanding rookie season, and without provocation from Xavier, the owners tore the contract up. The owners used fanfare and a press release at the arena when they publicly announced their offer of an unheard-of six-year $2.9 million contract. And behind closed doors, you could probably hear their champagne glasses clinking. Unfortunately, the complex details of the contract were cleverly disguised and buried deep inside the confusing and misleading legal jargon. When the six-year contract covers were pulled back, Xavier learned he would earn less than his original three-year rookie contract.

Xavier was outraged and beside himself as the deception became crystal clear. His rage stemmed from the fact that he trusted the owners. He had every reason to believe they were honorable businessmen and would treat him fairly. He thought, "Why wouldn't they treat me fair? I was their most valuable asset. I could help generate unprecedented revenue for years to come. So why would they disrespect me?"

The speculative contracts balance was to accumulate from a long-term annuity investment, which allegedly and contractually binds Xavier to the organization for an additional ten years beyond the contract years. To make matters more excruciatingly painful, the 10-year service obligation could be in any capacity of the owner's choosing, including but not limited to driving one of the company's moving trucks. This was a disgrace and disrespectful to the highest proportions.

Further, to add insult to injury, the deferred income was not guaranteed, so if the franchise or the ABA went out of business or Xavier was traded, he would not be entitled to the contract benefits. The team owners held all the leverage in the contract arrangement and could remove their liability of future payments simply by making a single trade, better known as "I win, you lose."

After digesting the contract details, Xavier, devastated and heartbroken, felt terrible. A profound distrust consumed him, but he rationalized that there had to be a reasonable explanation for the contract to be drawn up in such a manner. The following morning, he called the team office, seeking an immediate answer from the two principal owners. The office secretary, acting as the gatekeeper, told Xavier that one of the owners was out of town on business, and the other owner was unavailable or unwilling to take his call, which infuriated Xavier even more.

Finally, after contacting multiple sources for agent recommendations, Xavier received referrals that set the wheels in motion for someone to examine and explain his contract situation. He narrowed his list of agents down to those who could provide him with immediate service that would also not cost him an arm and a leg for their service. After meeting George Kennard in his Los Angeles office, Xavier came away impressed. George is a reputable agent and lead attorney for First-Team Sports Management Group.

Xavier appreciated George's openness and frankness and considered him a straight-up guy who didn't bring all the usual judgmental "BS." At this stage of his life, Xavier could ill afford to hire a self-serving attorney or someone kicking him when he was already down. So, after a meal and a handshake, Xavier decided to hire the services offered by the Kennard team.

As president and lead attorney of First-Team Sports Management in California, George maintained an affiliation with a team of four additional West Coast law firms, which he relied on for additional legal support.

A tall, slender, soft-spoken man, George keeps his athletic build courtesy of a Baldwin Park LA Fitness Center club membership. He was a New Jersey native living in the affluent Baldwin Hills (Black Beverly Hills) neighborhood in Los Angeles. After he graduated from Camden's Woodrow Wilson High School at the top of his class, and despite multiple East Coast academic scholarship offers, George chose to attend Stanford University in Stanford, California, on a track scholarship. It turned out George wanted to continue his friendly, now bitter (who's the best) high school rivalry against his friend, Camden High School's All-State track star, Benny Bailey, who a year earlier chose to attend UC-Berkeley in Berkeley, California.

After earning his degree from Stanford, George completed his Masters in Sports Law and Business at Arizona State University. But, two years of baking in the Tempe, Arizona sun was enough for George. He returned to Southern California to attend the University of Southern California Gould School of Law, with a program emphasis on entertainment law.

His First-Team Management group successfully manages elite athletes in various sports, including the NBA, NFL, MLB, and International Soccer Leagues.

They provide many client-friendly services, including contract negotiations, sponsorship deals, consulting, endorsements, career planning, and brand partnerships. In his approach to clients, George reminds them that retaining such services is part of the cost of doing business as a professional. Whether they like it or not, most athletes will eventually need professional help navigating contract complexities and surviving in what many refer to as 'the den of wolves'—commonly known as professional sports.

After a preliminary look at Xavier's contract, George and his associates decided to challenge the validity of the Mountaineers contract, which, if found fraudulent, would make Xavier a free agent. But that's a big if that needed to be proven. In the meantime, the law team went to work looking deeper into the contract's fine print details.

The lawyers scrutinized every line in the contract and found one particularly disturbing paragraph. Even with a very generous return, the owner's investment of $100,000 in the annuity would likely yield $1 million less than the Denver owners claimed. The lawyers told a furious Xavier, "Based on our interpretation, there is no way you can expect to receive the contract's full value."

After repeated phone calls to schedule a meeting failed, George and his team of attorneys finally persuaded the owners to meet.

Fearing possible legal action, the reluctant and reticent Denver owners sat down for a face-to-face meeting.

Ignoring the traditional pleasantries, George and his team opened the meeting by pointing out specific inaccuracies in the contract, especially the investment paragraph. George was miffed at the notion that his client would be compensated based on stock market performances. Although familiar, this payment method was different from a typical form of payment associated with a performance-based business like professional basketball. George asked the owners to justify the contract or simply restructure it so that the total amount as proposed would make sense and be realized in the six years as promised.

In less than thirty seconds, and looking like they owned the world, the owners uttered words that translated to a refusal and maintained that the signed contract was legitimate, valid, and binding. Disappointed in Denver's callous disregard for fairness, Xavier stood up from the stable and declared, "I'm out." The owners responded, "What do you mean by that?" When Xavier chose not to reply, they angrily looked at each other, then at George, and said, "Tell that boy to get his ass back in here. He's not going anywhere." As they waived the contract in the air, they said indignantly, "Don't you know we own you? We have a signed contract." Shocked at what they just heard from the team owners, George, and his team huddled at the end of the table while they gathered their material.

In their conclusion, the lawyers realized they were dealing with owners who were mere backwaters holding on to deeply rooted racial issues. Their attitude exposed them as nothing more than small-minded shysters more interested in skullduggery than being honorable business people. As they walked out, Xavier's attorneys told the owners, "See you in court."

The ABA season has started, but because of the contentious back-and-forth negotiation between Xavier's team and the Denver owners, Xavier was advised by his attorney/agent, George Kennard, not to suit up to play until the contract situation was resolved, one way or another. As a result, Xavier missed out on the first two months of his second professional season. He had worked hard all summer to prepare for a repeat of his MVP rookie season, but now all he could do was sit and wait.

The ABA league commissioner and his lawyers knew of the impasse between the league's brightest star and the Mountaineers owners. So, he was brought into a hastily called meeting to help resolve the contract situation. His concern was Xavier, "We don't want to lose him," he said to the Denver owners. "So, let's make this right for all parties concerned," were his last words before departing for another league meeting the following morning in New York. Denver held the position of having a signed contract and insisted the contract was equitable despite the claims.

"Imagine offering someone $2.9 million but only obligated to pay them $400,000, mused Xavier. If I were devious, I would dig my heels in the sand and maintain a similar staunch position." Denver, however, was determined to find Xavier at fault and portray him to the public as the bad guy for challenging the legitimacy of their contract and countered with a breach of contract lawsuit.

Although Xavier was contesting in court through litigation over the contract's validity, he was still technically obligated to the Denver Mountaineers. Ironically, however, Denver was clueless to the fact that at least nine NBA teams and several more in the ABA, including league officials, expressed an interest in signing Xavier. Those teams went so far as to make Xavier contract offers.

Interest in Xavier's services was growing day by day. Even though he was only three years removed from high school, George and his attorneys concluded that the long-drawn-out litigation was going nowhere. Instead of wasting their clients' talents, it might be time to look away from the ABA. George told Xavier, "We should consider the pros and cons of moving on from Denver and formulate plans to jump to the NBA." The decision to jump, however, would put Xavier on a collision course that directly challenged the NBA's long-standing four-year player eligibility policy. George reiterated to Xavier when he said, "I want to be upfront. If we make a move to jump, the NBA, in all likelihood, will vigorously defend their eligibility policy in a court of law, and we could lose that fight.

Feeling boxed in by the stubborn Denver owners and with no other recourse, George and his First-Team Management partners decided to take the Denver owners to court. After weeks of deliberations, the District Court judge found in Xavier's favor and considered the contract fraudulent, thus making Xavier a free agent, eligible to negotiate with any team of his choosing.

Denver's small-minded owners were outraged and refused to accept the court's decision, vowing to continue fighting for the validity of their contract.

The owners counter-sued to stay the lower court's ruling, saying to the media, "Those bastards have not heard the last of us." But this didn't stop Xavier and his lawyer/agent from pursuing the idea of jumping leagues.

29

JUMPING LEAGUES

"Section 2.05 of the bylaws of the NBA rules stipulated that a person who has not entered college shall not be eligible to be drafted or to be a Player until four years after he has been graduated or four years after his original high school class has been graduated, as the case may be, nor may the future services of any such person be negotiated or contracted for, or otherwise reserved. Similarly, a person who has entered college but is no longer enrolled shall not be eligible to be drafted or play until he would have first become eligible had he remained enrolled. Any negotiations or agreements with someone during such period shall be null and void."

FIRST-TEAM SPORTS MANAGEMENT principal agent George Kennard arranged a meeting with the owner of the NBA Seattle SuperSonics. The SuperSonics, interchangeably referred to as the Sonics, are among the nine teams that expressed an interest in Xavier during his hotly contested litigation with Denver.

Sonics team owner Samuel Bluestein, a respected member of the

NBA Board of Governors, had been outspoken about his desire to sign Xavier to an NBA contract and was anxious to discuss terms.

Despite the league's "four-year" rule, Bluestein was hopeful that he would be able to sign Xavier without a bitter fight.

Bluestein's confidence in signing Xavier stemmed from his earlier work on behalf of the Board. He was the lead negotiator who induced another superstar, Conrad Dawkins, to leave the ABA for the NBA. Therefore, he felt he would be entitled to a star.

His fellow owners were not thrilled when Bluestein went before the Board to request approval for the Xavier signing. They frowned on his attempt to circumvent league policy and ruled in a 14-3 vote against Xavier becoming an exception to the four-year rule. The ruling should have ended Seattle's quest to acquire the young superstar. However, the Board underestimated Bluestein's tenacity and willingness to battle the league to sign the coveted superstar.

It was mid-December, and Xavier, fresh from three months of contract war with Denver, was mentally exhausted and needed a break. All the shenanigans and deceptions Denver used in court took a toll on Xavier and left him mentally and physically exhausted. So, to decompress and take his mind off the legal matters, Xavier informed George to relay a message to the Sonics owner about his plans to pause negotiations so that he could spend the holiday in his family's company. Although Xavier appreciated Seattle's interest in him, he was just worn out. However, he agreed to meet after the break, but it was time out for now. The battle to play basketball and earn a living was just beginning.

Soon after turning in her law school research project, which she had worked on the entire semester, Sophie returned to her apartment, gathered her travel bags and the roundtrip ticket Xavier had sent, and headed to LAX International Airport. She boarded an American Airlines nonstop flight to join Xavier in Jamaica for a well-deserved holiday break.

Also visiting Jamaica were Xavier's pals, Willie and Vernon, who, on short notice, accepted his invitation to come to the island. This small but intimate group was just the antidote Xavier needed to give him temporary relief from the mental strain of legal disputes. Xavier often traveled quickly to Jamaica whenever he felt the need to seek refuge from the high-profile life that now claims him. Jamaica also granted him time to lay down his armor and chill while in the friendly confines of his family.

Despite the contract issues brewing in Denver and Seattle, Xavier relaxed in his parents' home and reflected on the fact that there is still much in his life to enjoy and be thankful for. While the guests enjoyed each other's company, KeShawn shared stages in his life that put into perspective how life wouldn't be life if there weren't ups and downs. He emphasized his point by saying, "Life can throw you curveballs or fastballs without warning. So you have to be prepared."

KeShawn went on when he talked about what it was like growing up in the Deep South. "The South had its particular issues and challenges, but our family was tight and so full of love that we looked at those issues as just a way of daily life." He continued when he said, "Maybe it was because we were just children and didn't know better, but life seemed straightforward. After we moved to Chicago, things began to change. I came of age in Chicago and started to see things differently."

Sensing he was getting too deep in thought, KeShawn changed the conversation and reminded his guest about the time in Chicago when he was the man. As the family sat comfortably in the den, Sophie, Willie, and Vernon, considered part of the family, sipped ginger beer and munched on banana chips and coconut drops. KeShawn shared anecdotal events about his life. "I was always the King" brought laughter to the tall tale he sprouted. "For real," KeShawn reiterated, in disbelief that there was doubt about what he was saying. "I'm not kidding. Just ask Uncle Freddie; he'll tell you."

He went on to say, "When we were growing up, I would beat everybody in all types of races and games, so they just started calling me The King." The family was still amused as KeShawn continued his story, "When we got to Chicago, nothing changed. I was, as I said, a bad man." Willie and Vernon laughed and slapped high-fives and said to Xavier, "Man, your Pops is a good story-teller," Xavier quickly replied, "Ya Mon, as kids, we enjoyed listening to his stories, but you know what? His stories are true, not some made-up stuff." Vernon looked at Xavier and said, "What?" Xavier continued validating his dad's story. "Before he got hurt, Pops was killing it in Chicago, and he was "The King." I'm speaking the truth; check it out when you get back." KeShawn replied, "But the family's storyteller is not me; it's Papa James. His stories will blow your mind."

Laughter was coming from everyone, filling the room with amusement and good times. Sophie, who was not accustomed to such storytelling, sat in awe but was thrilled to see her boyfriend laughing, his mind far removed from his legal issues. These were the moments that Xavier had in mind when he invited everyone to join him in Jamaica. Still on a roll, an animated KeShawn told one more story about how when he moved to Jamaica, he crushed the hearts of the locals when he swooped in and stole Dorothy right from under their noses. Amidst the laughter, Dorothy slapped her husband on his knee and said, "You didn't steal me. You were the hunter, and I was the game, but I captured you." In response, KeShawn could only hug his wife as the room continued its lit laughter.

The elephant was still in the room, though. As much as they tried to avoid discussing the court battles and the possibility of Xavier playing in the NBA, Vernon went ahead and asked KeShawn his thoughts about Xavier jumping to the NBA. Never at a loss for offering advice, KeShawn replied, "God has watched over Xavier his entire life, and I believe he will not abandon him now." There was a dead silence in the den as KeShawn broke it down like only he could do. "In his new professional world, Xavier must be aware of undetectable landmines and wolves disguised as sheep who lurk in the shadows, waiting to catch the unsuspected asleep at the wheel. "Wow! Too deep," replied Vernon.

KeShawn continued, "Papa James was a sage man, and he

taught us years ago that to survive tough times, you must stay true to your faith and find an inner strength to overcome obstacles and stay focused on your goals."

The living room was eerily calm as KeShawn continued, "Papa believed that when you combine belief, trust, and determination, you have the tools to navigate most of life's challenges. I can't tell my son what to do or predict what will happen, but I believe in God's will. So, whatever happens, and whenever it happens, it will be in God's hands and in God's time. And in God I trust."

After a long pause, Dorothy said, "I don't mean to interrupt, but Honey, that's enough preaching. I'm sure everyone is hungry, so why don't we go out and get something to eat." On that note, Xavier stood and, using his long reach, pulled Sophie up from her comfortable couch seat and said, "How about we go over to the Pier?" Dorothy immediately agreed but laughed after KeShawn said, "I know a good seafood place." In reference to the restaurant where he and Dorothy first met.

The Christmas Holiday Xavier spent in Jamaica enjoying his family and friends, away from the bitter cold that had a grip on most of the U.S., was just what the doctor ordered. Xavier's time in Jamaica was invigorating and provided him with a renewed sense of well-being. Bidding his mom and dad goodbye, he and Sophie boarded a nonstop flight to Chicago. At the same time, Vernon coerced Willie to fly back to Milwaukee to see his family. Afterward, they would make the hour-and-a-half drive back to Chicago.

30

——————

RETURN TO CHICAGO

When Xavier and Sophie deplaned in Chicago and walked outside the baggage claim area, they were immediately greeted by falling snow and a brisk wind blowing westerly off Lake Michigan. Those conditions, better known as the "hawk," were in far contrast to the island weather they enjoyed in Jamaica. The Luxy Black Car Limo Service driver, wearing a Vintage Newsboy Chauffeur Hat, recognized the stunning couple standing curbside and called out Xavier's name. "Yes, sir, your car awaits you." Two limo doors were quickly opened, giving Xavier and Sophie respite from the hawk. The luggage was quickly and carefully loaded into the back without assistance, and off they went. The Limo driver, a young woman who looked old enough to know better but young enough not to care, weaved effortlessly away from the arriving passenger terminal and headed east-southeast toward the city center. After the driver, a person of few words welcomed her passengers to Chicago, she suggested they sit back and enjoy the ride. She made the thirty-minute ride to the downtown Langham Chicago Hotel, where a penthouse suite awaited them, a pleasurable experience. The ride was long enough for Xavier to identify a few points of interest that helped make Chicago unique. The Art Institute is one of the oldest and largest art museums in the United States; the Magnificent Mile stretches along Michigan Avenue; Lincoln Park, home to the Lincoln Park Zoo; and the Chicago History Museum. Xavier then revealed to Sophie the evening's surprise he had quietly pre-arranged.

Displaying a veteran move while still in Jamaica, Xavier contacted the Langham Hotel concierge to secure two VIP tickets and transportation for an evening of food and relaxation at one of Chicago's leading jazz venues. The Jazz Showcase's glowing reputation for its great atmosphere and sofa-style VIP seating offered an excellent dinner menu. To have an opportunity to sit back, out of winter's reach, and enjoy a bottle of Caymus Cabernet Sauvignon while listening to the sounds of the renowned Ahmad Jamal Jazz Quintet was a nice welcome home treat.

Excited to return to Chicago, where he made a name for himself in high school, Xavier wanted Sophie to take in as much of the city as time allowed. So, after a romantic evening in downtown Chicago and a good night's sleep in Langham's California King bed, Xavier woke the following day to some not-so-surprising news. Xavier's plans included visiting friends and family when news about a potential snowstorm interrupted the regularly scheduled TV program. An additional foot of snow was forecast to blanket Chicago and the surrounding area. Residents were advised to use caution if they had to leave home. Otherwise, the recommendation was to stay indoors. This was not the type of news Xavier expected nor wanted to hear. Consequently, his short to-do list to visit his Uncle Freddie and Coach Parker, whom he hadn't seen since the Olympics, became shorter.

Xavier was forced to develop a contingency plan because weather was a factor, and his visitation plans were compromised. He had to use his limited time in Chicago wisely, but more importantly, he had to stay alert to flight departures out of Chicago.

The threat of unfavorable weather conditions would not be in their best interest. Xavier had to factor in flight delays or cancellations and how that would affect his scheduled meetings in LA and potentially Seattle and Sophie's classes resuming at UCLA.

To stay one step ahead of the weather, Xavier asked Sophie to contact the airlines and confirm their options for departing Chicago for Los Angeles. Despite the forecaster's best intentions, the weather in and around Chicago has a history of sudden and unexpected changes. As Xavier learned while living in Chicago during high school, staying nimble and ready to act was the first rule of travel.

Coach Parker was highly regarded as a mentor and a friend, so it meant a great deal to Xavier to find time to visit him, even if for an hour. However, Xavier knew that if the coach learned he was in Chicago and didn't at least call or try to stop by to visit, weather notwithstanding, figuratively speaking, there would be hell to pay.

After breakfast, courtesy of room service, Xavier talked to his Uncle Freddie and explained that if the weather allowed, he and Sophie would like to come over for a visit.

Adorned in their Chicago winter clothes, Xavier and Sophie ventured downstairs to assess the weather firsthand, and much to their surprise, the snow had stopped falling. Downtown Chicago was active as usual. Pedestrians and street traffic coming and going appeared business as usual. So, as the mid-morning got underway, Xavier accepted assistance from an ever-so-helpful doorman as they boarded a Yellow Taxi for the 20-minute ride to Oak Park to visit his aunt and uncle.

The precious time Xavier and Sophie spent having lunch with his Aunt Claudia and Uncle Freddie was refreshing and meaningful. They talked about pro ball, Chicago, and his Dad. But the threat of snow still loomed.

Aware of the unpredictable Chicago weather, Uncle Freddie told his nephew, "It's getting late in the afternoon, so I don't think you should mess around with the weather. The possibility of snow and maybe freezing rain can make travel on the streets tricky, real fast, especially after dark." Uncle Freddie continued, "So, you might want to find out if Coach Parker would be available to meet tomorrow."

Following his uncle's advice, Xavier repeatedly called Coach Parker's office, but his calls went unanswered. Frustrated that nobody had answered the phone, Xavier grew worried. He attempted again to contact the coach, hoping to learn he was safe. Finally, in his familiar baritone voice, Coach answered the phone, relieving Xavier's mind that all was well.

Coach assured Xavier that if the weather got any worse, he wouldn't be offended if they didn't meet, but Xavier was having none of that and offered a suggestion. "Why don't we try and have lunch tomorrow, somewhere downtown, at a place of your choosing." After a brief pause, Xavier asked, "The weather can't keep this up all night, or can it?" Coach Parker laughed and told Xavier, "You've been away too long, son; this is Chicago," that gave them both a good laugh. They ended their conversation in agreement to meet for lunch, weather permitting, at the Renaissance Hotel, one of Parker's preferred downtown hotel bars and restaurants and only a 15-minute walk from Xavier's Langham Hotel.

Although draped in a wool knee-length winter coat, Sophie was not thrilled with the bitter cold. However, she found the snow somewhat of a novelty compared to the weather in Los Angeles. Even growing up in Paris, where winter temperatures can dip into a cold range from 37-47 degrees Fahrenheit, rain was more prominent than snow.

Darkness was slowly creeping upon daylight as snowflakes continued to fall. Uncle Freddie insisted Xavier take a pass on the taxi ride back to the hotel and instead take the L-Train. "I will take you guys to the Oak Park transit station; it's not far from the house." Even though the transit station was not that far from their house, the intensity of the snow was increasing, which concerned Claudia. Out of her concerns, she suggested that Xavier and Sophie stay overnight and return to the hotel in the morning. Despite his wife's safety concerns, Freddie was steadfast. The falling snow did not phase him as he prided himself in having the skills to drive on snow-covered streets. So, after convincing Claudia, Freddie took a few minutes to sweep snow from his front steps. Then, he slowly backed his car out of the garage, where Xavier and Sophie took the back seat and jokingly asked Uncle Freddie, the chauffeur, to take them to the transit station.

The 24-hour Oak Park rapid transit Blue Line departed for downtown Chicago every 15 minutes. In his effort to time the train's departure, Freddie left his house in enough time to drive cautiously through the snow-covered streets. The last thing he wanted was to put a scare into Sophie with a black ice spinout. The lack of road traffic made the fifteen-minute drive to the transit station simple, while the back seat front seat conversation seemed to hasten the ride time. The sound of the rapid transit L-Train could be heard in the distance. So, after a warm and heartfelt embrace, Uncle Freddie watched as Xavier and Sophie purchased their one-way train tickets from the transit platform's Ventra Vending machine.

Taking the Chicago L-Train, another novelty for Sophie to experience, was a much quicker and safer alternative to risking the 30-minute taxi ride on snow-covered streets. Barring unforeseen circumstances, the train ride would have them back downtown in fifteen minutes.

Blaring from the TV in his hotel suite, Xavier sat up and listened as The National Weather Service interrupted a rerun of the Cosby Show with breaking news. Another winter snowstorm advisory warning for the entire Great Lakes Region was issued. Motorists were advised to limit their roadway travel, while pedestrians were advised to shelter at home. In anticipation of the storm

City officials and the Illinois Department of Transportation alerted their staff to assemble snow plows and move their rock-salt truck crews to the ready.

But in the meantime, the grey skies over Chicago were not revealing their true intentions, and the outside temperature was mysteriously pleasant. This calm before the storm gave Coach

Parker a small window to trek downtown and meet Xavier for lunch.

The bay window table at the Renaissance Chicago Hotel, a setting quite familiar to Parker, was an excellent choice. Parker and Xavier haven't been together since the Games of Mexico City. They finally get the face time they both have welcomed. Before engaging in business conversation, a waitress, who Parker knew by name, took their lunch order.

Just before meeting Parker for lunch, at Sophie's insistence, Xavier stopped and placed her lunch order at the Langham restaurant, requesting that the food be delivered to her room within 30 minutes of placing the order. The initial topic of conversation between the coach and Xavier was the weather forecast, which only raised Xavier's growing concern about the safety of his coach, who still had to make a thirty-minute drive back to his home.

Then, there were concerns about the status of flights out of O'Hare International Airport. These open-ended questions made the lunch meeting a bit unsettling.

Even so, Xavier tried to show calmness and maturity when conversing with his coach. He asked the coach not to worry about his flight schedule because, as they spoke, Sophie was on the phone working on a plan to leave Chicago as soon as possible. Xavier told his coach, "Remember what you taught me when I first moved to Chicago?" Parker looked at Xavier, trying to recall one of his many teaching moments, and replied, "And what was that?" Xavier answered as he tried to conceal his grin, "When traveling in and around Chicago, stay nimble and be flexible." Parker smiled and then laughed at the fact that his star pupil remembered that important lesson. However, Xavier didn't know that O'Hare International had made plans to get ahead of the approaching snowstorm by rerouting many of their outbound flights, including the Chicago to Los Angeles flight. While some flight departures remained pending, others that couldn't be rerouted were being canceled.

The waitress approached their table carrying two well-prepared lunches. Parker ordered a bowl of Clam Chowder, perfect for this time of year, and a Caesar salad and baked salmon on the top. Xavier opted for the Pan-Fried Chilean Sea Bass topped with Lemon Garlic Herb Sauce, Asparagus, and a bowl of Clam Chowder. Although Xavier was confident Sophie was enjoying her Caesar salad and Salmon lunch, the weather and the flight departure weighed heavily in the back of his mind.

Sophie was gracious enough to give Xavier and the coach the space they needed for a one-on-one conversation. She knew Xavier needed his mentor's counsel, so she chose to eat lunch in her room and continue her efforts to secure tickets for their departure from Chicago.

While they talked over lunch, Parker expressed grave concerns after learning about Xavier's plan to jump leagues. Parker, who'd been around long enough, knew a thing or two about the legal battle that was sure to ensue. "Challenging an institution as deeply entrenched as the National Basketball Association won't be easy," he said to Xavier.

He advised Xavier, "If you and your legal team pursue signing the Seattle contract offer, expect the worst. They will come after you in court, the media, and the league. They will try to cast you as an outlaw. As someone who's trying to ruin the game. Parker continued, "The league will try to turn players against you." While he listened to his coach recite the cons, Xavier thought, "If I go ahead as planned, this could be a war." Parker continued, "Plus, the league has in place qualified attorneys who are well paid and prepared to put down anyone who dares to challenge their authority and their archaic policies."

As Parker paused to sip his lemon-infused water, Xavier shared an earlier phone conversation where his attorney, George Kennard, informed him that the Sonic's owner was eager to meet and discuss a contract proposal. George also told Xavier that he had the framework of the proposed contract and wanted to meet as soon as possible. George also stated a word of caution when he said to his client, "I want you to know that if we get this deal done, it won't be without a fight. You will be attempting to break an age-old league policy." Then George added, "But Seattle seems sincere and has indicated they will commit whatever financial resources it takes to make and keep you a SuperSonic."

As Parker listened to Xavier's words, he knew a war was coming. Xavier told his coach that he agreed to meet his attorney in LA to review the preliminary contract details. Then, Xavier emphasized, "They want me, and I want to play in the NBA." Both men then smiled, stood up at the table, and embraced.

A glance out of the bay window caught Parker's eye. The intensity of light snow had picked up, and if the snow continued at this rate, it could pose a travel problem for him. Simultaneously, Sophie entered the restaurant shaking snow from her Estate Faux Fur trimmed winter hat. She greeted Coach Parker with a warm embrace and said to him, "Bonjour, comment allez vous." And to her surprise, Parker replied, "Très bien, merci." Then Parker said, "Sophie, you look wonderful," She retorted, "Merci."

Sophie returned a smile at Coach Parker and replied, "Excuse me," she then turned her attention to Xavier and kissed him before she reached into her crossbody Dooney & Bourke Satchel to pull out her airline flight notes taken between eating lunch and taking notes from the extremely, helpful ticket agent. She handed Xavier the notes, anticipating the type of reaction he would have. At the top of the note paper, Sophie wrote, "This requires immediate attention." Glossing over the notes, Xavier looked concerned. He repeated out loud Sophie's handwriting, "No nonstop flights to Los Angeles. We can leave Chicago for LA, but this requires a connecting flight out of Atlanta. The flight leaves in three hours." After reading from Sophie's notes, Xavier noticed Coach Parker putting on his coat. Parker embraced Sophie and Xavier one more time, and as he walked toward the exit, he turned and said to Xavier, "You need to get ready to leave, but know that "I'm here for you, son. Also, know this: war is coming." Xavier exhaled deeply, and as his eyes stared out at the Chicago streets, a thousand thoughts about the war reference raced through his mind as he watched his mentor/coach walk away under the falling snow. Then Xavier returned his attention to Sophie and said in a quiet, almost sad voice, "We better get going, babe."

In two days, one will resume studies at UCLA Law School, and the other will engage in life-altering meetings that could forever change his life and possibly the landscape of professional sports.

Hurriedly, Sophie and Xavier loaded their bags onto the elevator that descended non-stop to the first floor as the weather outside worsened. Slapping the bellman a high-five, he handed him a nice tip before the couple took their seats in a roomy Yellow Taxi driven by the veteran taxi driver and ex-hoopster known around Chicago as Edward J (J was for jump shot). The drive to O'Hare International Airport for a flight bound for LAX by way of Atlanta's Hartsfield-Jackson International Airport was the start of a future just as uncertain as the weather in Chicago.

Surprisingly, despite the falling snow and rush hour traffic, Edward made good time. However, driving to the upper-level departing passenger loading zone was a nightmare — the endless cars trying to maneuver to the curbside added to the confusion. The standstill traffic remained backed up despite efforts by the airport police to move cars along. In addition to the weather conditions contributing to the slow go, impatient drivers left their cars parked along the curb unattended while helping their passengers check their luggage.

Meanwhile, as the annoying sounds of car horns blared, snow continued to fall. The few passengers fortunate enough to move forward toward the terminal drop-off loading zone ended up parked three cars wide of the curb. Instead of waiting for space along the curb, passengers decided to unload their luggage from essentially the middle of the street. Anxious passengers rushed inside, clueless if their departing flights were being re-routed, delayed, or canceled. Flight information, announced over the public address system, was either sketchy, ignored, or difficult to hear. Requests for special assistance were out of the question. Even the reliable airline's kiosk screens were difficult to read, as flight and gate departure information changed as rapidly as scrolling mid-day stock market prices in Times Square.

Panic-stricken travelers joined the long lines of disgruntled passengers trying to negotiate their multiple pieces of rolling luggage. The wait time to get to the counter was agonizing. People were going nowhere in a hurry. Those fortunate enough to reach the ticket counter encounter a zoo. Passengers trying to make connecting flights became impatient and resorted to venting their frustrations at the ticket agents. Those needing wheelchair assistance were just as frustrated at the lack of available wheelchairs. While airport customer service agents, in a hurry to accommodate passengers, slipped and slid in the snow. At the outside ticket/baggage check-in counter, aggressive passengers pushed and shoved, trying to barge their way to the front.

Meanwhile, Edward, no stranger to driving his taxi in these extreme situations, finally reached the terminal drop-off loading zone. He informs Xavier and Sophie not to worry about the chaos because he knows a guy. After Edward delivers their luggage to the curb, he says to them, "Wait here for a second; I'll be right back."

When Edward returned, he was accompanied by a slender young man showing a ponytail underneath his winter beanie that covered his ears. Prominently displayed on the left chest of his buttoned-up overcoat was the company name, Alliance Ground International (AGI). "This is Xavier Coleman and his wife," and "This is my cousin, Murph," Edward said as he made the introductions. Murph asked Xavier, "Didn't you play ball in Chicago and the Olympics?" Xavier laughed and said, "Ya Mon, something like that," which caused Edward to laugh at Xavier, who downplayed his stardom. Edward said to Xavier, "I already filled Murph in on you. I told him to take care of this superstar and his lovely wife." Sophie looked at Xavier and smiled after hearing the words 'his lovely wife.' "Murph, you know what to do? We've been through this before. Just make sure you get them through all this madness; they've got a plane to catch," exhorted Edward.

Despite all the traffic coming and going, a voice could be heard coming from the direction of Edward's parked taxi. "Who's taxi is this? You've got 60 seconds to move it or lose it, cried the airport curbside patrol officer. Edward turned hastily and winked at Murph, then said to Xavier, "I've gotta go before they tow my livelihood. But if you ever get back to Chicago, hopefully, I'll get lucky and catch you and the Misses again." Not wanting to detain Edward any longer, Xavier shook Edward's hand, and for his service, he gave him a healthy tip, then wished him well as he hustled back to his taxi.

Xavier and Sophie made their way to the designated departure gate, thanks to help from Edward and Murph. While walking to the departure gate, Xavier couldn't help but notice that as he looked out through the terminal windows, airport maintenance crews were cleaning snow from engines, de-icing windshields, and plowing snow from runways. Unsure of what might happen with their scheduled flight, Xavier and Sophie sat in the boarding area and quietly waited, knowing the situation was out of their control. They inquisitively looked at each other's expressions but said nothing. Despite the ongoing noise and confusion, they suddenly heard an announcement from the overhead intercom. The boarding agent said through a hand-help microphone, "Those passengers holding first-class tickets, you may prepare to board."

The sweet sound of those instructions was music to their ears. Xavier and Sophie, for now, could breathe a little easier as they displayed their boarding passes and walked to take their first-class seats. Sophie preferred an aisle seat, but because legroom in first class was not an issue, Xavier was good sitting next to the window. Soon after buckling their seat belts, they gladly accepted a complimentary glass of white wine from the stewardess. As passengers in the second cabin filed through the door, the flight attendant, in a clear and distinct voice, emphatically announced over the intercom instructions for those passengers standing in the aisle to be seated as quickly as possible. She continued, "The captain is trying to get ahead of the impending storm, so please take your seats and fasten your seatbelts. Thank you."

Delta Flight 1137, with assistance from the ground crew, began to slowly back away from the gate and take its place in the line of waiting planes. From his window seat, Xavier noticed the intensity of the much-anticipated snowstorm had increased. To ease his passengers' anxiety, the captain confidently announced over the intercom that the LAX-bound flight with a stop in Atlanta was fifth in line for takeoff and would wait on the tarmac until instructed to proceed.

While the plane sat on the tarmac, passengers chatted and made themselves comfortable. But as wait time lingered and snow conditions worsened, passengers on the Delta flight to Atlanta became suddenly quiet. Then the captain announced they had been cleared for takeoff, but not before a scare. As he continued to look out the window, Xavier noticed airport trucks and their swirling orange lights approach planes that sat directly behind his Delta flight. They were directing those planes to return to the terminal gate because their flights had been canceled. Delta Flight 1137 was the last flight allowed to depart O'Hare International Airport.

31

BATTLE IN THE COURT

Soon after his Los Angeles meeting, Xavier's agent called Seattle owner Samuel Bluestein. The call was the first time Xavier had spoken to the Seattle owner. Bluestein reiterated his intent to sign Xavier to a fair contract during the call. After they ended their conversation, George asked Xavier if he could take anything away from the conversation. Xavier told George, "I'm going to trust my gut. I got a good vibe from Samuel. He sounded sincere about his interest in me as a person, then as a ballplayer." Xavier continued, "I picked up on his intent, enthusiasm, and willingness to include the court cost. In my book, that type of commitment is real." George nodded in agreement as Xavier added, "I like it, so let's see if we can come to a contract agreement."

Right before New Year's, Samuel Bluestein invited Xavier, George, and their team to meet him and his group for lunch in his downtown Seattle office complex. A sprawling complex with multiple offices ranging from 200-400 square feet and a dining area over 600 square feet. Bluestein intended to give Xavier a taste of Seattle by having lunch catered by Ivar's, a popular Seattle seafood restaurant.

On the menu was a variety of fresh choices, including White

Clam Chowder, Caesar Salad, crispy fried calamari, Crab-Stuffed Halibut, Wild Alaskan Coho Salmon, Red-Skinned Potatoes, and a choice of Desserts: Key Lime Pie, NY Cheesecake, and Snoqualmie Ice Cream.

After the meal was devoured, Xavier looked at George and Bluestein and said, "Ya, Mon, are you kidding me? I can get used to this real quick." While they laughed and nodded in agreement, Bluestein said, "That was just a taste of what Seattle can offer you."

Defying his colleagues on the NBA Governors Board and their objections to overlooking the four-year rule policy, Bluestein, on December 30, threw caution to the wind and audaciously signed Xavier Coleman to a fully guaranteed six-year contract worth $2.5 million. In addition, Bluestein, in writing, agreed to pay all associated court costs and attorney fees necessary to make Xavier a SuperSonic.

Exhibiting a big smile, Bluestein, in an attempt to avoid any misinterpretations, asked Xavier and his agent to take the contract back to their hotel, read the fine print and the small print, and highlight any unclear or ambiguous language that might concern them.

Even though the contract language satisfied George, he suggested to Xavier that if he chose, he could sign the contract but be given 24 hours for discovery to challenge any part of the contract. Confident in what his lawyers had drawn up, Bluestein agreed to the suggestion, vigorously shook Xavier's hand, and said, "War is coming, Xavier, so I hope you're ready to fight this fight because I am?"

Feeling encouraged and relieved, Xavier, the foreign-born, twenty-one-year-old superstar, three years removed from high school, agreed to the terms and signed the Seattle contract, thus putting himself into the crosshairs of the NBA.

Upon learning Seattle had signed Xavier to an NBA contract, NBA Commissioner William (Moochie) McCloskey, acting on behalf of the Board of Governors, issued a statement condemning the signing and rescinding the contract. Moochie ruled that Xavier was ineligible to play in the NBA because he had not yet been four years removed from high school, thereby violating the NBA's "four-year" policy.

In addition to that ruling, the league also threatened to impose several penalties against Seattle for knowingly signing Xavier to an illegal contract, including the possibility of disenfranchisement. Consequently, the war had begun.

Xavier's legal team did not take the NBA's ruling quietly. They countered the NBA's position and filed an antitrust lawsuit against the league in District Court. The court issued an injunction to prevent the NBA from rescinding the contract, which prevented Xavier from playing and earning a living and penalizing the Sonics. The bottom line of the injunction was that the NBA and its four-year policy essentially prevented Xavier from earning a living.

THE SHERMAN ANTITRUST ACT, named after U.S. Senator John Sherman of Ohio, was the first federal law in the United States to prohibit trusts and monopolies. It was first enacted by Congress in 1890 and signed into law by President Benjamin Harrison. The Sherman Act comprises two main provisions: it prohibits interferences with trade and economic competition and illegal attempts to monopolize any part of trade or commerce within the United States.

THE APPEAL to the District Court was the beginning of Xavier's antitrust (competition) action against the NBA. The suit alleged that the NBA's conduct was a group boycott, citing previous cases such as Fashion Originators' Guild v. FTC, 312 U.S. 457, and Klor's v. Broadway-Hale Stores, 359 U.S. 207, per se, a violation of the Sherman Act.

The presiding justice in the Denver Mountaineers case, who was also the judge hearing the Seattle case in District Court, granted an injunction pending litigation, which allowed Xavier to suit up and play for the Sonics until a verdict was rendered. The injunction also prohibited the NBA from imposing sanctions against the Sonics.

The federal district court ruled, citing several examples, including that if Xavier were not allowed to play, his career would suffer irreparable injury, and his acceptance as a superstar would deteriorate.

Xavier suited up as a Seattle SuperSonic for the first time on the same night he was notified of the injunction. Although he didn't play, just being in uniform and going through warm-ups was a welcome relief from sitting in a courtroom, something he's done for the past four months. Even so, drama followed when the Sonics traveled on road trips. In anticipation of his arena arrival, Xavier was widely booed, harassed, cursed, and spit upon.

On many occasions, just before the game started, a PA announcement was made saying the game was being played under protest because the Sonics were using an illegal player. The announcement only served to escalate the tensions of a frazzled crowd even more, which brought down a rain of boos, expletives, and the N-word. There were other times when the Sonics arrived at the arena, Xavier was physically denied entrance. He was forced to wait outside in the snow, wearing only his warmup uniform, or to sit on the team bus without a way to stay warm. This cruel and unusual punishment was knowingly inflicted with the league's blessings. Even fellow players shunned him and considered him a pariah for upsetting the league's status quo, which allegedly risked their playing careers. But this was his chosen path, and Xavier had to fight like hell to survive and save his career.

As his case proceeded through the courts, Xavier played in only 33 games. He would start, stop, and start again as each temporary injunction and legal entanglement began to take a toll on him. The Sonics head coach, a 15-year NBA veteran, and the rest of the team grew increasingly sympathetic to the mounting strain on their young teammate. This prompted them to create a cocoon of support and encouragement that helped insulate him from the increasing hostilities.

It wasn't until an early January game in Milwaukee, when temperatures outside hovered just above freezing at game time, that Xavier got significant playing time, and he delivered. Playing only the second half, he scored in double figures and was close to getting double digits in rebounds. By his performance in Milwaukee, Xavier gave a glimpse of what would come later.

Over the next 21 games, Xavier displayed the talent that teams had feared; he was a beast. He blocked shots, rebounded, and unmercifully dunked on opponents while showing a skill set the NBA had never seen from a power forward. In those 21 games, Xavier averaged nearly 20 points per game.

Not surprisingly, the NBA appealed the injunction, arguing that the trial judge had made an error on the case's merits. After all, no antitrust violations had occurred. So, in early February, while still playing on the road in Detroit, the joy and excitement ended when the Court of Appeals for the Ninth Circuit Court agreed with the NBA and ordered the injunction to stay (temporarily suspended). In its conclusion, the Ninth Circuit held that the NBA has permanently excluded young players from entering the league, citing the league's four-year rule or status quo. It added that if Xavier were allowed to play, the league and the public would be harmed because of a disregard for order and regulations.

The Court stated, *"Having considered the status quo existing before the District Court's action and the disturbance of that status resulting from the injunction, the nature, and extent of the injury which continuation of the injunction or its stay would cause to the respective parties; and the public interest in the institution of professional basketball and the orderly regulation of its affairs."*

The Appeals Court ruling put Xavier at a crossroads. He had nowhere to go and no place to play, putting him at a perilous point in his career as the ABA, NBA, and NCAA pursued legal action against him. Xavier couldn't move forward and couldn't move backward, so he leaned on his head coach, who was doing all he could to console and advise his depressed superstar.

Days would pass, and all Xavier could do was look out from his apartment window in downtown Seattle at the ever-present gray skies and the falling rain that peppered Puget Sound Bay. He tried to gain solace from the tranquility of the rain and trust in the words of his coach, who said to him, "Better days are ahead."

Xavier and Sophie talked daily, and her kind words brought him moments of comfort during those difficult days. However, because her time at UCLA was consumed with finishing her law school coursework, Xavier didn't want his legal entanglement to burden her. Still, she told him, "I can't be there right now, but know that I love you and will do anything to help you get through this." She continued, "I follow the case as much as possible through news outlets. I'm trying to understand how lawyers and judges reach their conclusions."

Sophie added, "If I get enough information, I will assemble my summations and submit them to my professor as a project paper and a teaching moment for contract law classes. But besides that, I want to know how you are holding up under this tremendous strain." She added, "I am praying that God will give you strength. I love you, dear."

One NBA executive was quoted in the media saying, " Coleman is causing an unbelievable stir around the league. He has everyone scared to death over what it means and where this might lead. Nobody knows how it will play out." The quote added, "The case is viewed as threatening for the entire league."

Xavier's concerned parents, KeShawn and Dorothy, made plans to fly to Seattle to be at their son's side. They wanted to bring family love and comfort because that's what the Colemans do. But Xavier politely asked them to hold off a bit longer. He appreciated their gesture, but his time was spent either in court or preparing for court. So, out of respect for their time, he asked that they pause their trip. However, the love he felt from his family brought him peace and steadied his resolve.

Xavier's agent recognized that his client was nervous, scared, and stressed. George was sympathetic to his client, whose professional career was hanging in the balance between two competing legal teams. Sadly, all Xavier could do was sit, wait, and worry.

During and between court proceedings, George and Xavier stayed in constant contact. They talked not only about the case but about life in general. George also reiterated to Xavier the importance of maintaining a positive and confident presence in court. He advised Xavier, "If their lawyers can see the case getting the best of you, they will smell blood in the water and will tighten the screws even more."

The stakes were as high as they could get, and Xavier's professional future was in the hands of the judicial system, as both sides threw punches and counterpunches at the judge.

In a candid conversation with his attorney, a stressed-out Xavier explained how he felt while he sat in the courtroom. "The way the arguments were flowing, I thought perhaps we had a chance to win, but I didn't know for sure. He added, "What if they permanently ban me from the league?" As he continued, the stress on Xavier's face, the toll on him physically, and the panic in his voice were more evident than ever. "Everything is on the line. I've probably burnt bridges on both ends. I have no recourse. I have to win," Xavier said to George.

At this point in the court challenges, there was nowhere to go but up, so Xavier and his team of lawyers, joined by the Sonics, appealed the Ninth Circuit Court's stay of the injunction to the highest court in the land: the United States Supreme Court.

32

THE SUPREME COURT: THE DECISION

oleman v. National Basketball Association:
Xavier Coleman challenged the NBA's rule that no player can enter the league until four years after his high school class graduates. His attorneys believed the rule violated Section One of the Sherman Antitrust Act, which prohibits restraint of trade. They argued that the NBA excluded an entire class of people (a group boycott) not four years beyond high school and that the group boycott was illegal and unethical and should be overturned by the courts.

Time was of the essence because the NBA regular season was coming to a close, the playoffs were about to start, and the Sonics were in a battle to secure one of the last remaining spots.

The league, however, had other ideas. They were determined to prevent Xavier from playing in the playoffs, and the Sonics, knowing that Xavier was critical to their chances of playoff success increased dramatically, were equally determined to have Xavier participate.

The full Supreme Court only hears cases that have been fully adjudicated, which often can take years; as such, this would undoubtedly damage Seattle's playoff aspirations. However, there have been occasions where appeals on parts of a case or an injunction needed a quick decision, and to allow room for that quick decision, each member of the Supreme Court served as a circuit justice. Circuit justices were empowered to decide the merits of an appeal individually and expeditiously for a specific Court of Appeals circuit.

Supreme Court Justice Earl Duncan was the circuit justice in February for the Ninth Circuit Court of Appeals; therefore, he was assigned to decide if the district court's injunction, which allowed Xavier to play, should be reinstated or if the Court of Appeals stay, denying his eligibility, should remain in place. As it stood, Xavier's professional career would be in the hands of the circuit justice.

On the first of March, in a three-page decision, Justice Duncan, writing as a circuit justice, summarized the facts of the case and the prior history of the lawsuit and ordered the District Court injunction reinstated. Justice Duncan's words made Xavier feel like a baby boy on Christmas morning. He, Xavier Coleman, could officially play in the NBA.

Justice Duncan wrote that the integrity of the playoffs affected his decision. At the same time, he also wrote that the antitrust lawsuit against the league could proceed.

When the news about the ruling leaked, Xavier, the Sonics, and the entire city of Seattle were thrilled beyond imagination. The Sonics immediately began to acclimate Xavier back into the lineup for the stretch run to the playoffs.

Eight days later, as the entire Supreme Court sat in session, they voted 7-2 to uphold Justice Duncan's decision without comment and remanded the case back to the District Court for further proceedings. As he sat in the courtroom, nervous and shaken, knowing his professional career was hanging in the balance, Xavier anxiously awaited the Supreme Court's vote. When the verdict was announced, Xavier stood and raised his arms in jubilation. Overcome by joy, Xavier could not contain his emotions and reacted by lifting and embracing each of his lawyers. He swung George around like a merry-go-round as they both shed tears of joy. Xavier was overheard saying to them, "Wow, wow, wow, this is f…ing incredible, we won. Man, not only do I feel vindicated, but I also feel liberated. Thank you, God, thank you, God!"

Soon after the Supreme Court's decision, the NBA, Xavier, and his attorneys reached an out-of-court settlement that allowed him to stay permanently as a Seattle SuperSonic.

Thanks to the battle waged and won by Xavier and his team of lawyers, the Supreme Court decision opened the door to giving many high school graduates and college basketball players the option to become eligible for the NBA draft before completing four years of college. "Will there be gratitude or recognition for the pain and sacrifice I made for this decision to become a reality?" Xavier asked his attorney. Before he replied, George paused and contemplated Xavier's question, and with a look of uncertainty, George replied, "Only time will tell Xavier, only time will tell."

When the court's ruling was announced, there were widespread rumors, speculation, and anxiety that the verdict threatened the existence of the NBA draft. So, in an attempt to get ahead of the unknown and quell the rumors, the NBA compromised by establishing a hardship rule allowing players to leave college early if they showed financial need. The compromise by the NBA was partly necessary to level the playing field in the fight against the upstart ABA over a college pool of players eager to turn professional.

In late March, Judge Charles C. Ferguson of the Federal District Court in California awarded Xavier summary judgment (a pretrial motion in favor of Xavier and against the NBA exclusive of going to a full trial), declaring the NBA's four-year rule violated Section One of the Sherman Act.

He noted in his summary that the NBA was not exempt from antitrust laws. The league and its members collectively agreed not to do business with players not four years beyond high school, which amounted to a group boycott.

The NBA had no policy or procedure for considering exceptions to the four-year rule. The judgment only emphasized the enormity of the group boycott and thus made it illegal. It allowed Xavier and other young players to enter the NBA without a challenge.

In addition to the Supreme Court decision, two more lawsuits were still pending. The Denver Mountaineers were suing Xavier and Seattle for breach of contract and tampering with a player under contract. Not long after the Supreme Court's historic ruling, the Mountaineers rescinded their breach-of-contract lawsuit against Xavier, which paved the way for an out-of-court settlement. Seattle agreed to pay Denver a fine in exchange for being able to keep Xavier, and after that, Xavier was officially a member of the Seattle SuperSonics.

Several days later, during a Seattle Sonics press conference, still looking tired and weary, Xavier addressed the news media,

"I can't begin to describe how relieved I am to have all the court proceedings done and behind me; the relief of winning the case often overshadowed my sense of joy. At age 22, nothing in my wildest dreams could have prepared me to handle the firestorm brewing in the NBA and the torment I faced. But I survived in large part because of the fans in Seattle. Your support meant a lot to me, and in the face of adversity, your support gave me strength and kept me upright when I could have easily folded under the weight and pressure of the court proceedings. The energy from your love allowed me to endure the taunts and ugliness and walk into court each day holding my head up high, and for that, from the bottom of my heart, I sincerely want to thank you, the fans of Seattle."

In the end, due to the court's decision and notwithstanding his substantial cost in legal fees, Seattle owner Samuel Bluestein agreed to drop his pending lawsuit against the NBA, which argued that the NBA draft system violated the antitrust laws. The magnitude of the court battle was monumental and promised to reverberate for years to come.

It took one superstar, his team of lawyers, led by George Kennard, and a willing owner, also a member of the NBA Board of Governors, for whom the fight was against, to stand up and fight for a player's right to make a living. Thanks to Xavier Coleman, the archaic doors that barricaded an unfair system have been challenged and dismantled. They have been replaced by modern pillars of hope and opportunity that stand tall, welcoming all to step forward and seek their dreams. But be reminded when passing through these modern pillars to pause and recognize that they were forged from sacrifice, courage, resilience, and a collective effort that upheld the promise of progress.

33

APRIL IN PARIS

The Sonics were thrilled to have Xavier back in the lineup, reflected by a different mentality and a renewed sense of purpose. They competed hard during the final stretch of games and put themselves in contention to challenge for a playoff spot. However, they ran out of time when the host Golden State Warriors prevailed in a thrilling overtime game that saw seven lead changes in the final three minutes. Despite early foul trouble, Xavier was magnificent down the stretch, including his driving one-handed cuff-dunk over two defenders with a minute left to tie the score. The dunk was so incredible that it brought the home crowd to its feet in awe. However, the Sonics were forced to foul to preserve time on the clock, and the Warriors obliged by making all their free throws, thus ending any chances the Sonics had of extending the game.

There was nothing the Sonics could do to pass the Warriors in the standings for the final playoff spot, even with a victory in their final home game against Portland. Despondent Sonic fans lamented their misfortune, blaming their superstar forward's on-again, off-again court hysteria. "Had Xavier played for the entire season? Wait til next season. The league was out to get us." Those were just a few of the dozens of comments leveled by the team's disappointed fan base."

Meanwhile, Xavier appreciated the fans' unyielding support. He promised the Sonics fans he would return more determined than ever to deliver the city its first-ever playoff. He had the entire offseason to prepare to make good on his promise.

By the time the NBA crowned the L.A. Lakers as league champions, Xavier and Sophie had already taken a romantic River Cruise on the Seine River in Paris, where they enjoyed time away from all the fanfare and drama surrounding his history-making transition to the NBA.

The River Cruise's tranquility brought Xavier peace and calmness, which he had not felt since spending the December holidays in Jamaica. The Paris getaway and time on the cruise also allowed Xavier and Sophie to cement their blossoming relationship.

The two have been in each other's lives, starting as early as the lost and then found Olympic Village badge encounter in Mexico City. Then, there was the separation after the Olympics when they attended college in two different parts of the country.

The legal shenanigans in Denver cascaded into a war of attrition, followed by an NBA season filled with uncertainty that almost ended his career. Still, Sophie remained in Xavier's life.

After spending considerable time together in Denver during his rookie season, they were both in agreement that once she finished law school and his professional life had a semblance of clarity, taking the relationship to another level, including the thought of starting a family, would be the ultimate commitment for them to make.

The fascinating views of Paris while cruising on the city's iconic river and learning about the city's unique history from the cruise guide were the equivalent of two semesters of history classes. Equally enjoyable was the time he and Sophie spent doing the French-like wine, cheese, and baguette picnic by the River. Unfortunately for them the picnic was prematurely cut short by the April in Paris unpredictable rain showers.

The two are in Paris not only for an R&R but to visit Sophie's family, whom Xavier first met in Mexico City during the Olympics. Her step-father, Thomas Brown, was born in the U.S. but raised in Montreal, Quebec, Canada; attended Syracuse University on a football scholarship and played professionally with the Montreal Alouettes of the Canadian Football League before retiring. Sophie's mother, Vivienne Alice-Dumas, a French native, worked full-time for the Minister of Higher Education and Research, assisting the ministry in overseeing university-level education.

Vivienne and Thomas have been together for fifteen years and raised Sophie as a child after Vivienne lost her first husband, a consul in the French government, in one of Europe's most deadly train accidents. When the horrors of the accident are brought up in conversation, minds in all of Europe are still boggled as to how the reliable high-speed TGV commuter rail train lost control and jumped the track as it entered the Brussels rail station. The lives of over a dozen passengers were lost, and countless others were injured. The tragedy was so horrific that officials have not closed the investigation.

Despite Sophie's parents' insistence that they stay in the family's West Paris 16th arrondissement home, Xavier and Sophie opted to stay at the charming 17th-century Hôtel d'Aubusson. The boutique hotel was nestled in the heart of Saint-Germain-des-Prés, a neighborhood known for its intimate character.

Paris is one of Europe's largest cities, and Sophie's excitement bubbled over. She couldn't wait to share her vibrant and diverse cosmopolitan home city with Xavier. Like New York City's flare, Paris exhibited a vibe that Sophie hoped would be another fantastic way to distance him from basketball.

Although Sophie was no stranger to Paris, she knew her biggest challenge was choosing from its many options. There are over 40,000 restaurants, 20 arrondissements, 400 parks, and 2,000 museums; deciding what, when, and where to go would take a lot of work.

While spending an afternoon in her parents' company in their three-bedroom apartment in the Chaillot neighborhood of the 16th arrondissement, Sophie brought up ideas for her and Xavier to do while in Paris. That's when her dad reminded her when he said, "Paris is best enjoyed if you let it come to you." He continued, "You can spend a full day moving about in the 16th District. Besides the views of the Eiffel, you have the first aquarium in the world to exhibit over 10,000 species, plus the District has over a dozen museums you might enjoy." As they listened to Thomas explain, Xavier was stunned by what he was hearing.

Sophie's mother, Vivienne, interjected with laughter and offered, "I agree, your father made a good point. Let's not make this complicated. Ditch the typical routine, and instead, let Paris surprise you." She added, "You can stroll and indulge in people-watching from one of the local restaurants or go to the flea market. Remember, Paris is more than a city; it's an emotion." Sophie then replied, "I think you guys are right." Xavier nodded in approval, then said to Sophie, "I'm good; we'll just take one bite of Paris at a time." It was time for Xavier and Sophie to leave and experience this wonderful city. Sophie hugged her parents and followed that by kissing them on the cheeks, and she and Xavier bid them a good day.

They were traveling along the cobblestone streets in the 16th District in a rented Citroën. Xavier couldn't help but be amazed at the exquisite architecture; then, he looked at Sophie in amazement. He wondered silently, as the Eiffel Tower suddenly came into his view, about the historical nature of this fascinating neighborhood and how it contrasted with the neighborhood of his youth in Jamaica.

At the Hôtel d'Aubusson, Xavier stood and looked out from the balcony as a light rain fell. He was temporarily mesmerized in thought about the painful reality that a few weeks ago, he was sitting in a courtroom, miles away, fighting for his professional livelihood. Although those thoughts occupied his mind, they were quickly dismissed and replaced by the specter of the beautiful cityscape he looked out on.

The captivating rain alleviated his worries and gave way to the allure of a city that embraced romanticism. Turning, he gestured for Sophie to join him in the window to look over the majestic city. But she remained seated on the edge of the bed, grimacing in discomfort as she rubbed her neck. Not getting the sympathetic response she expected. Sophie pulled Xavier from the window and said softly, "Wait until you see the breathtaking charm of the city at night." That suggestion rendered a light chuckle from Xavier before he replied, "You know we don't have to see all of Paris in a week. I'm pretty sure we'll come back."

As Sophie tilted her head back, revealing her beautiful eyes, she continued rubbing her neck, but the smell of the rain created a different effect. She quietly asked Xavier if he would rub the tension from her neck and shoulders. More than eager to oblige, Xavier retreated to the bathroom to soak a bath towel in hot water. While he waited for the towels to heat, he removed the comforter from the bed and asked Sophie to lie face down as she placed her head on the oversized pillow. But, before she descended face down, she removed her Sonics sweatshirt that exposed her neck and back.

As she lay there, prone on the bed, the soft Paris breeze from the balcony's open window gently moved the curtains back and forth; while the soothing sound of the rain comforted her, the warm towel relaxed her shoulders. Under the touch of Xavier's hands, Sophie melted into the bed, vulnerable to each touch. Xavier's tension massage soon gave way to soft, tender touches, prompting Sophie to roll over. The sensuous caresses of her body rendered her helpless, and as she trembled, she moaned in affection as the rush of desire overwhelmed her.

That feeling of April in Paris in a hotel suite on a rainy midmorning, in the arms of that special someone you love, seemed to have been the elixir that accelerated the relationship Sophie yearned for. The emotional connection and deeper appreciation of what's important in their lives moved them to talk about taking their relationship to the next life-altering step.

There was no sign of the rain letting up, so taking a walk to the market was off the table. Xavier reminded Sophie of the hotel's evening jazz lounge and suggested they do something they always enjoy: having a nice meal and enjoying the sounds of jazz. So, as Sophie blow-dried her hair, Xavier searched his luggage for something appropriate to wear for an evening of food and jazz in Paris.

34

THE HALL OF FAME INDUCTION

Xavier James Coleman, his immediate family, and close friends were seated in rows three and four just right of center stage. Tonight, by invitation only and reserved for the special few, was the pinnacle of basketball excellence: the Naismith Memorial Basketball Hall of Fame induction ceremony, where six individuals would be immortalized forever in the Hall.

By contrast, disappointment loomed yearly for hundreds of players and coaches who toiled in their craft, dreaming, wishing, and maybe hoping to one day be recognized.

In attendance to show love and support for Xavier and witness this historic occasion were his wife, Sophie; his three children, Angela, Morgan, and Miles; his father, KeShawn, and mother, Dorothy; his brother and sister, Jabari and Ania and their families; along with the family's of Freddie and Claudia Coleman; Moe and Gladys Banks, Charlie and Trina Parker, and numerous cousins, friends, and associates, including lifelong friends Willie Mitchell and Vernon Akquia; "The Golden Knights" high school teammates; DuPont University teammates Shafee Jefferson, Lawrence Moore, and Thomas Richardson; and Olympic teammates Silas Ford and Mohamed Caldwell.

The weekend festivities were magical, especially for those who were impactful to the growth and development of this extraordinary and talented human being.

Preceding Xavier to the stage, dressed in a Ralph Lauren gray and black pin-striped suit, was Tara Hall, an Olympic gold medalist, two-time college basketball player of the year, and a WNBA champion. Before speaking, she removed her tailored suit coat and, as a visible testament to her legacy and to a standing ovation, put on the custom "Reveal Suits" Hall of Fame jacket received at the Awards Gala the night before. A standing ovation followed Tara's emotional ceremonial speech. Next to be introduced was Xavier Coleman, whose career highlights and accomplishments played overhead on three video screens.

Wearing his newly awarded Naismith-Orange Hall of Fame Jacket, Xavier was presented on stage by Hall of Famers Bill Callahan and Tariq Jamerson. As he gracefully approached the podium to a one-minute standing ovation, Xavier touched his heart to recognize the love being shown to him. He cleverly tried to disguise his emotions by adjusting the podium microphone several times. But before he could say thank you, his emotions got the best of him, and the tears of joy flowed uncontrollably. Just as quickly, however, Xavier pulled from his inside coat pocket a white handkerchief, and as he wiped away the tears of joy, his shirt cuff revealed, stitched in the Jamaican colors of black, yellow, and green, the initials XJC followed by the words 'One God, One Love.'

The understanding and appreciative crowd gave him another round of applause. The cheers and applause were thunderous as Xavier gathered himself and addressed the audience. His Hall of Fame speech began paying homage to his Jamaican roots when he spread his arms wide and said to the crowd, "Ya Mon, One Love." The crowd responded in unison and repeated his words, "One Love," followed by another round of thunderous applause.

Xavier continued by giving Glory to the Creator for his blessings and for making this day possible. He then discussed the challenges of his cultural transition from Jamaica to the States before recognizing those whose impact on his journey was memorable. "I can't say enough about the unconditional love I received from my wife, Sophie, and my three children, Angela, Morgan, and Miles; my loving Jamaican and Chicago parents, especially my mom, whom I love dearly, as he blew her a kiss. Thank you, big brother and little sister; we had a ball, didn't we? as they smiled and laughed at hearing the truth. The dedication and love of Coach Parker: Who saw in me what others didn't and kicked my butt to make sure I got here. My good friend Willie has been with me since the start of this journey. My Olympic teammates: "We got the gold medal when everybody doubted us. Of course, my boys from Carter G. Woodson Prep Academy we were the first Prep Academy to win State; it was priceless. And thank you to the countless others who helped in some way." But he saved for last a moving and lengthy tribute for his dad.

Xavier acknowledged his dad's precarious journey and sacrifices, saying, "The sacrifices my dad made for me to be here were immeasurable. Because of him, I stand before you tonight." As Xavier dabbed his eyes, his voice quivered. Still, he continued, "If not for an unfortunate and untimely injury sustained while running track in college, my dad would have been inducted into the track and field Hall of Fame years ago." The audience responded by giving a heartfelt applause. Still fighting to control his emotions, Xavier shared with the audience some extraordinary numbers he put up while playing professionally. However, Xavier emphasized a particular point he wanted the young collegiate stars in attendance to understand.

As they sat in balcony seats, Xavier purposely directed his comments at them when he said, "Many, most, all, of you didn't have the opportunity to watch me play." Xavier continued, "The video footage shown during my introduction, although powerful, didn't begin to show the magnitude of my impact on basketball." Xavier noted his ridiculous rookie year MVP stat line when he said, "I'll leave you with this. After two years of college basketball, I entered professional basketball as a 20-year-old. During my rookie season, I played over 82 games, averaging 30 points and 19.5 rebounds per game." The entire audience gasped in amazement to hear those video game-type numbers. Then Xavier said, "None before and none after have been able to repeat those words." Xavier concluded his speech when he offered the audience a salute and a bow, and to a standing ovation, he returned to his seat, where his wife Sophie embraced him while his children waited to do the same.

The enshrinement ceremony concluded after Xavier's powerful speech, and those fortunate enough to be in attendance were invited to a VIP reception at the Marriott Springfield Hotel.

The Knights, joined by Xavier's University of DuPont teammates, still basking in the afterglow of seeing their friend enshrined, felt the energy and euphoria of the day slowly slipping away and decided to retreat to the cozy semi-private lounge adjacent to the Marriott's grand ballroom where they plopped down on the plush, oversized, burgundy sofa couches. The continuous handshaking congratulatory pats on the back from the overflow crowd of well-wishers was enjoyable but drained and exhausted them. They removed their shoes and slung their coats loosely on the back of chairs, and the neckties were next to go. The timing to kick back and chill from mingling couldn't have been better as another wave of fans jammed into the ballroom.

Xavier, followed by his three children, Angela, Morgan, and Miles, and still looking delighted, sat on the end sofa and joined the group for a well-deserved pause. "Here we are, fellas, what a ride," he said. Willie interjected with a bit of humor, "All made possible by the discipline of coach Parker. He demanded that we strive to be special, and we responded." The fellas extended Xavier a congratulatory high-five in appreciation for the invitation to attend the ceremony, including transportation and lodging. "Much love, Xavier, Curtis shouted from the other end of the sofa. Xavier replied in his Jamaican tone, "Ya Mon, much love."

Air transportation for the Knights was provided via a jet named "Eagle One," a private G550 Gulfstream beauty known for its reliability and comfort. The jet was courtesy of an illustrious but anonymous Chicago benefactor group known as the "Friends of Chicago." For years, there was talk and unsubstantiated rumors that this generous group was responsible for establishing the Carter G. Woodson Prep Academy and arranging for coach Parker to move from Detroit.

Though Xavier and Willie remained close friends and foundation partners, the "Knights" collectively had not been together as one since those high-flying high school years. The beauty of this mini-reunion was witnessed by the ease and flow of the conversations and the exaggerated stories. Stories that grew into fantasy tales as the evening moved on. The Knights's penchant for joking around was a testament to the chemistry and love the teammates always enjoyed.

The MC for the evening's event was none other than classmate JJ "the spin master" Hanson. His voice was heard through the walls when he introduced the legendary pop band Earth, Wind, and Fire. The live performance by the band was the main attraction for the overflow crowd jammed inside the grand ballroom. Xavier told his sons, Morgan and Miles, to go with their sister and find their mother, who should be seated up front and enjoy the band's performance. Shortly after those instructions, the band's music could easily be heard as it blasted through the ballroom speakers.

Vernon said to the guys, "Check that out. You hear that?" It was the song, Do You Remember. Silence fell upon the group as they listened to the song's lyrics. Reflection and introspection had replaced their banter. The Knights were suspended in thoughtful silence, reflecting on the evening's events and their journeys. Was it fate or the Creator's master plan that brought the Knights together years ago at Carter G?

Suddenly, the quiet in the room was interrupted by a gentle knock on the door. Coach Parker and Uncle Freddie entered the room, unaware of the thoughtful silence that just transpired. "Coach P, Uncle Freddie, what's going on?" asked Xavier. Coach Parker replied, "I've been working on something I think you guys will enjoy." He knew the Knights, especially Xavier and Willie, had a love for listening to Jazz just as much as he did. There were occasions when the coach unknowingly stopped by the pre-game quiet room to find the team listening to jazz music. One could tell that Parker loved that about his team's pre-game ritual. Blocking out the noise to focus on the task was an admirable trait that the coach appreciated about his team. This form of pregame meditation was initiated by Willie and Xavier and set the standard for future teams at Carter G.

Coach Parker has connections all across the country. In this case, he secured tickets to downtown Springfield's afternoon Jazz & Roots Festival. "But wait, there's more," an excited coach Parker said. "I've also arranged three tables at the Bohemian Downtown Jazz Lounge." Parker continued, "Before they return to New York, Blue Note recording artist Kenny Terrell and his band are in town for a weekend gig promoting their award-winning and newly released album, Blue Moon Over Yazoo City, featuring the hit song Chitlins con Carne.

"Kenny and I go way back," the coach said, and "his bandmates are some bad cats." The band featured Felix Turrentine on tenor sax, Ray Chambers on bass, Calvin Jones on drums, and Bobo Barretto on congas. Then he added, "The weekend is sold out, but between Kenny and the owner, Louie, I was able to swing something, as he smiled." Parker said, "If you want to take your family to either event, I've got you covered."

Standing and slapping high-fives, the guys shouted: "Thank you, coach." Xavier looked at his coach, then at his uncle, and said, "My dad is going to love this; thank you so much, coach."

EPILOGUE

During the first week of August, Andre Newman of the Philadelphia 76ers, by vote of the players union, was unanimously elected President of the National Basketball Players Association (NBPA), the union for current professional basketball players. He replaced Jamal Longley, who held the position for eight years.

It wasn't long after assuming the presidency that Andre, who entered the league before completing four years of college, expressed an idea he wanted to share with the association's Board of Player Representatives at their quarterly meeting. It was an idea that would finally allow him and his colleagues to make things right. Andre wanted the association to propose a measure to eliminate the redundant terms of hardship, early entry, and one-and-done and establish one term known as the Xavier Coleman Rule.

Even though such a bold move would require a two-thirds approval vote from the union membership, Andre wasn't worried about any potential fallout.

This was partly due to the positive feedback he had received from an earlier sit-down discussion. The Union's Executive Director, Harvard Law School graduate and practicing Attorney Marie Casteel, gave him positive feedback on the proposal.

Andre was confidently optimistic the measure would solicit positive responses from the association members. Marie, who already had preliminary discussions on the matter with the league office, told reporters, "Although the league office and I have had discussions, we have not yet held any formal meetings on the name change issue, but I expect that to happen at the highest level rather quickly." However, before Andre could put the vote to the union reps to gauge their support, a team representative from Cleveland, joined by the representative from Dallas, objected to the measure's quick action and recommended they table the action until the next collective bargaining agreement. To do so would essentially put the measure on ice for two years.

The objections were valid but became worrisome when additional representatives raised concerns. After a boisterous back-and-forth discussion elicited strong opinions, Andre called for a vote among the player reps. A show-of-hands vote to move the measure to a complete union vote passed 28-4. Andre instructed the Reps to take immediate action and initiate a vote among their teams. To accommodate those who may be difficult to reach, the results of the team vote count were extended. Team representatives were given ten days to report back their results.

In an unexpected twist, the votes from all thirty-two team Player Reps were recorded in just one week, and the results came back unanimously in favor of the proposal. One Player Rep reported that his team vote was enthusiastically 100% in favor of the proposal. But, there was still a tiny faction of players who wanted more time for discussion and preferred to table the measure until the current collective bargaining agreement expired.

Regardless of their concerns, the measure passed overwhelmingly. So, the next step was to have the Executive Council draft the proposal and send it to Marie, the Union chief, who would ratify and sign off on it. The proposal would then be presented to the league commissioner, Moochie McClosky, from her office.

In some ways, Andre felt the fight for this proposal was personal. As NBPA President, he was armed with a ratified majority endorsement and anxious for Commissioner McCloskey to respond.

Support from his Executive Council allowed Andre to speak openly and candidly with the commissioner about the growing percentage of players who take advantage of the Coleman ruling. He cited the fact that each year, roughly eighty-five percent of NBA players take advantage of the four-year rule the U.S. Supreme Court ruled illegal in Coleman v. NBA and entered the league before being four years beyond high school graduation. He felt that initiating an amendment to change the name was a no-brainer because the early entry percentages continued to grow.

In addition to the proposal, the NBPA and Union Chief included in the cover letter a request for an immediate response from the commissioners' office once the measure was reviewed. As chairman, Andre said during a brief press conference, "We wouldn't be here this early in our careers had it not been for the fight and the sacrifices that Xavier Coleman made. And as we reaped the benefits, we owe him a great deal of gratitude for doing what he did." Andre continued, "I don't know many other players who would have or could have withstood the torment and stress Xavier endured." Andre said, "And let's not forget, he emerged from all that court drama as a superstar baller. So yeah, making this recommendation was personal and an obvious decision. Andre added, "So that we're clear, we prefer the league office take immediate action on this proposal now rather than sit on their hands and wait for later."

Three weeks after receiving the NBPA's recommendation and the endorsement of union chief Marie Casteel, equipped with the endorsement of the Board of Governors, NBA Commissioner William (Moochie) McCloskey scheduled a press conference at the Hilton Towers in Manhattan.

After a choppy eight-hour, non-stop flight from Charles de Gaulle Airport in Paris, where the fasten-your-seatbelt sign stayed illuminated throughout the entire flight, Xavier and Sophie breathed a sigh of relief as British Airways flight 1922 touched down safely at JFK airport in New York.

It was early afternoon in New York, and as the limo rolled into Midtown Manhattan en route to The Peninsula New York Hotel on 5th and 55th, pedestrian activity slowed traffic considerably. The sounds of honking horns, sirens from emergency vehicles, and street vendors pitching their products welcomed Xavier and Sophie to what was unmistakably New York, where dreams and reality collide. C'est la vie!

There was only one thing on Xavier and Sophie's mind after checking into their Grand Suite hotel room that overlooked 5th Avenue, and that was to check on their children who were visiting their grandparents in Jamaica. While Sophie unpacked the suit-cases, she hung their clothes in the large, dreamy walk-in wardrobe closet, which had polished wood shelves, soft robes, and ample mirror space. Xavier unwound using the walk-in shower features to knock off eight hours of flight dust. After the week's clothes were sorted and hung, Sophie called Jamaica. Tossing her travel slippers off to the side, Sophie wiggled her toes in the carpet as she waited for the call connection. Grandma Dorothy answered the phone, but before she could begin the conversation, the sound of music and laughter forced her to retreat to the quieter bedroom. "Bonjour, Sophie! How are you? I am so sorry about all the noise, but KeShawn and the boys are having a good time in the den, talking and listening to music," explained Dorothy.

A laughing Sophie replied, "Well, from the sound of things, it does sound like fun." Before Sophie could ask how the boys were doing, Dorothy explained that Angela was at the library studying for her law school exams but would be home before dark.

Angela, a business major from UC-Santa Barbara, was finishing her law degree program at UCLA. She has aspirations of becoming a contract law attorney. At an early age, after learning about her father's contract trials and tribulations, she became inspired to learn more about the intricacies of contracts. She was determined to one day make a difference in the lives of aspiring athletes who rely on contracts and agents to fashion their occupations and shape their futures.

Angela wanted to implement monetary programs to help athletes avoid the pitfalls of unscrupulous contract agreements and pie-in-the-sky investment deals. She was interested in helping educate athletes, starting at the high school level, about personal budgets, contracts, legal obligations, money management, and fiscal responsibility.

After he emerged from the bathroom smelling fresh and with a new outlook on the day, Xavier immediately inquired about the family in Jamaica. "Dorothy, just a minute, someone wants to talk to you," said Sophie. As she handed the phone to Xavier, she said, "My turn," and walked into the marble bathroom to relax in the deep-sunken tub.

"Hello, Mom, how are you?" Xavier asked. Happy to hear her son's voice, Dorothy replied, "I'm doing just fine, and so are the boys. I told Sophie that Angela was studying in the library; it's much quieter there. But don't worry, she and her friend will return before dark." Dorothy continued when she asked, "How are you?" Xavier replied, "I'm good, tired, but good." Dorothy replied, "Your dad is having a great time doing what he enjoys: telling stories about Grandpa James down to you, and the boys are just eating it up." Bursting into laughter, Xavier replied, "I can just imagine." Then he added, "You know, Mom, Morgan is doing well in college, but one of the reasons he makes friends so easily is because of his special ability to captivate his friends by telling stories." Xavier laughed as he looked at Sophie relaxing on the bed after soaking in the tub. He sensed she wanted to get back on the phone. "I won't keep you, Mom, but it's good to know everybody is having a good time."

Before handing the phone to Sophie, Xavier explained, "You can probably expect us in a couple of days after our meeting in New York. Tell Pops to take it easy with the stories. Love you, Mom, but hold on, Sophie wants to talk to the boys." While Sophie was talking on the phone, Xavier took a call from NBPA president Andre Newman. "Ya Mon, what's up, Dre?" Xavier said as he walked away from Sophie's Conversation. "I want to confirm that we are still on for dinner," Andre said. Xavier replied, "Yes, Sir, but how about if we have dinner here at The Peninsula? I understand the menu is good, and we'll sit at the top of the hotel, where we will have an awesome view of the New York skyline." Andre, who respects Xavier tremendously, agreed to the suggestion. He was so excited about what he wanted to discuss over dinner that he struggled to stop speaking too soon.

Upon arriving at the 5th Avenue Hotel, Andre was struck by its opulence and grandeur. After he was directed to the front desk, the clerk handed him a special elevator access card, courtesy of Xavier, to gain access to the top-floor restaurant.

During dinner, Andre, seated across from Xavier and next to Sophie, did his best to keep the news of the recent Union vote under wraps but was undone by his excitement. The Xavier Coleman Rule was out of the bag. Andre explained to Xavier that Commissioner Moochie McCloskey had taken action on the Union's proposal and scheduled a press conference for a few VIP folks in the media.

After visiting Sophie's parents in Paris, Xavier explained to Andre that they would have a few days to spend in New York before leaving to rendezvous in Jamaica. Andre assured Xavier that he would have his office staff provide any assistance to him and Sophie as needed regarding accommodations, ground and air transportation, and any necessary ticket adjustments to leave New York for Jamaica.

Xavier accepted Andre's offer and expressed sincere appreciation for how he moved forward with the long-awaited rule name change. He said to Andre, "Man, it made me uncomfortable knowing that some of the players who are currently benefiting from the Supreme Court ruling all of a sudden have a so-called memory lapse about the rule's history." Xavier continued, "It feels like they don't want to know their history, and that to me makes no sense."

Xavier asked, "Why would you not want to know how you got to the league and who was instrumental in making it happen? But I get it. When I was fighting to break down those barriers, the league turned the players against me." As Xavier sarcastically chuckled, he continued. "So, the guys today, I don't know, perhaps their agents are filling their young minds with the same voodoo B.S. spread by the league during my time. But, you know what, I'm good. I'm at peace. My deed is done." Then he added, "The Creator has blessed me and watched over me my entire life. Now, I have a loving family, and I have my health. So, yes, this is what I mean when I say I'm good."

As Andre listened in stunned silence, he rose from his seat, embraced Xavier, and said, "Brother Xavier, I knew you were deep, but what you just shared, man. Andre explains, "Let me say this: we and I speak for most players. We appreciate what you did on and off the court." Andre continued as his emotions became exposed, "I'm just glad after years of delays and posturing, we could finally pass on to the commissioner the long-awaited and much-deserved recommendation to make the rule name change." Andre added, "Which is to give credit where credit is due." Looking and listening, Sophie smiled and said to the talkative men, "You guys are going to make me cry."

News services had already leaked parts of a story about a proposed amendment to the current NBA Collective Bargain Agreement (CBA). The circulated story, but without a named source, mentioned that the NBA and its player's union had agreed to change the existing early entry designation before the current CBA Agreement expired. Like wildfire, the news of an NBA press conference was spreading. Instead of a few invited media guests, the news conference was initially planned to be held in a small meeting room at the New York Hilton Midtown. But, it was suddenly moved to the main ballroom to accommodate the invited and growing uninvited guests. Many in attendance included league personnel, Union representatives, current and retired players, scores of news media, and Xavier and Sophie Coleman. Everyone had heard the rumors about an amendment change, but nobody was willing or able to share details until today.

After introducing and recognizing those who took the time to attend the press conference, Commissioner McCloskey got right to the point when he announced, "The league will be adding an amendment to the CBA. Effective this year, the league has adopted the NBPA proposal to change the hardship, early entry, and one-and-done classifications to the Xavier Coleman Rule."

Before taking questions from the crowd of eager media, the commissioner offered these comments, "Although controversial and unpopular at the time, in hindsight, we can all now agree that Xavier and his team of lawyers compelled us as a league to look internally and accept the reality of the times. He caused us to pause, think about the league's future, and ask, "What direction are we headed, and how do we get there?" The commissioner continued, "Today, on behalf of the league and its players, I stand before you to recognize and express the sincere gratitude we owe Xavier Coleman. He was willing to risk his career to fight for something bigger than himself, and we fought back in defense of what we believed to be a fair and just system."

The commissioner continued as news cameras flickered and reporters adjusted their handheld recording devices. "But like all things in life, if you don't evolve, you will end up in an unrecognizable world; simply put, all things will, must, and should change. Consequently, today, most of the players in the NBPA are here due to the evolution Xavier forced upon us."

As he pointed at Xavier, the commissioner added, "Thanks to Xavier, NBA revenues and player salaries have grown exponentially along with worldwide exposure, arena attendance, and TV viewership." After Commissioner McCloskey asked Xavier to join him at the podium, he continued by saying, "So, as we adopt the Xavier Coleman Rule into the NBA lexicon of early entry players, the league is proud to announce the establishment of the Xavier Coleman Early Entry MVP Award. The award will be given annually at the end of the season to recognize the most outstanding player who entered the league less than four years after high school graduation.

My wish for creating this award was to bring attention to the moment that caused the NBA to grow worldwide. I want players who enter the league early never to forget the player who made all this possible." The stunning and surprising announcement was met with rousing approval and a standing ovation that caught Xavier off guard. Xavier was now in the crosshairs of the news media cameras as Andre and members of the Players Union besieged the podium to congratulate him and shake the commissioner's hand.

The commissioner turned back to Xavier, pointed to the podium mic, and said, "All yours." After composing himself amidst the celebration and as the players circled him, Xavier, always willing to thank others for his success, touched his heart, humbly bowed his head, and placed his two hands together, symbolic of a prayer.

After thanking the Creator for this blessed honor, he thanked Andre, the Players Union, and the Commissioner for making the early-entry name change a reality and for establishing the Early-Entry MVP Award.

As Xavier adjusted the mic, something he had done many times before, he said, "My day in court was bittersweet because all I ever wanted to do was play ball and earn a living to help support my family, but when I was denied that right by the very league I wanted to join, I had no choice, I had to stand for something or fall for everything." The players erupted and clapped in support.

Xavier continued, "I couldn't go back to the ABA or college, so I had no choice but to fight for what I believed to be right." Another applause followed as he continued. "My lawyers and I weren't trying to make the league look like bad guys; we just used the law so that I could make a living doing what I love to do," and another round of applause ensued, followed by shoutouts from Union members, "Thank you, brother, we won't forget, and statue, statue." Xavier concluded his remarks by saying, "What I did in challenging the NBA in court was just the beginning of an evolu-tion-revolution. These changing tides reflect not only on the NBA but all professional sports, the NCAA, and high school associations."

Xavier continued as Sophie looked on proudly. "Athletes are the lifeblood of sports and the engine that drives the billion-dollar sports entertainment business. The time is now for athletes to not only sit at the table but to get a cut of the financial pie. Why shouldn't they? There will come a time very soon when fair labor compensation will be the norm." The players surrounding Xavier were overjoyed to hear his visionary words as he continued. "The next step in this evolution will allow all parties involved, or all stakeholders contributing to the success of a franchise, college, or business, whether as a player, coach, custodian, security or whoever else contributes, to have a percentage of ownership." The press conference turned silent as Xavier's words echoed. Then he continued, "I know what some of you might be thinking, "He's crazy! But stop for a second. Can you imagine how that person who now owns a percentage of the company they work for will treat the company?" All eyes and ears hung on to his words as Xavier continued. "But trust me, this is the age of evolution-revolution, so wake up everybody, no more sleeping in bed."

The reactions to Xavier's comments were jaw-dropping. His words reverberated throughout the room as he put something heavy on the minds of all in attendance. After a deafening silence, the room erupted into applause once again. Commissioner Moochie McCloskey and NBPA Chairman Andre Newman, awed by Xavier's forthrightness and vision, invited him back to their New York offices to discuss further his vision and how they could assist his foundation.

On the drive back to the hotel, Andre told Xavier, "I've had discussions with the Executive Board about instituting an automatic percentage contribution of one percent from all players who have entered and from those who will enter the league under your rule." Andre continued, "The contributions would be made in the name of your non-profit foundation." Xavier smiled and nodded his head, accepting the idea as sincere. But he explained to Andre that his current focus was on his family in Jamaica. "I plan to encourage my children and continue to support them as they pursue their dreams; I owe that to them." He continued, "After we return to the States, I will call you so we can expand on the foundation contributions idea." Then Xavier said, "The work of my foundation is powerful, and I would like you and the Union Board to learn more about our vision."

Back at the hotel, and before going their separate ways, Xavier said to Andre, "My Pops always gave me good advice, but there were two thoughts that remain in my consciousness to this day: Don't give up the fight, and all that glitters is not gold."

Xavier, the trailblazing Hall of Famer and a man finally at peace, confessed, "For reasons unknown to me, I was chosen to fight this fight, and I now know that I was truly blessed to do that." After looking at each other, the two friends embraced, shook hands, and walked away.

ABOUT THE AUTHOR

Wiley is a retired community college educator living in Arizona with his wife, Roberta.

He and his siblings were raised in the Conant Gardens neighborhood of Detroit, Michigan. As co-captain, he played on their state championship basketball team alongside NBA star Ralph Simpson and Naismith Basketball Hall of Famer Spencer Haywood at Pershing High School. He was a lifelong educator, teaching, training, developing, and coaching college students for over 40 years from Everett, Washington, to Phoenix, Arizona. During the 10 years following retirement, Wiley served in various positions, including chairman of the George Gervin Prep Academy Advisory Council and Board Chairman of the Gervin Prep Academy in Phoenix. In addition, Wiley served as an executive member of the Spencer Haywood Non-Profit Foundation in Las Vegas. A foundation whose mission is to support nonprofits pursuing social justice initiatives and organizations that provide health counseling, educational welfare, and sports development opportunities in marginalized communities. Wiley was also a 30-year classroom volunteer for Career Concepts for Youth, a 6th-grade Stay-In-School and Achieve Program in Phoenix, Arizona.

He was the head men's basketball coach for six years, where his teams reached the playoffs for four consecutive years. He was the women's head coach for one year and coached the men's golf team for four years. He was also an adjunct sociology faculty member at Maricopa Community College District South Mountain and GateWay campuses. After moving to Southern Arizona, he enjoys listening to music, has an active fitness lifestyle, and golfs several days a week. After turning his attention to writing books — the Flight of A Thousand Songbirds was his first, with several more currently in the works. Turning an idea into a story is gratifying and rewarding, yet not without its challenges.

www.ingramcontent.com/pod-product-compliance
Lightning Source LLC
Chambersburg PA
CBHW032357310726
48973CB00007B/2059